Somersham Boy

JAY D. WAVENEY

First published by Cranthorpe Millner Publishers (2025)

ISBN 978-1-80378-288-1 (Paperback)

www.cranthorpemillner.com

Cranthorpe Millner Publishers

For Jane

CHAPTER ONE

June 2020

Somersham Court

'What the hell is going on?'

Miles had been staring out of one of the windows on the south side of the house, his thoughts lost in admiring the view when a tradesman's expandable ladder appeared over the top of the wall just to the left of the wrought iron gate in an archway. He was transfixed. His companions had moved on into other rooms, their footsteps echoing in the empty building.

It looked like a young woman with masses of long, curly black hair in a ponytail. She was leaning over the wall, extending the ladder and climbing down. He thought about rushing downstairs to confront the interloper, but she would have had sufficient time to scrabble back over the wall before he could intercept her.

The window was grimy and he was just about to clean a patch on the inside of the window for a better look but decided against it as the movement might catch her eye. There was nothing to steal from the house, nothing left in the garden; why was she breaking in? Her actions were baffling. She came right up close to the house but seemed disinterested in it, her attention focused on the large broken statue of a stag, the garden gate and the view across the meadow. The same view he had been admiring. Walking backwards and then forwards, she stepped left and right, as though matching the angle to some image on her phone.

Obviously, she had found what she wanted. Believing she was alone, she jigged up and down with excitement, like a child who had found the last chocolate egg on an Easter trail. She appeared to take some photos facing the gate and then scrambled nimbly back over the wall and out of sight. The ladder disappearing after her.

'Mr Mortimer.'

An impatient voice regained his attention. He turned to face the carefully selected group of people, consisting of a conservation officer, surveyor, architect and specialist builder, keeping an approximate two-metre distance from one another due to the COVID-19 rules.

He indicated that they had his attention. Their eyes peering over the top of their masks showed impatience.

Since moving to East Anglia, Miles Mortimer had heard the expression "Normal for Norfolk". He had assumed it was a local joke, but he was beginning to think he could be wrong. The girl's behaviour would have been considered bizarre anywhere else.

§

'I found it; I know where it is. I was right, it *is* Somersham Court!' Lucy burst into the studio, disrupting the calm atmosphere her brother Adrian cherished. He patiently put the cleaning swabs he was using down on the table beside him. Before he could reply, she said,

'I'll put the kettle on, make tea and tell you all about it.' With that, she left the large airy studio room as fast as she had entered.

Adrian loved his twin sister, not identical in every way but bonded through birth and life experiences. She was as extroverted as he was introverted. Her colouring was as Italian as their father's, whilst his was as English as their mother's; Lucy was passionate and vibrant, whereas he was quiet and thoughtful. But despite their differences, they had a fierce protectiveness for each other. They often disagreed, both stubborn and opinionated, but all quarrels were put aside if either was in trouble.

The tea arrived, two teapots, one with Earl Grey in it and the other containing Assam, they couldn't even agree on what type of tea to drink. They had tried half-and-half, by mutual agreement; it tasted horrible.

'I took the Land Rover and drove down the track from the road to the other side of the house. The garden gate was padlocked and looked too rickety to climb over.' She gulped down a large mouthful of strong Assam tea. 'But I stood on the back of the Landy, tied a rope to that extendable ladder you left in the back, lowered it over the wall and climbed over!' There was a triumphant note in her voice. She waited for his applause.

It did not come.

'So if you were spotted, then it is my registration number that the police will identify and me who has to offer an excuse for trespass.'

Lucy ignored his comment. 'Well it is the right place, if you stand near the house on the southeast corner and look out, it is right: the edge of the house, the iron gate, even a statue of a stag. The only thing that isn't quite right is, you can't see clearly over the wall.' Lucy's face crumpled with annoyance; she did not like inconsistencies.

'Maybe the view is from a higher window?' Adrian offered.

'Yes. I should have tried to get inside.'

Adrian made a resigned sort of laugh and suggested that adding housebreaking to trespassing was going a bit too far to prove the provenance of a painting. He pointed out that the auction for the property was only in a few days maybe the new owners would give her permission to investigate rather than risking breaking her neck over the wall. But he was quietly excited about his sister's exploits.

'Well, let's see if you are right.'

§

Miles had decided to sit apart from his lawyer at the auction house. He had not wanted to bid himself as he didn't trust himself to stick to his limit. So he sat by himself at the back, but with a clear sight line of his representative. The auction room in Ipswich was full, though not as packed as it used to be; COVID-19 social distancing put paid to that despite the government's recent downgrade of the alert system. The chairs had been moved closer to accommodate more people, but this had been unnecessary as many were happy to stay at home and bid online. There were spare seats near him, including the one to his immediate left.

Miles had arrived early and, having read the catalogue from start to finish, was doodling on the front. His mother, whilst thinking him an idiot, had phoned earlier to wish him well at the auction and pointed out that the date being 24th June was Midsummer Day: one of the traditional quarter days when rents were collected and properties were bought and sold.

The chair nearest to him suddenly took on a life of its own as a latecomer collapsed into it. A handful of papers escaped her hands and slid across the floor, scattering on the polished wooden surface. Without thinking, Miles got up and started to gather them together, his attention caught by the late arrival's footwear, beautifully tooled and stitched leather cowboy boots with silver bits on the toes and around the heels. *Completely incongruous with the place, outrageously over the top and yet rather magnificent*, he thought.

Miles straightened up and turned to see that the owner of the boots had been watching him.

'I see you are admiring my boots. Or are you just showing bourgeoisie disapproval?' she challenged him.

Before he could reply, the auctioneer called the room to silence, giving him the opportunity to think of a response.

'I think they are unusual, but I wouldn't be seen dead in them!' He had meant it to sound flippant, but it didn't come out right and he mentally winced at the sound of his voice.

'They wouldn't fit you. Besides, they already are a dead man's boots,' she retorted.

The auction started with lower-valued houses. In the room was a cross-section of bidders including seasoned developers and young couples hopeful of buying a property in their limited price range. What Miles found saddening was some of the reasons for selling such as repossessions and probate cases. The object of his interest was not dissimilar: probate for an elderly lady who had soldiered on in the house living in a limited number of rooms for years and leaving the rest of the house to sink into genteel decay.

There was a break in the auction.

'Are you here to bid for anything particular?' Miles asked the boot-clad woman.

'No. I want to find out who buys the property I am interested in,' came the bland reply.

'Next, Somersham Court, a fine Queen Anne house,' the auctioneer's loud voice ended the break. 'The details are in the brochure. There has been a lot of interest in this property…' The auctioneer's following words were lost to Miles due to the rather loud muttering next to him.

'Bollocks! It isn't Queen Anne, it is early Georgian, in the style of William and Mary.'

'And you would know because…?' Miles asked.

'Because I know what I am talking about.'

Miles ignored her, his eyes fixed on the back of his lawyer's head. He could see he had joined the bidding as the auctioneer's eyes kept flicking backwards and forwards between the interested parties. Miles could hardly breathe. He hadn't realised just how much he wanted this decrepit house. After what seemed an interminable amount of time, the hammer came down.

'Sold to…' The auctioneer leaned forward and looked directly at Miles' lawyer who had done the bidding.

'Mortimer.' Loud and clear was the response.

Miles leant back in his chair, both excited and daunted in equal measure. He noticed that his "knowledgeable" cowboy boot wearer had just written *Mortimer* on the top of the catalogue as well as the hammer price. Then it dawned on him.

As he stood up to leave, he leant towards her and in a quiet measured voice said, 'Next time you want to visit, try knocking on the front door rather than climbing over the wall. Besides, it's a better view from the rooms upstairs.' With that, he walked out.

'Shit, shit, shit,' Lucy muttered under her breath and picked up her shoulder bag. Without stopping to think, she jumped to her feet and rushed outside.

She looked up and down the pavement trying to spot him. Then she noticed him with a companion, just turning into an office block at the end of the street.

She sprinted along the pavement, frantically waving at people to get out of her way and barged through the front doors to a very plush reception area, just in time to see him standing by the lift.

'Wait, wait, please, I have to talk to you.'

The buzzer announced the lift had arrived. Miles indicated that his companion should go up without him. 'Yes?'

'Look, I'm sorry I climbed over the wall. But that's no reason for you to get arsey with me as you didn't actually own the place at the time.'

An interesting form of an apology, thought Miles.

'I am trying to research the provenance of a painting and I needed evidence about its setting.'

Miles did not respond.

'I think, I need to be higher up to get the angle right.' She was getting the cold stare treatment, and it was beginning to work.

'Phone and we can discuss this further, and if necessary make an appointment for you to visit, when I would expect you to be punctual and come to the front door.' He handed her a business card.

She wanted to tell the supercilious, rich bastard where to put his card but restrained herself. 'Thank you.'

She was still holding the card when she left the building. Barely reading it, she snorted with derision, but just as she went to throw it in a litter bin mounted on a streetlight, she changed her mind and put it in the hip pocket of her jeans.

A couple of days later, when Adrian was sorting the washing out into piles by colour and temperature, he checked the pockets of her jeans. Too many times all sorts of weird and wonderful things had failed to survive the cycles of a cotton wash because of her tendency to stuff everything into her pockets, especially dog treats. He found the card and put it to one side for safekeeping.

When Lucy saw the card, having been wondering where it had got to, decided it was time to phone. The telephone conversation to arrange the visit had been brief and business-like.

§

Now several days later, Miles was having second thoughts. Why did he agree to it? Why should he care about some painting or other? He had higher priority things to do with his time. However, despite his reservations, he was looking forward to seeing her again.

The previous day, he had been out exploring and strayed over the border into Suffolk and discovered Halesworth with its pedestrianised high street and lots of little shops. There was a somewhat eccentric delicatessen which had a narrow shop frontage, but once inside it was an Aladdin's cave of things to buy. He bought all sorts of cold meats, quiches, cheeses and irregularly shaped bread rolls to be able to offer his visitor for lunch. Knowing his luck, she would be a vegan on a diet, so only bought things he knew he liked in case there were a lot of leftovers.

That morning, he felt unusually nervous. He chose his clothes carefully; he didn't want to look too tweedy in baggy corduroys like something out of a *P.G. Wodehouse* farce, nor did he want to look like a city boy out for the day to antagonise the rustics. He worried that at thirty-eight he was getting too old for jeans.

He waited for her, not even convinced she would turn up, watching out of a window overlooking the driveway, not sure what to expect. In many ways he was not surprised when a pale cream Morris Minor convertible, with its faded red canvas roof folded down, turned in. As well as the driver, the car contained two rather imperious-looking greyhounds sitting upright in their harnesses on the back seat, giving the impression of a pair of querulous great-aunts coming to visit, determined to disapprove of everything. She had asked him on the phone if he would mind her having her dogs with her.

Lucy climbed out of the driving seat and shouted up at Miles, who now stood on the top step by the front door.

'Can I let the dogs out?' Not getting an immediate response, she added, 'Don't worry, they are perfectly docile;

their nuts came off years ago.'

Miles smiled and nodded. What crossed his mind was that he doubted any male managed to hang onto their nuts for any length of time with her around.

'The big brindle is Ozzy and the smaller black and white is called Marble,' she announced, unclipping the harnesses, then pushing the driver's seat forwards to let them out.

Miles watched the dogs trot around making a thorough inspection of the driveway. He was struck by the elegance and effortlessness of their movements, such graceful creatures. He loved dogs, but his London-based work and lifestyle had excluded them from his life, but soon, very soon, that would change. Whilst Miles was admiring the dogs, Lucy had gone to the boot of her car and taken out something wrapped in a felted cloth.

'I really like the Morris Minor.'

'It was Mama's. And it's cheap and simple to run. Also, Adrian hates driving it.'

Miles was taken aback. Who calls their mother that these days? And who the hell is Adrian? *Of course, she'd be married or partnered*, he thought; she is a very attractive woman, if somewhat prickly and defensive. Whoever lived with her would never die of boredom.

They all went inside. The dogs did not like the hall and trotted quickly past the base of the stairs to explore the rooms, still smelling of the elderly previous owner. Miles and Lucy went into the drawing room whose many windows had sunlight streaming through them, despite years of not being cleaned.

She could not be anything else but impressed by the

obvious quality of the building. 'Why did you buy this place?'

'Why did you climb over the wall?

His response rather took her aback; she had expected him to go into a monologue about wanting to restore the house to its former glory and prestige. She had heard it all before.

'I will tell you why I bought the place if you explain why you climbed over the wall.'

Lucy walked over to the mantelpiece and unwrapped a relatively small oil painting set in a non-descript gilt frame from the cloth.

Miles walked over to look at it carefully, then jolted into life. He strode over to the window nearest the corner of the building and stared out.

'Bring it upstairs!' he barked.

Lucy, taken aback by his reaction, picked up the picture and followed.

Miles climbed the main stairs right to the very top of the house into the little tower perched in the middle of the building above the roof line. Lucy had enough experience with old buildings to be very cautious about tramping about on old, neglected floorboards.

'It's a wonderful view, but the belvedere is too high, we need to be on a lower floor,' remarked Lucy.

'The what?'

'Just a fancy name for a room in a tower that allows a 360-degree view of the grounds.'

'OK. Let's go down a level.' With that, he was off, back down the narrow staircase.

'Good God, what is that stink?' Lucy had opened one of rooms.

'Apparently that was the chickens' winter quarters! If you think that's bad, try the one over there. It was used for keeping rescue hedgehogs!'

'Look at this view.' Miles was now in the southwestern room on the first floor, which by comparison only held the smell of a neglected and decaying building. He tried to open the sash window but without success. Layers of paint had sealed the window tight many decades earlier.

'That's it, that's it exactly, well, apart from the state of the garden,' he announced triumphantly.

'That's not all. The woods have changed shape and the tree line is not as long as it is now. I reckon that centuries of felling and replanting have caused that,' Lucy added.

'Obviously, the woodland would look different, but the angle of the wall, the arch over the gate with the monogram over the top, even that stag is in the right place.' He turned from the window and his face was beaming with excitement.

'So what now? You know the subject of the painting, but how do you find out who painted it and why? After all, why would a view be painted from an upper floor room which was probably a bedroom or dressing room?' Miles, an analyst by nature, was firing off the questions without expecting or waiting for answers.

'And there's no signature, only a couple of Roman numerals. Is that unusual?' He stared down at the picture, as though willing it to speak to him.

Lucy was taken aback by his enthusiasm, considering it was about a painting and not some investment opportunity. She had done her research on him: grammar schoolboy with a first at Cambridge, gone into merchant banking and then into specialist fund trading. She had not even tried to understand the strange financial dealings that resulted in such obscene amounts of money changing hands and huge bonuses being paid. None of it seemed real, like a giant game of Monopoly. She had expected him to be cool and calculating, as though playing poker all the time, evaluating every move. Instead, he was standing before her, holding the painting in his hands, grinning. She had failed in her efforts to establish any personal background; he seemed to keep his business life to a minimum in the media and his private life came across as off-limits.

'This is really exciting. Do you fancy some lunch?' He didn't wait for an answer. He handed the painting back to her and headed off down the series of back staircases that took them into the lower ground floor where the kitchen was.

Lucy was excited to see the original flagstone floor still in place and she had started exploring the other rooms when Miles called her.

'It is still quite warm in the sun, so I suggest taking lunch outside. If are you OK with that? There is a bathroom down here if you want it; it's a bit primitive but functional.'

Miles sat at a brand-new wooden table with two long benches on either side. The carefully planned lunch was laid out ready; it just needed the protective cover removed. Lucy wondered which caterer he had used, or if some invisible and silent housekeeper was lurking in the shadows, like Du Maurier's Mrs Danvers.

'This looks wonderful.' Lucy really meant it as she eyed up the roast beef rolls; she hadn't bothered with breakfast and the little individual quiches looked very promising. Ozzy and Marble certainly agreed with her as their long inquisitive noses and greedy eyes appraised the possibility of pickings later.

'I didn't know what you would like. I was worried you might be vegetarian or even worse, vegan.'

'That roast beef looks delicious. Can I have some, please?' Lucy had allayed his fears and his relief was palpable. She helped herself to one of everything but was taken aback when lifting the lid off a bowl to find remnants of the beef, cubes of cheese and broken digestive biscuits. She looked quizzically at him.

'I wasn't sure if the dogs were allowed scraps, but I brought them out just in case.'

'Oh, thank you, they'd love them.' Her words were accompanied by a beaming smile.

Between mouthfuls of food and homemade lemonade, Lucy explained her interest in the place; how Adrian had bought the small oil painting at a local auction because he was taken with the quality of the artist, even if the subject matter was a bit bland. His intention had been to subject it to a gentle restoration with a new frame to sell at a later date at a different auction, hopefully making a decent profit. But he was stumped as to its subject matter and provenance. That was where she came in.

'I'm a researcher, paintings, houses, families, you name it, I can probably ferret out its history.'

'Did you research me?'

'Yes, though I didn't understand all the financial gobbledygook. Also, I couldn't find much about your personal life. I came to the conclusion that you are very wealthy, very clever and very private.'

'Correct on all counts!' Miles then asked her to expand on her research into his house.

Now she was in her element, she went into a monologue about how to "read buildings". He learnt about the difference between vernacular and polite; the idea that a building might be polite rather than rude amused him. He also learnt very quickly not to tease her; she was passionate about her subject and seemed to lose all sense of humour when talking about it. He asked her opinion of Somersham Court.

'First impressions, it's a classical post-Restoration box built probably in the early eighteenth century, taking symmetry to the extreme with its external design and fenestration. Set over four floors, the main rooms are sandwiched by domestic usage, the lower ground floor for food preparation and storage, and the attics for servant accommodation.' Lucy checked that Miles was still listening, then continued.

'The interior is more interesting because, unlike the country houses that preceded it, the rooms are light and airy with high ceilings and they have a flow about them. Under all the grub and grime, there are some interesting original features. The shuttering and panelling look kosher to me, as well as the fireplaces.'

Lucy stopped herself there, then added, 'Personally, I think it looks like a doll's house but once restored, it will be a nice place to live. If you don't mind rattling around like a pea in a whistle.'

'The size of the building is interesting: not large enough for a permanent country residence for the landed gentry; more likely to be a small country retreat that could be managed by a minimum number of servants. Difficult to say without more research. Basically, neither one thing nor another.'

'Are you always this brutal with your clients?' Miles was both intrigued by her assessment and rather miffed by her opinions.

'You aren't a client, and you did ask.'

'What if I was a client and wanted you to do a full research project on this property, would you be a little gentler with your opinions?'

'No.' Lucy answered feeling chastised, which annoyed her.

'Well, if you were to research further, use John Matthews as a starting point; he is believed to have built this place in 1721.' Miles recounted the information given to him by the auction house.

'Wrong.' Lucy had a somewhat triumphant look on her face. She offered him an explanation.

'I was in Norwich Records Office looking for other records, which are proving elusive. But curiosity got the better of me and I looked up the manorial records for Somersham.' Lucy did not go as far as mentioning to Miles that she had spent hours researching the information she was about to casually impart to him. She continued in a nonchalant manner.

'The land was owned by Sir Stanley Jacks in 1719 when it is described as "with a house newly built" but he surrendered it to John Matthews in 1720. Obviously, it doesn't say why.'

'What would make him surrender his house?'

Lucy laughed at Miles' misunderstanding and explained that surrendered just means either sold or inherited, a simple change of ownership.

She glanced down at her watch and was surprised at how

quickly and pleasantly the time had passed. 'I have to go now, but if you *are* interested in me researching the house, I will email you some information about the work I do.'

Lucy opened her car door for Ozzy and Marble to resume their imperious positions on the back seat. Miles and Lucy exchanged pleasantries and Lucy assured Miles that she would not climb over the walls in future.

Miles watched the little car disappear through the gates and turned to look at the house. As though the building could comprehend and reply, he asked,

'Well, Sir Stanley, what did happen here in 1720?'

Chapter Two
Late September 1720

'You are without breeding or social consequence.'

John Matthews' face failed to betray any emotion from the scathing retort. Sir Stanley Jacks' insipid blue eyes glared out of his corpulent florid face hoping to have hit home with his barbed observation. He was disappointed and unnerved by the steely manner of his visitor, who paused before making a reply.

'You are quite correct, sir; I am as you say. However, I am in a position to be of considerable service to you and that is my purpose.' John spoke quietly and calmly, but Sir Stanley interrupted again.

'Damned impertinence! Insisting upon entrance and then suggesting that I should sell my country house to the likes of you!'

'Indeed, it could be considered such. I am willing to leave now if that pleases you; if you have confidence in settling your debts before the bailiffs arrive to arrest you and incarcerate you in the Norwich Debtors Prison within the next few days.'

John Matthews was very certain of his ground; he had in the previous days spoken to the merchant bankers in Norwich and brokered a deal with them. If he concluded a purchase of Somersham Court before the end of the month, they would hold off any incarceration and proceed with legal proceedings to seize Sir Stanley Jacks' assets.

'How dare you speak to me in that tone and with abject falsehoods? You will be the one in prison for slander… peasant.' A large amount of spittle accompanied his final insult.

'Sit down and hold your noise. You know I speak the truth.' John rose from the flimsy brocade-covered chair. He walked across the light airy room and stood by the door, as though to leave. He actually wanted the steward, Carver, to hear, convinced there was a pair of ears in the hall straining to hear every word.

The ageing aristocrat felt panic for the first time. He was not acquainted with John Matthews of Old Manor Farm but was now aware that this sturdily built, middle-aged man in plain but quality country clothing, was privy to his problems.

'Your pride will be the undoing of you and your family and that is of no consequence to me. I have no affiliation. I suggest you listen to my proposal more carefully this time. Your failure to appreciate how beneficial it could be to you will result in my leaving your property, never to be heard from again.' John watched the aristocrat's inalienable sense of superiority seep out of the old man as he slumped into a chair, his long, curled, powdered wig shifting forward over his forehead.

'My understanding is that you borrowed heavily from merchant bankers in Norwich using Somersham Court as collateral. The funds were then invested in the South Sea Company that offered more than substantial, if unrealistic rewards,' started John, but he was interrupted.

'I was not alone in this; Sir Robert Walpole and other

high-ranking members of society were too. Even the King invested! I was wrongly advised; it is not my fault this so-called "bubble" burst.'

'Indeed, sir, many people have lost a great deal of money. Mostly because greed blinded their reason, but most investors only used capital they already possessed.' John doubted that, unlike Sir Stanley, many had borrowed a vast sum against collateral as valuable as Somersham Court. But Sir Stanley, like most people who had been gulled, had not seen through such a scheme, that to get rich that easily was obviously a deceit on a massive scale.

'News of the financial turmoil caused by the South Sea Bubble has reached even Norwich's community of financiers. The situation is simple: your creditors there are calling in their loan. If you cannot pay, you will forfeit Somersham Court and lose your reputation and standing in the county.'

'Who cares what a bunch of country bumpkins think? I do not favour the area. I will return to London. My steward will sort out the details.' Some of Sir Stanley's bluster was returning.

'Do you think your steward will stay in your employ whilst you are in Norwich Prison? Do you think your wife and daughters will be queuing at the gate daily to take you privileges, by which I mean food and make payment to the guards to ensure your safety?'

Sir Stanley just stared at him, so John continued. 'There is a warrant made out to take you to Norwich to attend court where, without doubt, you will be detained until the debt is cleared, unless there is proof of repayment within an acceptable period of time. It is that proof I am offering to you.' John paused to see if Sir Stanley had understood. No haughty reproof, just silence from the armchair. John knew this was the time to force the point home.

'As soon as knowledge of your predicament is known, all your other accounts, such as tailors, dressmakers, wine merchants and suchlike, will cease credit and now press for payment in a very public manner. You need to consider your wife and daughters, who I believe are of marriageable age. Society doors will be closed in your wife's face and if your daughters have advantageous suitors, they will fade away like the morning mist. It is unlikely you will be received at court. So ruin awaits you.' Having knocked his man to the ground, it was time to pick him up and save him from ruin.

'I offer to buy Somersham Court from you, free of any lien or charge, at a reasonable price.'

'Your valuation or mine,' muttered Sir Stanley.

'The valuation will be what the land tax commissioner has given. I assume an assessor has been and the tax paid?'

Sir Stanley shook his head. John could barely keep the delight from his face. 'The price will then be discounted by the outstanding loan and the settlement of the accounts of tradesmen who worked on the property and whose accounts you have refused to pay.'

Before John could continue, Sir Stanley jumped to his feet and shouted, 'I will not pay the local scum! Let them whistle for their money.'

'Then, good day. I cannot do business on that basis.' John turned on his heel and strode out of the door, just in time to see Carver scarper round the bottom of the stairwell out of sight. John was pleased that the conversation had been witnessed, albeit in a clandestine way.

Carver, having regained his composure, reappeared carrying John's tricorn hat and cloak. He handed the hat to John who noticed that the money pressed into the crown was now missing, replaced by a folded piece of paper. The cloak had barely settled on his shoulders when he heard Sir Stanley call him back. He ignored the call and Carver opened the front door, only for Sir Stanley to call again, louder and more insistent.

'I agree to your terms. Can you proceed within the time available?'

'Indeed, sir. I have a draft agreement for you and your man of law to study.' With that, John pulled from the inside pocket of his frock coat several pages of a legal document. He went on to assure that he would make all the necessary arrangements without Sir Stanley having to leave the house; the conveyancing would be conducted at Somersham Court.

'I have one condition. There must be complete discretion about the whole situation and transaction. I must have your word on this matter.'

'I assure you, Sir Stanley, you do. As you pointed out, I do not have breeding nor social consequence, but I do have integrity and a social conscience.' With that, John turned his back on Sir Stanley and left through the front door.

What John could not see was the venomous look on Sir Stanley's face, nor hear the muttered threat to bring John Matthews down and make him regret his insufferable impudence.

Carver held John's horse whilst he mounted. Picking up the reins, he leant forward to flick a strand of the mane into position, when Carver took the opportunity to address John, unnoticed from the house.

'Everything you asked for is in the note,' Carver muttered.

'Well, I will keep that under my hat!' John's attempt at humour fell flat.

§

The horse seemed to sense the adrenalin still pumping around John's body and instead of its usual calm manner, it kept breaking into a bouncy trot and shying at invisible things in the hedgerow.

'Steady on, Parsifal, it's been a difficult afternoon; I don't require my teeth shaking loose.' He stretched out his hand and stroked the animal's neck until a steady rhythmic walk was re-established.

It was only then that John felt he was distant enough from Somersham Court to reveal what really was under his hat. He looped Parsifal's reins over his arm and inspected the inside of his tricorn hat. Indeed, the coins he had lodged inside had gone and they had been replaced by a piece of paper. Despite knowing he was alone, John double-checked: no other traveller on the bridleway, no sounds of carts or human voices. He opened out the paper. There, in Carver's neat handwriting, was a list of all Sir Stanley Jacks' creditors and the approximate value of his debts.

Despite this useful intelligence, Sir Stanley's scornful words had hit their mark. John had no ambitions for himself, but his eldest son, Thomas, could easily make the transition from yeoman farmer to country gentleman. Thomas had the education, the easy society manner combined with a natural wit and charm that would allow him to move into a higher social status. Somersham Court was not for John and his wife, Alice, it was for the next generation: Thomas and Constance and onwards, with Joseph their son. The time was right, it was the early eighteenth century and values were changing. Whilst lineage and connections were still paramount, merchants and traders were becoming wealthier than their landed counterparts and many a titled gentleman was taking a daughter of a wealthy merchant for a good dowry.

'Well, Parsifal, if this afternoon was stressful, I have yet to face Alice with this venture.' The horse snorted as though in sympathy, but more likely in reaction to John's heels in his flanks to speed up.

§

'Husband, are you out there in this cold air?'

John Matthews was indeed out in the twilight of the day, sitting on a bench in the orchard under an apple tree whose fruit had all been gathered in and put to dry for the winter by his prudent wife, Alice, who was now calling to him. He just wanted to listen to the sounds of the early evening and enjoy the smells of the land around him. He understood the language of the land, the calls of the birds and the indications of change in weather patterns. Old Manor Farm was where he had been born and lived with his family, but his horizons were widening.

'Aye, here under the apple tree.' He reached for his pipe and pouch when he heard her call again. He filled his pipe with fine Virginian tobacco, one of the few indulgences he allowed himself. The smoke from his pipe had a fine aroma. Alice had never found it pleasing, yet her own mother had enjoyed the occasional pipe herself. He smiled and thought fondly of his mother-in-law, a woman toughened by life and the hard work that had put her in an early grave.

'Come inside, the parlour fire is alight. What ails you?'

'Alice, bring your shawl and come sit with me, I would talk to you, I have need of your company.'

Alice detected the weariness and worry in his voice, so instead of arguing took her thick woollen shawl, wrapped it around her shoulders and walked out hesitantly into the semi-darkness. John stood and walked towards her to take her hand and guide her to sit beside him. He looked at his dear wife, not a business-minded person but so aware of the wickedness of the world and the failings of human nature. He felt compelled to share his news with her first as he hoped she would not question his decision, nor scold him. After thirty-four years of marriage, he still needed her understanding and support more than any other person.

'We live in times of great change, and we have to adapt,' he started tentatively, not sure where to begin.

Alice jumped in, 'I know, husband. You mean what kind of topsy-turvy world we do live in when our sovereign cannot speak a word of English.' Her indignation was clearly heard in her voice.

'No, Alice, I do not think that our foreign king only speaking German affects our lives. But if it makes you happy, I will avoid inviting King George to dine with us!' He turned his face to make sure she knew he was not mocking her, just jesting.

'We have good lives, we have two strong sons, a grandson, a good home and our health.'

Alice was painfully aware that he had glossed over their other two children, Martha and Henry, who lay in their cold graves but a mile away. An involuntary shiver ran through her body.

'Alice, are you cold?'

'No. I recall 1709.' It was all she needed to say. Those who had experienced the Great Frost in the early months of that year would not forget the toll it took on lives and livelihoods. There was a brief mutual silence as the grief surfaced once again.

John spoke first. 'We have made good money from trading ventures, from our tenants and the land, not forgetting the sale of grain through Yarmouth that made us a tidy profit last year.'

Alice was not impressed by him taking credit for what had been their younger son Daniel's work and certainly no thanks to the lazy indolence of her eldest son, Thomas.

'I am about to acquire a house as an investment.' John just got to the point; he was getting cold. He wanted to tell his wife separately from the household, but her impatience had started to show. He continued.

'Do you recall Sir Stanley Jacks? Owns land over Somersham way? Well, he has had a new house built. In the latest style with windows everywhere!'

Alice shook her head. She had no time for fancy folk, she being a yeoman's wife, however successful and wealthy her husband might be. She knew her station in life and was content with it.

'The fool went and borrowed money to invest in the South Sea Company thinking he would double, even treble, his investment. The company has crashed; his shares are worthless. In fairness, he was influenced by the likes of Robert Walpole and many other high-ranking personages.' What John really thought was that they had all been lambs to the slaughter, as a few select shepherds had thoroughly fleeced them. He allowed himself a slight smirk at his farming metaphor.

'Robert Walpole? He who brought disgrace on Norfolk some years back, I remember, you told me he was even sent to the Tower of London,' Alice interjected.

John felt this was neither the time nor the place to try to explain the intricacies of politics between the Whigs and Tories. So he ignored her comment.

'The situation is that Sir Stanley cannot meet his creditors' demands here in Norfolk, nor can the obligations he has to complete Somersham Court be met.'

'Well, he has other houses, other wealth. My thoughts are with the poor honest men who have provided goods and services. What about them? They are without blame and now without money.' Alice folded her arms across her body in righteous indignation.

'Indeed. So I have struck a deal with Sir Stanley. In exchange for the full title of Somersham Court, I will settle all outstanding debts, meet his commitments and give him a balance of coinage.' John waited for Alice's admiration and approval.

'John Matthews, you have lost your wits. I'll hear no more

such nonsense! You tell him on the morrow that you have changed your mind. Dear God, have we not already got a fine house and home? What would we want with another?' With that, she took to her feet, lifted her skirts clear of the now dampening grass and returned to the house, like a startled hen into the coop at the sight of a fox.

John was a little exasperated that his wife had not stopped long enough for him to explain that they would not be living there, it was to be leased out for additional income. He rose and followed her into the house. Nothing more was said about the subject, other than he assured Alice he would better explain in the morning.

§

Whilst John Matthews had been sitting in his orchard reflecting on his day's business, Martin Carver was hiding Matthews' coins amongst his possessions, keeping one to spend on himself. Knowing that Sir Stanley was dining with friends that night, he informed the housekeeper he was out about some personal business that evening.

He strode out in the cooling autumn air towards the village inn. There would be good pie, passable beer and, best of all, the sight of Sally Smith's ample bosom to welcome him.

''Evening! Getting chilled now the nights draw in.' Martin played down his Scottish accent to avoid too many questions about his background. The locals knew he was Sir Stanley's steward, but he was liked despite being an incomer as Carver appeared to be a fair and straightforward person. As long as he uttered, "Who will join me?" on an occasional basis, then the regulars were more than happy not to ask too many questions and just sup their free beer.

Carver, whose full name was Martin Carver Macgregor, was a Highlander and born into a clan so ill-favoured that a hundred years previously King James VI made it illegal to even use the surname. Martin was not initially drawn into nationalistic fervour like his brothers and distant cousin, the infamous Rob Roy. Martin had been a reluctant member of the Jacobite army that made an incursion into England as far as Preston in 1715, which ended in surrender to the English Government forces. Martin knew as a Macgregor he would have to flee to save his life as other prisoners may get pardons, but he would certainly not. Quick-witted, cunning and a good horseman, all he needed was a change of clothes and a fit horse, both of which he acquired without the English owner's permission and headed south.

Five years later, he was sitting on a bench in an inn in East Anglia, with coin in his pocket and even more coin in his savings.

Sally delivered the plate of steaming rabbit pie to his table. Leaning forward, she smiled encouragingly as her ample assets threatened to spill out of her bodice.

'Come sit with me, Sally, tell me all your news.' Martin patted the bench beside him. It never failed to amaze him the amount of intelligence that could be gained from the garbled chatter of a barmaid who loved to eavesdrop. His skill was filtering out the irrelevant and recognising the nuggets of gold; a skill he had honed over the years and made some useful coin over the years with one goal in mind.

Sally sat beside him, possibly a little too close for comfort judging by the stern looks from her father, the innkeeper. But her father thought a man with a steady steward's job would be a good catch for his daughter, so he reined in his paternal concerns.

Sally chattered away, sipping beer from his tankard and refilling it from the jug on the table. She had nothing new to tell him. He felt weary and wanted his bed, preferably alone. He had spent most of the early hours of the morning going through the account books in Sir Stanley's parlour, making a summary of his financial position. He was ready to sleep.

He took his leave of the inn; Sally came rushing out after him to scold him for leaving early. He obliged her with a good kissing, a bold squeeze of her bottom and a promise of more in the future.

§

True to his word the following day after breakfast, John, trying not to heed Alice who sat stony-faced concentrating on the sewing in her lap, called his family to the hall. Thomas had informed his wife Constance that this was family business and that women had no part to play. Constance was grateful not to be included but did wonder if Thomas dared exclude his mother in such a high-handed manner.

John spoke to his two sons, Thomas and Daniel, and their mother, Alice. Their reactions were as he expected, given their natures. Thomas took some cruel delight in another man's misfortunes, whilst feeling privately relieved that he had been unable to raise funds to invest in the "cannot lose" South Sea Company. Unlike his younger brother, Thomas was envisaging an elevated social life and his advancement in society.

Daniel was unconvinced at first by his father's decision, disgruntled, like his mother, that there had been no discussion on the merits of the deal or its impact on the other revenues. However, he could see that leasing out the house to create income with only an agent to employ had considerable merits though he feared having so much capital tied up in one venture.

John explained clearly to both Thomas and Daniel that the financial arrangements made with Sir Stanley were to remain privy to the parties. Despite this later that day, Thomas had his horse saddled and he rode out to pay a visit to Lady Adele Edgerton and take tea, her husband being unexpectedly at home that day had thwarted their true intentions. Unbeknown to him, Lord Edgerton's presence had prevented Thomas from sharing his exciting news with the biggest tittle-tattle trader in the county. He might have learnt the secrets of the lady's body, but he had never had the wit to see her true nature. Nor did he know that if he had broken his promise of confidentiality, the rapid social and financial advancement planned for him would have ended there and then.

As soon as his father had finished sharing his plans, Daniel made some excuse about visiting a tenant whose plough horse was lame. As for Alice, she left the room and went silently to her realm, the pantry and buttery, where the job of laying down enough provisions for the winter was uppermost in her mind.

John took himself off to the parlour and guided by the

intelligence provided by Carver, formulated his plans and incorporated them into the agreement on his terms. When he had completed his task, he drew a chair up close to the fire now rekindled with a couple of logs. He pulled out his pipe and unfolded a letter received that day. Before he reread it, he reflected on Daniel's concerns about having so much of the family's fortune tied up in one investment. He knew Daniel was right and the contents of the letter might be a start to some further financial diversity more to Daniel's liking.

The letter was from David Parker, a relative on the maternal side of his family. He lived on the Suffolk and Norfolk borders in the large village of Fressingfield. Like John, he was a yeoman farmer with a good amount of land. David's pride and joy was his flock of Norfolk Horn sheep from which he gained a return from the sale of the wool to the local weavers of worsted cloth and the sale of the sweet mutton. David and John had corresponded recently about how to improve their flocks, especially the killing-out weights. David had bought some new Ryland sheep from Leicestershire and in the letter invited John to visit to assess them, and to bring Daniel with him if he could be spared.

John decided to accept the offer once the Somersham Court surrender was complete.

CHAPTER THREE
Early September 2020

The conveyancing complete, Somersham Court had finally been transferred into Miles Mortimer's name.

He sat at his makeshift desk in the small cottage that formed part of the stable block. The house was going to be uninhabitable whilst the builders were working and the cottage, formally used as a holiday let, made a temporary bolt hole.

Miles opened his laptop and keyed in the actual costs of the purchase against the estimates, relieved there was little difference. The restoration was a different matter. Miles had never undertaken such a project in his life. His money market experience was of little use now, other than to generate the funds to pay for it. This situation made him feel vulnerable. He knew what he had to do: talk it through with his new "friend", Stan, who never interrupted nor contradicted him.

It was a cold day; the wind was from the northeast straight from Siberia. A local had told him that the winds in East Anglia were "lazy" as they didn't go round you, they went straight through you! He walked round the front of the house and across the forlorn gardens to Stan the Stag, who was where he had been for the last three hundred years, staring back at the house.

'Well, Stan, what do you think? I have a dilemma; I am

way out of my comfort zone here. Yes, I have engaged a firm of specialist builders and am paying through the nose for their expertise; I have the listed building conservation officer only too willing to give his opinions; I dismissed the architect, couldn't take any more of his brilliant yet unrealistic ideas and the surveyor and his arse-covering caveats are driving me nuts. All I want to do is restore the building to its original state but with all the home comforts of the twenty-first century. Is that too much to ask?'

Stan remained as silent as the stone he was carved from.

'I will get your broken antler mended but before those more important things like the roof, the plumbing and suchlike. I just don't know enough to know if the estimates are fair or I am having my leg lifted, to coin a phrase.' Miles wandered around the base of the plinth whilst he talked to himself. He stopped to look through the arched gateway and remembered the sight of the ponytailed woman climbing over the wall. Then the answer came to him.

'Thanks, Stan, great idea! I will phone that strange young woman with the painting. She appears to know a lot about building history and the local area. I can't imagine anyone daring to bullshit her.' Miles knew it was a sensible idea to make use of local resources, but whether he could cope with her bluntness… Only time would tell.

He found her number easily; she and Adrian had a website offering art restoration and historical research services. He spent some time looking at the website; it was stylish and impressive and gave him confidence in her ability to do a professional job.

He phoned and Lucy picked up. Before he could speak,

she launched into a defensive monologue.

'I know I haven't finished the estimate and sent the email, if that's what you're chasing. I have clients and commitments that make demands on my time.' What she really meant was that she hadn't taken him seriously.

'Hey, don't jump down my throat. I'm not chasing you for the proposal. Quite the reverse.' Miles couldn't help but chuckle as he spoke. Before he could continue, she said,

'Got bored with the idea now?' Lucy was shocked by her response. She was well aware of her directness, but she could not understand why she felt so defensive.

'I was going to offer you a job, but I'm beginning to think it wouldn't be a good idea.' Miles was not impressed with her attitude, but he needed help and he did rather like her. 'If you would do me the courtesy of listening before you interrupt again, I will explain. I *do* want to know about the house's history, but not now. What is more important is the work on the house, now and in the future.' Miles paused.

There was no interjection, so he continued.

'I want to hire you as a historic buildings expert; I want you to be my advisor when dealing with the builders and the surveyor, who speaks a foreign language to me. But most important of all, to keep under control that snotty-nosed little conservation officer who seems to know a great deal about bloody nothing!' Miles realised that she probably knew who he meant.

'Do you mean the little grey man? Grey skin, grey hair, grey suit, grey shoes and a grey Skoda?' Lucy could barely suppress a giggle.

'That's him.'

'He's an arrogant little man, way out of his depth. His head of department, who was very knowledgeable and reasonable, has just retired. Unfortunately, the grey man has been promoted above his capabilities. I've had several head-to-heads with him and won each one! Remind me to tell you about one of his ridiculous circular demands that nearly derailed a restoration near Fressingfield.'

'Can we meet?' No sooner had the words left his lips, than he doubted their wisdom.

They arranged to meet the following day.

§

'I'm in here. Come *parlez* in the parlour!' Miles had to project his voice to carry above the noise of workmen and their incessant radios. He had asked them why they had to have each radio tuned to a different channel and so loud. The reply was both obvious and annoying: they were in different rooms; they like different radio stations and they needed to have it loud because of the noise they were making. Miles consoled himself that it wasn't for ever.

Lucy strode into the smaller of the reception rooms. 'What a bloody racket, how do you put with it?'

'I just filter it out.'

'Anyway, I've got lots to tell you.' She paused, noticing that she didn't have his full attention. 'What are you doing?'

'I am crosschecking the workmen's timesheets with the builder's invoices and trying to make sense of why these demands for money are so high and so frequent.' Miles did not take his eyes off the paperwork in front of him straightaway but placed a ruler between the documents to mark his place. He looked up to see the amused look on Lucy's face. *Cheeky cow*, he thought, *she thinks I am running out of money.*

'Why are you cross-checking everything?'

'In my time working in the City of London, I learnt never to leave anything to chance. As the saying goes, the devil is in the detail. Also, I'm out of my comfort zone with the restoration work, so I'm being doubly cautious.' What he meant was that he thought he was being milked as an ignorant, super-rich plonker from London.

'I could help, if you like, by checking the work they say they have done. At least you will know if the worksheets are genuine.' Lucy knew what Miles was thinking; he was concerned that his enthusiasm and bank account were being taken advantage of. Then she saw the look on his face which she misinterpreted as him being doubtful about the idea.

She was furious. 'Well, I am a bloody sight more qualified than you! You probably didn't think it important enough to remember that I am a buildings historian.'

Miles suppressed the need to laugh, especially when he saw her aggressive stance and challenging glare. 'Steady, tiger. Even a condemned man gets the right to have the last word!'

She did not react.

'I hadn't forgotten. I don't know why I was subject to that outburst; I was just about to ask you to help but wasn't sure if you would be offended if I offered to pay you. But candidly, you are so sodding prickly and quick to offend, I couldn't make up my mind what to say next.' He paused, then sighed heavily. 'So... convince me of your qualifications and tell me your terms and conditions.'

Lucy was furious with herself for losing control and her fragile self-confidence was fading by the second. 'Sorry, I don't think it would be a good idea. I'm a fraud. I failed to complete my master's degree; never got past the 1750s as I bailed out halfway through.'

Miles could see the aggression melting, but the nervous energy was still there, making her shake. 'Let's go for a walk, away from this noise, and talk properly.'

§

When Lucy started work a few weeks later, Miles' initial concerns were proved wrong: she was a godsend. He had worried that her hot-headed personality would cause more problems than it solved. But he had enjoyed overhearing her cleverly win an argument with the builder who had now realised that her depth of knowledge of building techniques and history far surpassed his. The team of workmen had also enjoyed her besting their boss with her expertise, as Sean Mitchell could be an arrogant sod to work for. She scrambled up scaffolding and clambered across roofs to evaluate the problems and offer suggestions, made tea and even brought her homemade cakes for everyone.

She was so successful that it made Miles feel superfluous to requirements. He did the money transfers to suppliers and Sean; Lucy did everything else. Once Sean knew that Lucy went through his "time and materials" invoices in detail, the totals seemed to reduce. For Miles, one bonus was that Ozzy and Marble could not shimmy up ladders, nor did they know the difference between ashlar and asphalt. So the hounds thoroughly enjoyed themselves pottering around the grounds or being curled up in Miles' office, snoring and silently breaking wind.

A few weeks later on a quiet Wednesday afternoon, Miles had been distracted from his research, not money-making ideas but deerhound puppies for sale, when the door was flung open and Lucy shouted,

'You've got to come and see what I've found!'

Miles did not instantly move, only stared at her. Then thinking there might have been a dreadful accident and that someone had fallen off the scaffolding, he jumped up and nearly fell over the two, now animated, greyhounds.

'Come on, quick, come now.' Lucy was already out of the door and heading towards the house.

Miles followed her as fast as he could whilst retrieving his mobile from his jacket pocket, expecting to have to contact emergency services. Lucy bounded up the outside steps two at a time, then stopped and turned.

She bellowed at him, 'The back staircase, first floor.'

When Miles arrived, there was no dead or dying workman, no blood or gore, just Lucy on her knees carefully pulling out what looked like paintings wrapped in cloth from a gap in the wall.

'Come and look what I've found. Under all the layers of wallpaper, there's a small cupboard under the stairs. The handle must have been removed and the space papered over.'

'What made you suspect it was there?' Miles thought this a reasonable question.

'It's obvious that there was a cavity under the stairs.' Lucy was surprised he hadn't known.

'Why would anyone hide the paintings?'

'I reckon a long time ago, someone couldn't decide what to do with them, or just didn't like them. Then at a later date, the door was just papered over an unwanted storage space without checking inside.' Lucy made it sound like this was an everyday thing.

'Remember I told you about a restoration project in Fressingfield? Well, they found a boarded-up cavity that had once been a cupboard, next to an inglenook fireplace in the main bedroom. It contained several, now illegal, guns and the records for a local cricket club in the 1920s. Judging by the statistics, they were a really crap team.'

'What did they do?'

'Put the guns into feed sacks and took them to a local gunsmith who quietly chopped them up!'

'Surely they should have taken them to the police?'

Lucy gave him a withering look. 'Yes, these guns were dangerous; if you tried firing one you were likely to have half your face blown off. But that's not the point. The cavity needed opening up to check for rot or potential of leaking pipes, even dangerous materials like lead, asbestos or some such.'

Miles nodded his head in acknowledgement and refrained from commenting that if Lucy had thought there was a possibility of asbestos being present, she should have been wearing protective clothing.

He now watched her carry the large bundle effortlessly over to a trestle table and very gently unwrap three different-sized paintings, two of which had been removed from their frames. The largest one was a typical early eighteenth-century composition of the family, favourite dog and of course the ultimate status symbol, the country house. It was clearly Somersham Court in the background.

Miles and Lucy stood fascinated. The next was a medium-sized portrait of a boy and a greyhound accompanied by a separate gilt plaque with the title *Somersham Boy*, no other details.

It was the smallest picture that caught their attention. Lucy and Miles turned and looked at each other in amazement until Lucy broke the silence.

'It's another one, just like my painting, same size and style, but the view is into the wood from your meadow with a packhorse and two men leaving the wood. They must be part of a series of paintings.'

Very gently she wiped the face of the picture with her sleeve and then squawked with excitement. 'Look, look, it's got Roman numerals in the corner, just like mine.'

She stared at Miles, looking for a reaction.

He seemed to be struck dumb. 'Maybe they're dates? Your picture reads "twenty-one" and "five"; this one is "nine" and "five". Could it be that one was painted on the twenty-first of May and the other on the ninth?'

'Possibly,' Lucy replied. She thought it sounded nonsense but could not offer a better solution. 'Bugger, I have to go away for a couple of days. Could you take them to Adrian to clean them up?'

Miles did not think it the right time to point out that the paintings had been found in *his* house and were now his property. It was not up to her to decide what to do next.

'Of course,' he replied.

A couple of days later, having stopped by the temporary traffic lights by the Old Manor restaurant, Miles glanced over at the Elizabethan house. It was a large, attractive timber-framed house with black beams built in a haphazard pattern that contrasted with the pale and weathered East Anglian pink lime render.

Before the lights could change, he looked at the building again, it appeared to be in the shape of an H, the gable ends not quite the same size as each other. In fact, he thought, nothing is symmetrical about the place. So different from Somersham Court, yet beautiful and timeless. He thought about Lucy and wished she had been with him to give him chapter and verse on its possible history.

'If only you had a voice and could tell the secrets of the generations of people who have lived beneath your roof,' he muttered aloud. The sharp sound of a car's horn behind him announced that the lights had changed. His mind turned to that morning's telephone conversation with Adrian.

'My name is Miles Mortimer and I…'

The disembodied voice on the other end interrupted. 'Yes, I know who you are and I know where you live.'

Miles found his response rather sinister. 'No doubt Lucy has told you about the paintings that were found. I would like you to evaluate them. Could you come over?'

'No. Lucy has the Land Rover in Kent and I can't fit them safely in the Morris Minor.'

'Could I bring them to you?' Talking to Adrian was

like "drawing teeth" as Miles' father would have said. But after further brief exchanges, they agreed on 3 o'clock that afternoon.

So Miles found himself in the middle of nowhere trying to follow Adrian's directions relative to his satnav. Adrian's were more descriptive than functional; Miles didn't really need to know that the pub on the corner of the junction before the village is where the local bowls club met, but he thought it was worth noting that the pub apparently did excellent ham sandwiches.

Miles was curious to meet Adrian. It wasn't just the paintings; he wanted to find out what sort of person could cope with being Lucy's partner. He wondered if he had been neutered like Lucy's greyhounds! Adrian had the same Suffolk burr to his accent as Lucy, but the delivery was noticeably slower; Lucy spoke rapidly like a Gatling gun on full chat whereas Adrian spoke in careful measured tones. Miles had been warned that just because someone speaks slowly, it doesn't mean they are slow-witted; far from it. Many people moving to East Anglia had made that mistake.

Miles glanced at the clock on the dashboard; he was going to be early, which to him was as bad-mannered as being late. He pulled into a parking space in front of the village church, a great barn of a place probably built during the wool wealth of years ago when church attendance was compulsory and the clergy enjoyed considerable financial contributions in Norfolk and Suffolk.

He looked at the pub and imagined the ham sandwiches, great slices of ham cooked on the bone between thick "doorsteps" of bread with loads of English mustard. His stomach rumbled painfully at the thought. He should have had lunch earlier.

He had some time to kill. Unplugging his mobile from its cradle, he considered making some calls. Instead, he just held it in his hand and thought about the call from his former work colleague, Leonie, that morning. He had emailed her the previous day, making general enquiries about life and the universe for her and his former colleagues. His phone rang in his hand: Leonie. It was good to hear her strong, confident Cockney voice so full of intelligence and life. There were the usual office politics: Mark's wife had had a baby girl and they were all sick to death of looking at endless baby photos on his phone. She said there was a limit to how many times you could get away with, "Ah, bless!"

Leonie could no longer talk about industry news as he was not part of the team and she, regretfully, was no longer his researcher. After some general conversation about the restoration work, during which he realised it was probably as interesting to Leonie as baby pictures, Miles invited her to come up to Norfolk and see the house. She declined. He should have known better than to ask; it would take a combination of the Great Fire of London, the Black Death and alien invaders to get Leonie to leave her beloved London at a weekend, if at all.

Miles resumed his journey and soon his mobile phone announced that he had arrived at his destination. It was a small bungalow in the middle of nowhere in rather uninspiring flat countryside, with all the hedges grubbed out due to corporate farming greed. Not what he expected at all. A 1970s bungalow with large UPVC windows, about as historically uninteresting as you could find. Why on earth did this couple of obviously artistic people choose to live in such an unremarkable place? He had assumed, quite incorrectly, that it would be a listed cottage, with roses round an ancient door flanked by hollyhocks. It would be like the Victorian painting his parents had in their dining room of a timbered house, a brick pathway leading to the front door of a lovely cottage garden in full bloom. He remembered the signature, Thomas Tyndale, not that he knew anything about the artist.

A young man who came out to meet his visitor, Miles thought him about Lucy's age. His baggy corduroy trousers and Tattersall checked shirt were just visible beneath the large, functional apron, which showed the marks of years of paint. Wiping grubby hands on it, he introduced himself.

'Adrian Albini.' He offered his hand, then thought better of it. 'Come in, come in.'

Miles was so taken aback by the bungalow that small talk evaded him. Realising there had been an embarrassing silence; Miles broke it with a rather inane comment.

'Nice garden, I like the potted herbs.'

Adrian did not bother to turn round but beckoned Miles to follow him down a narrow path beside the house. 'That's Lukie's doing, she is the gardener and cook. Please, come in.'

Adrian opened a side door into a room full of light, colour and smells Miles easily recognised beeswax and turpentine. The studio appeared to be converted from a double garage; very ordinary looking from the front but extraordinary looking from the other side. The rear north-facing wall had been extended and was made up of huge windows whose panels bent back to form part of the roof, filling the room with natural northern light. There were different-sized easels, with small worktables beside them; everything was neat and orderly. A place for everything and everything in its place. The shelves were covered in jars, boxes and things wrapped in oilskin clothes.

'Sorry, Lukie isn't here; I'm sure you would rather talk to her.'

Miles detected a slight waspishness about his tone and feared that he might be getting in the middle of a domestic crossfire, but his curiosity got the better of him.

'Why do you call her Lukie?' Miles had thought he had misheard the first time, but that is certainly what he heard the next.

'Oh, I forget it's a pet family name. Everyone else knows her as Lucy. Her full name is Lucretia, but it's a brave person who calls her that! When I was little, I couldn't pronounce it and Lukie was the nearest I could get.'

'So you've known each other since you were children? When did you first meet?' Miles was amazed; he thought childhood sweethearts were a thing of the past.

'Er, yes.' Adrian was rather taken aback by Miles' ignorant question. He continued. 'I suppose in the womb, but we were never formally introduced; just sort of got to know each other after we were born.'

Adrian now realised Miles hadn't known that he and Lucy were fraternal twins and was grinning at the mistake.

'We are brother and sister. Lucy was born in the Land Rover in Ipswich Hospital's car park, and I was born on the hospital's delivery ward twenty minutes later. You could say she's been bloodymindedly independent from the start. And I have been quietly conventional ever since.'

'Is that the…'

'Yes, it is the old Land Rover she drives today. It was only a couple of years old then and it has been part of the family ever since. A sort of mobile womb she can retreat into.'

Miles was speechless. Adrian's casual way of describing things made the bizarre sound almost mundane.

'But you have different surnames, I know your sister as Lucy Moncreif,' Miles countered weakly. As soon as he spoke, he wished he had kept his observation to himself.

'Our mother was Suffolk born and bred but she was impregnated by an Italian student in Sienna while on an art scholarship. Brought home a couple of buns in the oven and named them Lucretia and Adriano, though please don't ask me why. She adopted our father's surname, Albini, despite him denying any responsibility. However, Lucy changed her name by deed poll some years ago when she was besotted with an older man who wouldn't marry her. Probably because he was already married!' Adrian's voice was cold and mechanical, just a little too controlled for Miles' liking. Miles adjusted his hold on the paintings; they weren't heavy but the purpose of his visit was not to discuss their family history. Adrian noticed his movement.

'Well, let's see these paintings. Bring them in for a closer look.' Adrian pointed to an empty easel. 'Pop the large one on there.'

Miles unwrapped the painting. The natural light made it look even dirtier and more neglected than on first inspection. He suddenly felt rather embarrassed at having brought it.

'Interesting. Stored in a hidden cupboard, I believe? Not

the worst condition I've seen. No obvious tears or cuts. The paint hasn't started to flake off too much. Possibly just a question of carefully stripping the layers of varnish and grime and a little touch-up here and there.' Adrian dragged over a stool on castors and became lost in thought as he pulled on a headset with a range of little magnifying lenses attached.

'Layers of varnish?' asked Miles.

'Oh yes, a common practice in the past. If a painting looked a little tired or lacklustre, rather than painstakingly cleaning it, a new layer of varnish was put on to refresh it. This can happen many times. But it traps the grime underneath.' Adrian continued to scrutinise the picture.

'Judging by the clothes of the sitters and the composition… I would hazard a guess at early eighteenth century. Typical of its type; painted to fill the gaps on the drawing room walls.' He paused, then continued.

'Two notable things: a signature, looks like "Millar" which is more than feasible, and secondly, there are numbers, but too indistinct at present. Even through the layers of grime, it looks like two artists have been at work here.' Adrian rolled the stool even closer, changed the lens on his headset and peered closely at the figure of the child.

'Do you know of an artist called Millar?' Miles' curiosity was thoroughly aroused now.

'Yes. There was a journeyman artist called Clive Millar who did the rounds of the new landed gentry, pumping out pictures of their families, houses and favourite horses and dogs. It was a transition period when a great deal of money was earned from trade and the wealthy merchants who wanted to buy instant heritage.'

'Oh, was he East Anglian?' Miles wasn't sure if Adrian had just made a monumental dig at him but gave him the benefit of the doubt. If it had been Lucy speaking, there would have been no doubt about it.

'I believe he came from the Trimley St Mary area near Felixstowe, but you would have to ask Lucy; she does all the historical research for me.'

'So what do you think?'

'It can be restored without too many problems. It will be time-consuming, which means costly, and the painting still won't be worth much. However, it is more than likely to be of the previous owners or residents of Somersham Court and therefore part of its history. More of interest to a historian than an art collector. Up to you. As for the boy and hound, same artist, but has some nasty cracking, as though the varnishing was not completed properly.'

'But this is the one Lukie and I are interested in.' Adrian picked up the small landscape found in the cupboard.

'Why?'

'I believe it is by the same artist as the view from Somersham Court; not just the quality of the composition and brushstrokes but they both have a Roman numeral where you would expect a signature.'

'Can you prepare me a quote for the restoration and framing of the family group and the boy with the hound? The landscape I want to talk to Lucy about.' Miles got up to leave, but could not resist asking, 'So where is Lucy? Is she likely to be away for long?' He tried to sound nonchalant, only mildly interested in the answer.

'She's staying in a village somewhere in Kent, strange

name, Boughton Mal… something. There's a farmhouse there that was once the wing of a huge Elizabethan manor house. She did some research on the place a few years back and has become friends with the barmy old coots who live there. She also delivered some restored paintings to a client of ours on the way.'

'More family portraits of the eighteenth-century *nouveaux riches*?' Miles couldn't resist the counter-dig.

'Indeed.' That was Adrian's final word on the matter. He walked Miles back to his car, making a mental sneering note of the vehicle's make, age and value.

Just as Miles' car disappeared down the road, his mobile rang.

Adrian recognised the number. 'How did it go?'

'Really well. James and Bunny send their love. The old ducks just love the painting. They can't wait for the next visit from Colin, their son-in-law from hell. They've justified the "cleanings" by telling him that I am doing them as a thank you for allowing me to use their house in a research project.' Lucy was prattling on.

'I've done my bit; it's up to you to arrange the contribution to the roof fund now.'

'All in hand,' replied Adrian rather tersely as Lucy always sounded as though he was likely to forget and needed regular prompting.

'Bunny has sent you some quails' eggs. Hadn't the heart to tell her you don't like them! But I do, so that's OK.' Lucy justified her actions.

Typical, thought Adrian.

'Moneybags Mortimer has just been here.'

'Did he bring his paintings? What do you think of him?'

'Yes. He's all right, but under all that good-natured veneer there is a ruthless bastard.' Adrian did not tell his sister that he found Miles dangerously attractive, for a very good reason.

It was several days later that Adrian started to look at Miles' paintings in detail. He chose to review the largest one first, the large typical family portrait of husband, wife, child and two dogs, with what looked like Somersham Court in a hazy background. He was certain it was by Clive Millar and would get Lucy to do some digging, but there was another hand in this work too. A finer, more naturally artistic hand had overpainted the face of the woman and the whole of the boy. Also, he suspected a child had been sitting on the woman's knee but later removed. Maybe the child had died during the course of the painting; not unlikely given the time period.

Then it dawned on him that he had seen a similar style and technique before and went off to get Lucy's landscape for comparison. There certainly were similarities, but the landscape had a natural feel about it whereas the portrait was very measured and precise; there was a touch of class to the landscape, unlike the mediocrity of Millar's work.

Adrian texted Lucy; it was the way they agreed to communicate when he was working even though he was in the same building.

The bungalow had a simple layout: a large kitchen/dining room; a good-sized sitting room in the middle, which was shared territory; two bedrooms on one side, which gave Lucy somewhere to sleep and a study lined with books and pictures to work in. Adrian's extended garage gave him the studio, next to another bedroom and bathroom. The unwritten rule was no entry to private quarters unless by invitation.

'You rang.' Lucy had lightly knocked on the internal door to the studio and went in.

'Yes. I want to show you something.' Adrian beckoned Lucy over to look carefully.

'Before you do, just to let you know James phoned to say, that just after you left Kent, the sale completed and our money has been transferred. He's excited that the roof repairs can now start. Except Bunny wants to restore the rose garden with the money! Please don't charge them a commission for selling; get your pound of flesh off that fat bastard in Scotland. God knows he has enough to spare! But they will need an invoice for the cleaning and reframing.' Adrian did not respond to Lucy's news as he was still absorbed in comparing the little landscape with the trees in the portrait painting.

'Don't nag; I'll do it later and email it to them,' Adrian replied, rather absent-mindedly.

Lucy laughed out loud.

'I don't think there's an internet connection available to James' typewriter!'

Adrian waved his hand to acknowledge he understood but showed no sign of amusement at Lucy's quip. 'I think your landscape is an apprentice piece done by the same hand that made these alterations.' He pointed at various areas on the larger painting. 'It was quite usual for a journeyman artist to use his apprentice, not just to mix paints and apply varnish, but if they were talented, to use them to paint the backgrounds, sky and suchlike too. Millar was nothing special, so unlikely to be well documented, if at all. But the apprentice is something else. I think I've seen similar work in Suffolk, around the Lavenham area. I'll go back through my paperwork and see if I can find anything useful. I keep thinking Edwards but am not convinced.'

'I'll see what I can find on Millar and an apprentice. Problem is, there are likely to have been more than one,' she concluded.

'I'm beginning to think there is a set of these paintings and they are centred on Somersham Court. But the Roman numerals are baffling. Can we put the two paintings side by side again?'

'Do you think the V indicates there are five in the series?'

Adrian just shrugged his shoulders at her suggestion.

'Adrian, could you look after Ossy and Marble tomorrow? I want to spend some time in Norwich, but don't how long I will be.'

'I suppose so. What are you working on?'

'More details on the surrender of Somersham Court and if I can find any conveyancing records. Miles asked why Sir Stanley Jacks transferred ownership to John Matthews.'

CHAPTER FOUR

Early October 1720

The wheels of the carriage and the hooves of the horses galvanised into action by the whip of the coachman, scattered the small stones on the driveway. The lawyer and his clerk representing Sir Stanley Jacks left Somersham Court for the last time.

John Matthews went back into the house to speak to Carver. There were matters of estate to be attended to, but most important to Carver was the money due to him.

John returned to where he had left his own lawyer, Michael Le Trobe, standing on the steps. They waited in silence for a few minutes until Carver brought their horses round. John instructed Carver to maintain the house with staff brought in from the village, whilst staying on the premises until plans were made for the future. Carver was given a pouch of money and told to account for all expenditures and to settle monies owing to him.

A mile or so away from the house, Michael broke the silence. 'Well, John, are you satisfied with your morning's work?'

John patted the leather satchel strung across his chest and grinned. The satchel contained the deeds to the house and other documents regarding the estate now bearing John Matthews' name as the new owner.

'I have been your friend and lawyer for many years. Permit me to offer advice.' Michael waited for John to object.

Instead, John just looked quizzically at him.

'John, beware. These men of noble birth, money, power and influence are not to be trifled with. They are not as the likes of us. They play by different rules. We know what is right and wrong, even what is within God's laws. Though most of them are honest, some are not. Once you have made one enemy, you will find you have gained a network of unknown, unseen, ruthless vipers.' Le Trobe was seriously concerned for his friend. Seeing no reaction from John he continued.

'Besting Sir Stanley Jacks and taking advantage of his stupidity was a risky venture. He will of course rewrite events and weave them into a tale of falsehoods and deception, and you, John, will not be the hero of the day but the villain.' Le Trobe knew that was only the start of the vile accusations Jacks would spread throughout the trading walks of The Exchange and the salons of the social elite in London to distract his peers from his foolishness.

'Can you imagine him recounting to the lords and ladies of court how a good, honest yeoman farmer saved him from the debtors' gaol in Norwich and the complete ruin of his family? How John Matthews completed the purchase of his folly house only two days before his arrest? I think not.'

'You make your point well, Michael, but why is it important to me? I do not frequent the salons of London; my trade is here in Norfolk and I certainly do not have connections with the court. The people whose good opinion of me I want will know the truth of the matter, so my reputation remains intact, where it is of importance to me.'

The naivety of John's response was not lost on Michael. 'John, Norwich may be many miles from London, but it is still this country's second city. Is it not through your contacts amongst the traders that you knew of Jacks' misfortune? It is Thomas who will suffer; he has aspirations above his birth. It is your ambitions for him that have fuelled this.'

'Enough!' The violence and volume of John's response made both the horses react and throw their heads up in the air, jangling the bits in their bridles. The two men rode in silence to the crossroads from where they would go their separate ways.

'Remember what happened to Icarus!' Michael Le Trobe shouted as he turned his horse's head to the right and urged it to break into a trot. As he rode away, he turned in the saddle and gave a farewell wave.

John held Parsifal in a stand as his mind raced. Did he hear correctly? Who Icarus was or even where he came from, he neither knew nor cared. He assumed he had misheard Michael and just dismissed it from his mind. His concentration was now on visiting the blacksmith.

John's good mood had totally evaporated by the time he neared the forge of Seth Brown. He could hear the rhythmic ring of hammer on molten metal and then the double tap on the anvil before he saw the large forge doors, left wide open to dissipate the heat of the furnace. Seth was quenching a horseshoe in a water bucket beside the anvil. The red-hot metal of a large iron shoe for a plough horse hissed and spat as it hit the cold water. Seth looked up and took the shoe out, resting it on the anvil.

''Afternoon, John Matthews. I had wondered if you would

be visiting your brother-in-law whilst in these parts.' Seth wiped his sweating brow with a filthy-looking rag hanging on a nail. He walked out of the forge into the cooler air of the autumn day.

John led Parsifal over to a tethering ring near a trough of water. 'Why's that, Seth Brown?' John walked towards Seth with his hand outstretched in greeting.

'Rumour has it that Sir Stanley Jacks has quit Somersham Court and the chances of our accounts being settled go with him.' Seth's voice was filled with bitter acceptance. He knew that there was one rule for the rich and one for the poor. Had *he* defaulted on any payments, he would be in a debtors' prison by now.

'Ay, part of that is true, he has gone, but the debts remain here,' John corrected him.

'We need no reminding of that. But if nothing is paid, there will be no bread on our tables, nor new supplies, nor paid men.'

'What if the debts could be paid? If not in full, but a good part?' John suggested.

Seth Brown folded his large, muscled arms across his chest with a snort of derision.

John waited a few seconds so his next words would have maximum impact. 'I know you and others have approached Sir Stanley and were, on his instructions, driven away by his steward, Carver, empty-handed. What if Carver were to visit every one of you with a good proportion of the monies owed?'

'Pigs might fly! Sir bloody Stanley has gone; what does a new owner care?' Seth had work to do and this was a pointless conversation. In normal circumstances, he would have passed the time gladly with his favourite sister's husband. But he needed to make up for lost time and earnings.

'The new owner does care.'

'Oh aye? And you know, how?' Another snort of derision from Seth.

'Because you are looking at him.'

§

Several days later, a subdued cavalcade travelled to Somersham Court, an open carriage with four occupants and two riders on horseback following. The only sounds came from the metal rims of the wooden wheels, the leather harness creaking and the rhythmic beat of the four horses' hooves on the compacted road surface. Each member of the party was lost in their thoughts.

Alice was still cross with John. For the first time in their married life, he had made a huge decision without seeking her views beforehand. She was not impressed that he had wanted to tell her first, the deed already done, rendering her views irrelevant. Her concerns went deeper than that though. John's obsession with Thomas becoming a country gentleman rather than the son of a yeoman farmer had gone too far.

The carriage driver turned the horses' heads to the left and entered a driveway marked by two, large pillars on either side. Each post was topped with a heraldic shield depicting three scallop shells. John made a mental note to have them removed.

'What are they?' Alice pointed to the top of the posts.

'They're from the Jacks' family crest. Sir Stanley was

overly proud of his Norman ancestry and naval connections,' explained John.

'Well, his ancestors would be rolling in their graves if they knew how he turned out!' snarled Alice.

All turned to look at her. For Alice to have a harsh or unkind word for anyone was unheard of.

It was a short driveway compared to other houses of status, but it did not detract from the splendour of the building. The brilliance of the new Portland stone quoins contrasted with the copper red bricks. Most notably, the sun reflected on all the glass in the windows set in a symmetrical pattern on each side of the building.

Alice stared in amazement.

'Here we are.' John stood up in the carriage with a beaming smile. In contrast, Daniel was stony-faced. He failed to mention he had already been there and had formed the opinion that it was a pointless house of no practical use. Daniel was sceptical that anyone would want to live in a purely decorative house with insufficient land to support it.

Alice was about to break her silence with a mighty scolding of her husband for his folly, when a man in his early thirties opened the front doors and walked down the steps.

'Good afternoon, sir and your family.' After a small bow, he continued down the steps to the carriage door and opened it, letting down the carriage footplate.

'Good afternoon, Carver.' John turned to his family now assembled at the foot of the steps.

'This is Carver. He was Sir Stanley Jacks' steward and agent but will remain in his duties here in my employ.' John took Carver to one side. 'Is there anything we need to discuss today?'

'No, sir. I have engaged a "maid of all work" to keep the house clean as you requested. She lives in the village and will visit daily,' Carver's assured voice reported. 'And there is the matter of the hounds, sir. Sir Stanley has left two greyhounds in the kennels. I have continued to care for them but did not know if you wanted to keep them or have them shot.'

'No! You must not,' Constance cried out in alarm. She turned to look at John, then Alice, but carefully avoided her husband's eye. She knew he would have them shot just to distress her.

'Are they dangerous?' Alice asked, horrified at the idea of the pointless and callous deaths of these animals.

'No, mistress, they are not. In fact, they are too soft even for the purpose for which they were bred. Which is probably why they were discarded.'

'I will care for them. If that is permitted?' Constance spoke up boldly.

'Carver, take my wife and daughter-in-law to meet these hounds. Between them, they can decide on the matter.'

John was impatient to show his sons his new acquisition. He liked dogs, but they were unimportant to him at that moment.

Alice hung back. Her curiosity about the house got the better of her and she let Constance go with Carver to the kennels without her.

The family inspected the house with little enthusiasm. It was so different from the Old Manor. Daniel knew that one day Thomas would get his hands on the place, so why waste time admiring it? However, it did cross his mind that it would free up the old family home to become his inheritance.

Alice hated it, not just because of John's behaviour over buying it, but she thought it ludicrously impractical. All those windows would need cleaning, the ceilings too high to be dusted, and she could not understand why a room should be called a drawing room. She had to admit that the lack of dark corridors, crooked door frames and uneven floors and walls could be advantageous. But the kitchens in a basement and the servants' rooms in the attic made no sense to her. Yet she reserved her fiercest disapproval for the gardens.

'John, I wish to speak with you.'

John had been worried that she might.

'God knows the house is ridiculous. But the grounds are beyond description.' Alice drew breath and continued before John could respond.

'There is no orchard, no vegetable garden, nowhere for the chickens. Just endless patterns of paths and tiny hedges, and for what purpose? And then…' Alice was so exasperated that she ran out of words.

'A gentleman does not have chickens running free in his grounds.' John's answer was both pompous and an unwarranted put-down.

She knew there was no talking to him, so turned her back and walked away.

Alice found Constance by the kennels where she had let the dogs out, probably not the most sensible thing to do, but they were enjoying the attention and stayed close to Constance.

As Alice approached, she could see the tears on her daughter-in-law's cheeks. 'Do not fear, child, we will not let these lovely hounds be shot. They will have to live here for a while and they will be company for steward Carver, but not forever.'

But Alice had misunderstood the tears. She soon realised that something else was the cause, and it pained her. Maybe this was the time to air the problem.

'Constance, you are a good and kindly soul and it pains me to see you cry. Could it be you identify with the abandoned hounds? Their loyalty and love ignored, put aside, unwanted?' Alice spoke as gently as she knew how.

Constance's body started to shake, her sobs juddering her whole body. Words came tumbling out in no coherent order, but it did not take Alice long to understand the root of the problem.

She was not surprised that her son was not just cruel and belittling in public, but also a physical bully in private, which included his marital duties in the bedroom. Constance was slight and she did not have what Alice's mother would have termed "childbearing" hips. Her pregnancy had been plagued with sickness; she had not bloomed like a woman with child should do. The confinement had been long and arduous, her spirit crushed when over-hearing her husband tell the physician to save the child at all costs. "I can always re-marry".

'I cannot be a wife to him, it hurts too much. I know he goes elsewhere but that does not distress me, for he only married me for the land left by my parents, not out of any sense of love or care.' Constance's voice grew calmer and she even smiled when one of the hounds gently licked the tears from her face.

Alice said nothing, hoping Constance would continue

unprompted.

'He wants more children, especially as Joseph is frail, and it is my duty to provide them. I accept my obligation. But the pain when…' She could not bring herself to say the words.

'Say no more, child, I understand. You are slight in body, you are frightened of him and any resulting pregnancy, and so your body will not respond to his needs.'

Constance nodded.

Alice took a deep breath and continued. 'You need to relax before your body can accept his member.'

Alice had never used that word outside her own marital bedchamber and shocked herself. But she had to help this fragile woman because she was a woman in a cruel world. Alice had had the fortune to have a body designed for childbirth and a husband who loved her with gentleness and passion.

'Keep a small decanter of fortified wine in your bed chamber and a small pot of goose fat under the corner of the mattress.' Alice blushed; it was her sister who had told her about that. 'If he comes to you at night, take a glass of port down as fast as possible. It will relax you. Take two if needs be!' Alice smiled at Constance, they both now blushing with embarrassment. 'Then, put a small amount of the goose fat on your finger and rub it on yourself, it will ease his entry and hurt you less.'

Constance stared wide-eyed at Alice.

'Quick, put the hounds away, I hear the men returning from their inspection. Wipe your face. Do not hide away your fears, come talk to me, let me be a mother to you. I fear you are vulnerable alone.' Alice had taken Constance's hands in hers and held them tightly, gently shaking them to reinforce each syllable of her words.

'Please do not make me live here with Thomas alone,' Constance's voice thin with fear.

Alice patted her hand and smiled unconvincingly. She knew exactly what her son would do.

The journey home was as silent as the journey there.

Later that evening, John sat at the table in the chamber originally called the counting house in his grandfather's day, and still the business heart of the family. What would his grandfather and his father say now? Would they think him a shrewd businessman or a fool? Well, he certainly knew what his wife and youngest son thought. But he also knew there was money and advancement to be made through the ownership of land and property. Had it not served his forefathers well? They had bought their tenancies, even the small manor and its manorial lands where he and his family now lived.

'I will be master in my own home,' such was the strength of John's thoughts he spoke aloud.

The door was ajar, and unbeknown to him Alice was standing in the corridor. She was holding a pitcher of ale and a small tankard for she knew he already had taken a full tankard from the buttery.

She pushed the heavy oak door open. 'You *are* master in your own home. But what you forget is that it is not just your home, other people live here too, and you are responsible for their welfare.'

John rose from the table with his tankard in hand, which he held out to be refilled. He settled in a chair by the hearth after he had put another log on the fire. Alice filled the small tankard for herself and settled on a stool on the other side of the fireplace.

'John, will you hear me out? I fear your ambitions for this family will cause more harm than good.' She sipped her beer. *It's good*, she thought. She had brewed well from the hops which had been gathered recently and their youthful flavour could be tasted.

'I understand that every man wants to improve his standing with each generation. I still remember your grandfather bringing his farm horses to the forge and lifting me up to sit upon their great broad backs. He left a good legacy to your father, who also worked hard to better himself and sent you to school to learn more than how to put a horse to plough.' She took another sip.

'You know I do not have the learning like you and am ignorant of the ways of business. Yet it does seem wrong to me to profit from another man's misfortune.'

'He was a greedy fool! And you forget there are many local men of trade who will now be paid thanks to my intervention.' John failed to mention this would be at a substantial discount, knowing it would incense Alice even more because she was a blacksmith's daughter and sister to Seth.

'You have always favoured Thomas, often at Daniel's expense, and that is wrong.' She hesitated because she expected a prompt denial. His silence confirmed her opinion. She continued.

'Thomas has, when he feels like it, wit, charm and intelligence and his good looks make people warm to him. Sometimes the wrong people warm just a little too much!'

'What does that mean?'

'Oh, John, surely you have seen Lady Adele Edgerton's

son, Robert? Many other people have. I have suffered several sly comments, drawing attention to how alike Robert is to Joseph. "Like two peas in a pod", was the last comment I got. Lord Edgerton is elderly and often in London at his business, his wife pretty but young and wayward. Thomas is known to dine at their house often.'

'Nonsense. I had never considered you a pedlar in tittle-tattle, Alice.' John had heard the insinuations also but had not wanted to pass them on to his wife. 'Alice, I want to make some things plain. I respect your ability to see into people's souls and judge their true worth. Many of the things you say are true, even I can see that. But I want you to trust me on matters of business.'

'There is more to life than just business.' Alice would not be silenced; she had more to say on the matter. 'Daniel is plain-looking, serious and mindful of his actions. He might make for a dull companion at times, but he will always be an honest one. Should God decide to take you before me, which of our sons will care and comfort me in my old age?'

She turned to look at him, wanting but not expecting a reply.

When none came, she continued. 'Do you realise that there is little bond between our boys? This horrible new house will only widen the chasm. Thomas is determined to have the house for himself and intends to move in without delay. He sees no need for that agent, Carver, to have free run of the place. He will, John. He will pester you, wheedle at you and then demand. You will give in; you always do.'

Chapter Five

November 1720

Alice Matthews' words did come true. Thomas got what he wanted, not because of his father, but as a result of an invitation three weeks later from Lord and Lady Edgerton. Alice was grateful that the invitation did not include her, unlike John, who was rather put out that he was not included.

Thomas and Constance asked to call upon the Edgertons at their residence the following afternoon.

'Welcome, come in, dear friends.' It was hard to tell which of the three other people present was the most surprised at Lord Edgerton's effusive greeting following the butler's announcement of their presence. Lord Edgerton rose from his chair and strode over to Constance who stood in the doorway and, after brushing the back of her hand with his lips, dry as parchment, he offered her his arm.

'I trust the journey did not tire you too much and my carriage was comfortable.' Edgerton escorted a bewildered Constance to a chair covered with pale yellow and dove-grey brocade.

'Oh no, the carriage was most comfortable. Your horses are so perfectly matched in looks and temperament; they are such beautiful creatures.' Constance's nerves had got the better of her as her words tumbled out.

Edgerton thought there was a rather attractive simple

charm about her that could be exploited.

'The two horses you saw today are called Opal and Emerald; they are half-sisters. In fact, I have another mare called Ruby also by the same stallion and last night she foaled a well-marked filly I shall call Pearl. Would you like to see her?' Edgerton watched her carefully, as Thomas' mousy wife responded with a smile brimming with pleasure and gratitude, accompanied by a vigorous nod.

'Geoffrey, you said you had business to discuss with Thomas.' A petulant Lady Adele felt snubbed that her husband was paying such unwarranted attention to Constance.

'Indeed, ladies. Would you excuse us? We will not abandon you for long!' Edgerton indicated to Thomas to follow him.

'Dear Constance, I have much I would love to discuss with you.'

Constance froze in the chair for she could not imagine what she had in common with this society butterfly.

Edgerton paused by the door to offer an explanation. 'Indeed, my wife has been to Norwich and has selected the best bolts of silk cloth in my warehouse. She will seek your advice on such matters, as is the nature of you ladies.'

Constance looked and felt like the proverbial rabbit in a poacher's lantern. She knew nothing of fashion, which would be easily exposed by Lady Adele whose smiling face had a trace of maliciousness about it.

Lady Adele knew exactly the impression she made on her lover's nervous wife. She had chosen to wear a dress of pale blue silk brocaded in silver, with a large-scale pattern of fruits and leaves on the fabric, the train carefully arranged around her to show yet more opulent brocade. A deliberate display of wealth and fashionable taste.

Constance just wanted to gather up the skirts of her plain, woollen dress and run.

Edgerton ushered Thomas into a parlour which was a large well-lit room with an eclectic mix of furniture and furnishings, as expected of a man of his status.

'Well, Thomas, I have a proposal to put to you.' Edgerton indicated that Thomas should take a chair by the large writing desk. Thomas was feeling decidedly uneasy to be in such proximity and intimacy with a titled gentleman whose wife he bedded at every opportunity. Edgerton was old enough to be his father and was certainly his social superior, so Thomas smiled politely and sat down, endeavouring to look nonchalant and amenable.

'I believe that we can offer each other a mutually beneficial service.' Edgerton pulled up a matching chair and sat opposite Thomas, so close that there were only inches between their knees. 'I would ask you to listen to my idea in full before you form an opinion.'

Edgerton then set out his carefully devised plan.

'To speak plainly with you, Thomas, you are a young man with all the social graces and tastes of the landed gentry, yet you lack the connections or capital to make your mark on society. Unlike myself as my face is well known in all commercial and society venues. My presence in any of the trading walks of The Exchange in London is noted; should I visit trading centres in Norwich it becomes a topic of conversation. I am in some respect a victim of my own success because I can no longer gather trading intelligence unobserved.'

Thomas stared in silence.

'However, you have a quick wit, a curious mind and excellent recall. You are ambitious.' Thomas felt like a small boy facing a tutor's report, expecting a damming punchline.

'I am an old man, but what I lack in physical health, I make up with mental agility. We complement each other.

'I intend to lease Somersham Court from your father. Install you and your family there on a retainer to act as my agent in some of my commercial interests.'

Thomas was so taken aback he could not remain silent and interrupted. 'On what matters? You have already listed my deficiencies quite clearly.'

'I have also mentioned the qualities I require. And I told you not to interrupt. I will instruct you to cultivate the acquaintances of certain merchants, financiers and traders. You will invite them to dine at Somersham Court, where they can be encouraged to discuss topics that I will instruct you on. You will make note of not just what is said but unsaid and the reactions of the individuals present. You will become my eyes and ears in commerce.' Edgerton looked at Thomas' face intently to gauge his reaction. What he saw was exactly as expected: ambition and greed.

'The majority of my interests are centred in London and, as you know, I have to spend considerable time there.' Lord Edgerton paused, then resumed.

'My good friend and distant cousin, the Earl of Pembroke in Wiltshire, is active in the expansion of his mills and their produce, which coincides with developments with other mill owners in Norwich. But more of that later. I only wish to know of your initial interest.' Edgerton knew his fish was on the hook, but now was not the time to reel him in.

'We will not go into any detail at this point; that will be drawn up in a letter of agreement. Of course, there will be conditions and clauses to the agreement. My lawyers will draw up the agreement and we can discuss it further, to our mutual satisfaction.' Edgerton leant back in his chair, inviting Thomas to speak.

'Well, sir, I am completely taken aback. However, I assure you that it is of great interest to me. I have concerns though.' Thomas was now bitterly resentful of his wife's background and nature.

'Let me guess, your dear sweet Constance? Such an appropriate name for such a devoted wife. Nothing must be done to upset her. I make no demands on her to be part of any business matters; she will not be burdened with the additional costs or trials of the entertainment of visitors, as both coin and appropriate servants will be provided. It is her quiet, retiring and private character that makes her most suitable. Please do not concern yourself on her part.'

Thomas wasn't in the least concerned for his wife's wellbeing, but Lord Edgerton had answered one important question: who was paying for this lavish lifestyle?

'My father will want to know why you would choose to lease Somersham Court for no apparent reason and then have his son installed as the occupier.'

'Your father is, for a yeoman farmer, a shrewd and discrete man with a mind for good business. Besides, he will be more interested in my lease payment than my motives! However, part of my agreement with him for the taking of Somersham Court will remain known only to the three of us.

'Thomas, you must understand that for this venture to

succeed, everyone involved must be sworn to secrecy.'

'Including your wife, sir?' Thomas thought the chances of her keeping such knowledge to herself minimal.

'My wife will not be privy to the arrangement, nor will yours. To society in general, what could be more natural than the eldest son of the owner taking up residence?

'And my involvement in this is to remain unknown and that, Thomas, must be at the heart of our understanding.

'Come, we have been away from the ladies too long.' Egerton rose and beckoned Thomas to accompany him back to the morning room and their wives.

Constance was rarely pleased to see her husband but, on this occasion, she truly was, for the conversation with Lady Adele had been both stilted and embarrassing. She had no idea, nor interest, in what the ladies at court were wearing; the names of the grand ladies to whom Lady Adele kept referring completely lost on her.

Constance's sweet nature had completely failed to pick up on the fact that Adele's intention was to belittle her lover's wife. But she had failed; Constance oblivious to her intentions.

Lady Adele was irritated that the mild-mannered woman sitting next to her was unscathed by her maliciousness. So when her husband returned, she was pleased to be able to make an excuse to end the charade.

'Geoffrey, you have been away too long. Master Millar has finished the portraits for you to approve and has some sketches of your hounds as you suggested. He is waiting on you in the parlour.'

She turned to Constance. 'I am so impatient to see these finished portraits. They have been painted by a well-connected artist recommended to us.'

It was Thomas who picked up on Adele's words rather than his wife. Once they returned to Old Manor, Constance fled to the sanctuary of her room, whilst Thomas went to find his father.

'Father, I must speak with you.' Thomas entered the parlour without knocking.

'Must you, Thomas? Is it of such great importance that you burst in and interrupt my concentration?' reproved John. The terseness was lost on Thomas, whose enthusiasm often overtook his discretion.

'I have just returned from visiting Lord and Lady Edgerton.'

John mentally winced, for he knew of the invitation to his eldest son to visit their establishment, but to be invited to take Constance with him bothered John. He knew of Constance's anxiety when faced with social engagements outside her sphere of society.

'They have the artist Clive Millar staying with them. He has painted pictures of them to hang in the panels in their drawing room. As he has nearly finished, I have asked him to call upon me at Somersham Court next week to discuss a similar commission.' Thomas took a step back, looking pleased with himself.

'Pray tell me, son, how do you know the future tenants of Somersham Court do not already have their own family portraits to display in those panels?'

Thomas knew a paternal putdown when he heard one and was about to withdraw from the parlour when his brother, Daniel, knocked on the open door.

'Come in, Daniel, you will not disturb me.' John gave Thomas a meaningful look, whose self-congratulatory smile had now dissolved into a sulky frown. However, his good mood soon returned as he explained Lord Edgerton's plans.

What he enjoyed the most was the look of loathing on his younger brother's face. Daniel was aware Thomas got all the attention from their father while he had to work hard on the estate. Conversely, Thomas just swanned around the county, tupping the bored wives of the gentry. His reward was a house to live in and leg-up in the world of commerce, where contacts and favours were the currency of the day.

'Now we have heard Thomas' extraordinary news, what did you need to say to me, Daniel?' John had picked up on the tension between the brothers. It must have been palpable if their father noticed.

'It can wait.'

Daniel left the room.

John leant back in his chair; he was trying to take in Thomas' news. It was almost too good to be true. The lease was to be taken and paid for and his son, Thomas, to live in Somersham Court and be introduced into the inner circles of Norwich commerce. He felt very uncertain about it; why was Edgerton doing this?

Chapter Six

January 2021

Miles was used to having razor-sharp clarity of mind and to be able to make quick, incisive decisions, but recently he felt decidedly adrift in a mental fog. Staring into the bottom of his nearly empty coffee cup at the sludge left behind, he could not understand his mental paralysis. The only conclusion was that he doubted the wisdom of buying Somersham Court.

He had enjoyed the Christmas and New Year break, visiting his parents and friends in London. However, everyone kept questioning the wisdom of his unusual decision to move to "the arse end of England", as his geographically challenged friends called Norfolk. They had undermined his confidence.

He walked across to the house, which was a hive of activity and a cacophony of sound. The noise of saws, nail guns and drills was fine, as was most kinds of building equipment, but he still could not stand the blaring radios.

He looked for Lucy. He knew she was there somewhere as Ozzy and Marble had come to the rooms in the stables to make their presence known, each demanding a biscuit. He found her on the first floor with the carpenter, imaginatively known as "Mick the Chip".

They both seemed fascinated by a hinge on a wooden window shutter.

'Hi. Come and have a look at this workmanship.' Lucy's

beaming smile cheered him up.

'What am I looking at?'

'Well, this shutter was damaged, with rot around the hinges, so Mick has cut out the damage and grafted in a repair. When it's painted you won't see any difference.'

Miles refrained from commenting that despite the outrageous hike in the cost of timber in the last twelve months, the cost of the time spent for a craftsman like Mick to cut out the rot and then fashion the repair was probably more than the inflated cost of replacement timber.

'That way, nearly three-quarters of the original shutter is saved. After all, this is restoration, not replacement work.'

It was as though Lucy had read his mind. Miles found this very disconcerting.

'Could we have a word?' Miles nodded towards the door. He thanked Mick for his excellent work but barely understood a word of the mumbled reply.

'I'd like to ask a favour. I want to go and visit a litter of puppies and would like you to come with me. I'd really appreciate your opinion.'

'Well, you can save your fuel. I'll give you my opinion now. Do not buy a puppy, take in a rescue dog. God knows there are enough of them available. By buying a puppy, you are just encouraging indiscriminate breeding, with only profit in mind. I will gladly come with you to any of the rescue centres.'

'For fuck's sake, Lucy, don't you ever get vertigo stuck up there on the moral high ground? Do you think I'm stupid enough to see a picture of a little fluffy creature on the internet and then rush off to exchange it for cash in a lay-by on the A12? Jesus wept, woman, I wish I hadn't mentioned it.

'So, at least you know the reason I won't be here tomorrow. I'm going to be in Kent.' Miles was cross with himself for overreacting and losing his patience, especially as he didn't like to swear at women, however provoking they might be.

What really niggled Miles was that he had already spent hours on his computer researching breeders, bloodlines and breed-specific health problems and spoken on the telephone to a selection of The Kennel Club's approved breeders. He had been alarmed by the number of dubious-looking deerhound crosses on popular websites. The number of pure breed litters available was reduced because of the impact of the lockdown and the COVID-19 pandemic. However, deep in the Kent countryside was a well-respected breeder with a litter, with six puppies available, two dogs and four bitches. They had emailed him a selection of photos, pedigrees and supporting information. Miles was smitten and no lecture from Lucy was going to make him change his mind. The only major decision was whether to buy a dog or a bitch puppy.

He did not return to the stables, but decided to walk off his annoyance, purposely striding out of the gate of the walled garden and across the meadow, along the old footpath towards the woods.

Lucy could see him from the window where she and Mick were still assessing and discussing the repair work to other window frames and shutters. She regretted her hasty words, not because she didn't stand by them, but because she rather liked the idea of spending a day with Miles and she was a pushover when it came to cuddling puppies. She tore a corner off a large sheet of protective covering on the floor and grabbed one of Mick's marking pencils to scrawl a note. Knowing he wasn't going to be in, she rushed over and pushed the note under the door. It read:

> *Sorry I upset you, but I think you might mean*
> *acrophobia (fear of heights) rather than vertigo*
> *which is a spinning sensation. I would like to come,*
> *if you can suffer my company for a whole day! Lucy.*

Miles arrived at the edge of the wood and was disappointed to see that the wooden stile was rickety and rotten. From what little Miles knew about public footpaths, everything seemed in breach of government guidelines. He could just about see the footpath through the wood which was mostly overgrown with brambles. He sighed at the prospect of further expense. It then dawned on him as to why he was in such low spirits: everyone around him had at least one practical skill and was working hard, whilst he wandered around just watching and waiting for the invoices to be presented. *He* would replace the stile, *he* would clear the footpath. He would show them all that there was more to Miles Mortimer than a bank account.

He was about to walk briskly back to the stables when he stopped and turned to look back. He asked himself whether it had to be a stile, could it be a gate? He would have to check the landowners' guidelines. He chuckled to himself, thinking that no doubt Lucy would demand he put in a gate so that three-legged lurchers and blind bulldogs could get through easily.

On his return, he read Lucy's note. He didn't know whether to laugh or swear. Even an apology from her sounded confrontational, containing as it did an opinion and worse still, a correction! He picked up his mobile and keyed in a short text:

§

Lucy watched Ozzy and Marble in the early hours of the following day crisscrossing the headlands around a huge stubble field yet to be ploughed, their natural hunting instincts were dulled by their advancing years and having already had breakfast. She wanted to give her boys a good run so that they would be happy to potter about the house and sleep. Adrian was not the most reliable of dogsitters and had sulked when she told him she was spending the day with Miles.

She rubbed the dogs down with old towels, after which they settled themselves on their dog beds. Adrian sat at the kitchen table in his pyjamas, eating something that looked to Lucy like sheep feed mixed with yoghurt.

'Why are you fussing about with a picnic? I would have thought Moneybags Mortimer could at least buy you lunch.'

Lucy ignored him. She loved preparing and having picnics. 'Well, if he does, that's your dinner tomorrow sorted then.'

Lucy picked up her bag and checked the contents before balancing it on top of a wicker basket. She walked round to the other side of the kitchen table and dropped a kiss on top of Adrian's head, saying goodbye.

Miles was, of course, on time and so was Lucy. She was standing on the doorstep as the grandfather clock could just be heard chiming in the sitting room. It had just started to rain, so she threw her bright red waterproof around her shoulders and walked briskly to the car.

Miles suppressed the desire to tell her she looked like *Little Red Riding Hood* with her coat and her wicker basket of goodies. But he was touched that she had thought of lunch because it hadn't crossed his mind.

It was not long before Lucy had to ask, 'Why a deerhound? Do you know anything about them as a breed?

'I'm going to tell you a story about my childhood. It's precious to me, so please be gentle with it.'

Lucy was taken aback. Wondering why he felt it necessary to say that; she made no response.

'When I was a young lad, I used to spend my summer holidays with my grandparents up on the west coast of Scotland. My grandparents worked for the eccentric lady in the "big house". Gran was the housekeeper, which was a polite way of describing her work as an indoor skivvy, whilst Granddad was the outdoor skivvy! But their needs were modest and the job came with a lovely cottage just by the western shore of the Gareloch. I loved staying there, despite the local children's jeering at me for being a Sassenach!

'A what?' Lucy had to ask.

'A less than polite term for someone who is English, I think. I'm not sure but it might be the Gaelic equivalent of Saxon.

'Anyway, the main point being was that Mrs McLachlan,

the lady from the big house, bred deerhounds. She used to talk to me about their bloodlines and let me help her groom them. I would often go for walks with her on an old drover's road which went over the hill towards Loch Long.' Miles broke off.

'Hang on a minute, I hate this junction.' Miles was indicating to come off the A12 to join the M25 and needed to change lanes. The wheels of the huge articulated lorry alongside them looked intimidating to Lucy who was not used to being a passenger in a low-slung sports car.

Having safely negotiated his way onto the clockwise traffic heading for the Dartford Crossing, Miles resumed his story.

'Well, one day we were walking up on the track, it was a wonderful sight: those five hounds sniffing and snuffling in the heather. Whilst trying to run through the heather with them, my right leg disappeared down a rabbit hole and I fractured my leg. Needless to say, Mrs McLachlan didn't have a mobile phone.' Miles chuckled at the idea of that old Scottish lady using modern technology.

'She thought for a minute, then pressed down a patch of thick heather, took her coat off and laid it on there like a nest. She helped me down onto it, then called to the dogs and commanded two of them to lie down by me. I can remember word for word what she said, "There you go, you'll be fine awhile, wee man. Archie and Hector will keep you warm and safe whilst I get help. Dinna fash yourself, I'll no be long". With that, she scuttled off down the track with the other dogs. Archie and Hector did not move, they only raised their heads to watch her go then settled back.'

'You must have been scared witless being left there.'

'No. I had total trust in Mrs McLachlan to get help and as long as Archie and Hector were there, I felt safe. I could feel the warmth of their bodies and Archie's head on my stomach. What was there to be scared of? My bloody leg was hurting like hell by this time though!'

'My granddad had been reading me Walter Scott's story, *Rob Roy*, at bedtime, so I pretended I was a persecuted McGregor hiding in the heather to avoid the Redcoats and had to remain absolutely still. From where I was, I could see a lone Scots pine tree silhouetted on the ridge whose image fixed in my mind.'

'Your company's logo is a tree. Is it that one?' Lucy was fascinated by his story and not surprised when he agreed it was the same.

Miles went on to explain that a four-by-four rescue vehicle with first aiders arrived and he was carted off to the hospital in Helensburgh. He also explained that up to now, he had neither the time nor space to own a dog, let alone a deerhound. To do so was a lifetime's dream.

'What an amazing story. You didn't make it up, did you?'

'Dear God, I am not Scheherazade!' Miles could not believe she'd asked that.

Nor could Lucy, who immediately felt awkward and remained silent until they were over the Queen Elizabeth Bridge and into Kent.

Miles put the radio on which was preprogrammed to Classic FM and it was Sibelius' *Symphony No. 2* which was a particular favourite of his.

Lucy just concentrated on keeping quiet.

It was well over an hour later when they arrived in

Appledore on the edge of Romney Marsh. Lucy proved to be a good, precise map reader and they found the kennels easily. Miles parked the car by a wonky handwritten sign stating: Visitors Park Here. A lady in her fifties came out of a side gate with four beautiful deerhounds whose coats were different hues of grey, silver and fawn. Lucy thought she heard Miles audibly whimper with delight.

'Mr Mortimer. And Mrs Mortimer, I presume?'

Lucy sniggered. 'No, Lucy Moncrief.'

'My mistake, welcome to you both. Meet the girls.' She turned away and, pointing in a rather random way, boomed out a list of names.

'The little one is Willow, the dark grey is Flora, fawn colour is Pip and the silver grey is Iona. Let's go and see Skye and her puppies and then we can have a little chat.'

They walked round the side of a very typical-looking Edwardian house that looked as though a little TLC would not go amiss. What surprised both Lucy and Miles was behind the house. There was an immaculate kennels complex, built in a horseshoe shape. It was constructed partly of breeze blocks painted bright white and timber lap painted a dark brown. It was spotless. Each kennel had its occupant's name on the mesh doors, which were all open except one in the far corner. This one was a different configuration from the others. It had an additional door at the back which opened out into a grassy area where Skye and her puppies were enjoying the sunshine.

'Oh, my god, she is beautiful.' But Lucy was a bit taken aback that deerhound puppies were not quite as cute as other breeds. With their little yet long noses, bright eyes and whiskers, they looked a bit like *Roland Rat*. Their long uncoordinated legs made their movements comical. But she would have loved any one of them unreservedly. She could hear the breeder not so much as questioning Miles but interrogating him whilst introducing the puppies.

'I haven't named them, so just call them by their collar colour. Purple and green are the boys. All are for sale except the yellow collar; she was reserved this morning.'

Miles sat on the floor and let the puppies come and investigate how edible his shoes were. Little white collar climbed onto his lap and when he picked her up for a cuddle, she pee'd on him. Lucy couldn't stop herself laughing and Miles couldn't have cared less, for he was in heaven. It was purple collar he was drawn to; the little puppy had a good white shield on his chest and the tips of his paws and tail both looked as if they had been dipped into a pot of white paint.

Lucy in the meantime sat next to Skye and was stroking the watchful mum. The bitch moved closer to Lucy and rested her head on her shoulder. It was love at first cuddle.

'I had thought of buying two puppies so that they are company for each other. But I have been warned off the idea as they bond to each other and humans play a secondary role in their lives, which makes them difficult to train.' Miles had decided on a dog puppy but couldn't face choosing between the two.

'Quite right,' the breeder confirmed. 'Anyway, I never sell two together.'

That's put paid to that, thought Miles.

'This is Skye's third litter, I believe. What happens to her after that?' ventured Lucy.

'She will be spayed and live out her days here. Why do

you ask?

'What if she could be homed with her son, after she has dried off and been spayed?'

'What an extraordinary question, young woman,' the breeder snorted. But the idea had its appeal as there was a limit to how many retired breeding bitches could be kept as pets.

The breeder watched Miles' face filled with indecision, and then she knew.

Miles quickly looked back and there in the middle was purple collar looking straight at him. 'Purple boy,' he decided.

'Good choice. Will be like his sire. I sent you the pedigree and photos.'

'Is he not here?'

'Unlikely, he lives in Sweden. His efforts came over in a phial!' The breeder barked with laughter at her own joke until she realised, they hadn't understood.

'Artificial Insemination. Got the wrapping paper if you would like to see that!' She was still laughing as she took them inside.

After some more questioning, paperwork and a deposit paid, purple collar had a new owner. When the details had been agreed, the breeder told him she would agree to Skye living with him and the reasons why.

'In the late '90s, I went up to Scotland to buy my first deerhound bitch. I had a shortlist of breeders to visit, but I chose a puppy from a litter whose sire had a wonderful temperament. There was a small boy of about twelve watching me very carefully as I looked at each puppy. Mrs McLachlan spoke to him and called him Miles. Was that you,

Mr Mortimer?'

'Oh, my God, it was my Rona with the blue collar you bought! She was my favourite and I wanted to keep her, but my parents absolutely refused. So are these puppies descended from Rona?'

Lucy thought Miles was going to explode with excitement.

'No, but she had a long and happy life with us. We called her Islay and she had three litters of pups. Some went on to become champions.'

The lump in Miles' throat felt like he had swallowed a toothbrush sideways. He vividly recalled the day when the puppies went to their new homes; he had cried his heart out. His grandfather had mocked him, calling him a "big girl's blouse" and told him that real men don't cry. He learnt then to bottle up his emotions and keep them private.

'Got any ideas for a name?' the breeder asked.

Before Miles could reply Lucy announced that she would put good money on it being Archie or Hector!

'Fergus. Unless I think of something else,' replied Miles laughing.

§

The Royal Military Canal was not far away, so they drove there and walked along its banks until they found a bench and unwrapped Lucy's picnic. Lucy had made tiny Cornish pasties and little quiches, her pastry as light as the proverbial feather. The game soup had kept just above lukewarm in the Thermos, washing down the pasties.

Miles was enchanted and didn't even mind when Lucy

launched into a potted history about the canal. He hadn't known it had been constructed in the early 1800s as a defence against Napoleon and local smugglers, nor that it was twenty-eight miles long. He was beginning to realise that it wasn't a need to show off; Lucy had a real passion about life in the past. However, he thought that it must be something about the present and the living she struggled with. Reluctantly, he suggested they make a move, now the Dartford Crossing would have cleared a bit by the time they got there.

They were driving back through Appledore when Lucy thought to phone Adrian to ask him if all was well. It was her way of reminding him that Ozzy and Marble needed feeding. If she asked directly, he would get irritable with her. However, no sooner had she opened the contacts app, than her phone came alive with a call and the name "Bunny" filled the screen. She answered.

'Lucy, oh Lucy, what am I going to do?' Letitia Boughton-Hay, known to all as Bunny, was in an almighty flap.

'Bunny, slow down, what's happened?' Lucy flipped the phone to speaker so that Miles could hear also.

'It's James, he is in hospital… I have burnt my hands… the firemen were so kind. Now I don't know what to do. They have sent me home and I am frightened,' the distraught old woman explained.

'Bunny, I'm in Kent, currently driving with a friend. If they don't mind, I'll ask them if they'll drive me to yours. We're only forty minutes away.'

'Of course, I will.' Miles leaned over to speak nearer to Lucy's phone.

'Is that the man Adrian calls Moneybags Mortimer? I

phoned your home and Adrian told me you were in Kent with Mo…'

Lucy cut in before she could repeat her social faux pas.

'Yes, Bunny and we're on our way. Do you want to stay on the line until we arrive? Bunny, can you hear me?'

'Oh Lucy, did he hear me?

'No.

'If the kitchen isn't damaged then go and sit by the Aga and keep warm.' Bunny had ended the call, so Lucy wasn't sure if she had heard her.

'Miles, I am so sorry about Adrian's rudeness and Bunny's blunder.' She looked over at him. Even though he was concentrating on the road, she could see he was chuckling.

'OK, Lady Penelope, punch the coordinates into the sat nav and *International Rescue* is ready for lift-off.'

'FAB., Virgil.'

They both laughed at their silliness.

Chapter Seven

Later the same day – January 2021

The sun was setting over the Weald of Kent as Miles' car wound its way up the narrow road to the top of the Greensand Ridge. He flinched every time his exhaust system scraped the tarmac where large oak trees' roots had created humps and bumps in the road. They arrived at a very old house that looked out of proportion, as though an architectural jigsaw had been put together without the help of a picture. Not at all what he had been expecting. No sooner had he parked the car than Lucy headed for the house.

Miles followed her and walked up to the weather-worn, iron-studded oak front door. Lucy called out to him and pointed towards the path leading round the side.

'They call that Death's Door because it only gets opened for funerals, as coffins can't get through the boot room at the back.'

The image and purpose of Traitors' Gate at the Tower of London came into Miles' mind. He was still trying to grasp the idea that a house had a door used solely for funerals when Lucy waved her hand impatiently for him to follow her.

'Must make for some strange delivery instructions for couriers: Please leave at Death's Door!' Miles' humour fell on deaf ears as Lucy was not listening.

The latch lifted easily on the back door and opened into

a large, low-ceilinged room with an uneven, tiled brick floor. There was an ancient butler sink by the window and hanging above the benches was a motley assortment of waxed jackets and coats worn by several generations. Under the benches were piles of boots and sturdy shoes of every size, shape and style, all having the dull grey look of age and neglect. Miles couldn't avoid wrinkling his nose and thought the place smelled like several damp Labradors had been hiding in the coats for decades.

Lucy had gone ahead through another door into a sprawling kitchen, where the old lady was sitting in a large armchair by an ancient Aga.

'Bunny, are you alright? It's bloody cold in here. The Aga is stone cold.' Lucy crouched down in front of the old woman.

'You told me to stay here.' Bunny's voice was a strong contralto and seemed out of place, coming as it did from such a small, frail body.

'Lucy darling, I am so sorry to spoil your day, but I've been a bit of a dizzy duck. It was hateful leaving James in that horrible big hospital, he will be lost without me. I just didn't want to phone Lottie.' Bunny stretched out her bandaged hands to grasp Lucy's, forgetting her burns and giving a little yelp of pain.

Bunny had been so relieved to see Lucy that she had completely ignored Miles. Realising her mistake, she turned to him but couldn't remember his name, so she just looked expectantly at him.

He broke the silence. 'Miles.'

'Yes, dear, I am sure you have travelled miles and I much appreciate you giving darling Lucy a lift.'

Lucy giggled and threw Miles a look which begged his forbearance of Bunny's response.

'First things first, dizzy duck. Let's get a warm drink into you and some heat into the house. Just rest; leave it to me.'

Bunny smiled her appreciation.

Lucy went into organisational mode; Miles would probably have described it as just being plain bossy. He was sent off with instructions on where to find old newspaper, kindling and a scuttle full of anthracite fuel. He watched, intrigued, as Lucy rolled newspapers into quills, then was astonished when she opened one of the doors of the ancient Aga to reveal the solid fuel burner. But this was nothing compared to the amazement he felt when she marched him off to the boiler room to restart the central heating. He thought he was looking for some kind of pilot light to rekindle, so when Lucy explained that the boiler needed riddling, the ash removing and a fire lighting in not a dissimilar way to the Aga, he laughed. He rose to the challenge and the old boiler roared into life, eventually.

Miles returned to the kitchen triumphant, only to be given a shopping list and directions to a local supermarket. It was described to him as some "odds and ends", but it was quite a long list. He obediently disappeared off into the night on his errands.

'Well, Bunny, time to tell me what happened.' She listened patiently to the old lady's explanation.

Apparently, James had been up a stepladder trying to take a picture off the wall, lost his balance, fell and banged his head on something on the floor. He must have lost consciousness because he was unaware that the falling stepladder had sent the paraffin heater flying, which in turn started a fire amongst the papers strewn across the floor. It was the burning sensation on his legs that brought him round and he screamed for Bunny. She burnt her hands beating out the flames with cushions from one of the armchairs. She assured Lucy that they had both suffered only superficial burns which would heal, but James was being kept in for observation in case of concussion.

'Why was he taking the painting down?'

'Guess! We must get the old boiler replaced. It is so temperamental and unreliable. James just can't manage it much longer. We had a quote to remove the old boiler and install a combo one, so we wanted to sell the painting.'

'Bunny dear, you must stop being vain and use your hearing aids. They're called combi boilers not combo; it's short for combination as it provides hot water and heating.'

They both chuckled at her mistake.

'Is the painting damaged?'

'No, it's hanging skew-whiff on the little sitting room wall. It's the one with lots of animals.'

Lucy left her and went to investigate the picture and the fire damage. She took some photos and sent Adrian a short email from her phone:

Hi,

Bunny and James are relatively OK. Nothing too dramatic. Want to sell what I think is a Hunt, probably Charles Jnr. Usual thing: yokels in a cottage full of domestic animals. Good anatomically, strong use of light. Your chap in France? Approx. 25cm x 35cm. They need in excess of £8K. Phone you tomorrow. Big hugs to Ozzy and Marble.

L xx

Miles' expedition was successful and he unpacked the shopping onto the kitchen table. The radiators still felt tepid so went back downstairs, only to find the boiler had gone out and he had to start it again.

Lucy made little squares of toast and put on them smoked salmon and scrambled eggs for Bunny, considering the dish light on her stomach and full of protein but easy enough for her to pick up with the tips of her fingers, which poked out of the bandages.

Bunny was thrilled when Miles poured three glasses of red wine. 'Oh goody, Ribena! I love Ribena.'

Miles wasn't sure if she was joking or just bats in the belfry.

The kitchen was cosy, the tiny glass of red wine combined with painkillers knocked Bunny out. Bunny was frail in body, but strong and stoic in mind, which had stopped her from mentioning that her hands were in agony and that the pain was draining her energy.

Lucy tried to rouse her from her sleep to get her to bed and attempted to lift her. Miles bent down and picked up Bunny easily in his arms; she felt like a limp ragdoll. He followed Lucy up the wide, oak staircase and gently deposited the exhausted woman on a four-poster bed whose curtains had seen better days.

He left Lucy to put Bunny to bed. On the half-landing of the staircase, he paused and looked out of the large, mullioned window that overlooked a considerable sized pond in the garden, the smooth surface reflecting the moonlight.

A great wave of loss washed over Miles. The last time he had held such a frail body in his arms was a few days before

Helen's death. It also had been a moonlit night when she had asked him to carry her to the window so that she could see the moon. The unspoken phrase "one last time" weighed heavier on his heart than her body had in his arms. He had carried his wife to the window of the hospice which overlooked a large lake. It had been so beautiful in the moonlight it brought tears to his eyes just thinking about it. The old anger started welling up inside him. Why did cancer have to so cruelly end the life of his wife, whose beauty was more than just skin deep?

His introspection was cut short by Lucy joining him on the landing. He snapped himself back into the present when he heard her speak.

'Full moon tonight. Looks lovely from here, especially over the pond.' Determined to change the subject of his thoughts.

'Why is she called Bunny? I can't believe she was christened that. The upper class give their children loads of forenames but then call themselves something silly like Pongo, Fluff and suchlike.'

Lucy explained, 'Her real name is Letitia, but like me, she hates her official name. When she was very little, she had a porcelain baby bowl and cup with the character Bunnykins painted on it. They are still made by Royal Doulton. I think they have an image of a running rabbit around the rims. Well, she wouldn't be parted from it, so the nanny started to call her Bunnykins and it sort of stuck.'

Miles restrained himself from making a merry quip that in his family, a nanny was a female goat.

'It could go back to when the boys were marched off to boarding schools at very early ages. They were all addressed by their surnames and forenames were never used, so they invented nicknames to give themselves some sense of individuality.' It was just a guess on Lucy's part as she had never been to boarding school.

They settled down in the kitchen and ate the ready-made pizzas, which tasted better than Miles expected, washed down with even more red wine. The plan was that in the morning a car would be hired suitable for getting bandaged oldies in and out and have it delivered to the hospital so that Lucy could drive James home from hospital. Miles needed to return to Norfolk the following day but offered to take the animal painting to Adrian and collect Ozzy and Marble, who would stay with him.

'How did you meet Bunny and James?'

'As part of an agrarian history course, I wrote a dissertation about the impact of the introduction of the Whig Government's Death Duty Tax Act 1894 on country landowning estates. So many landowners were asset-rich but cash-poor, so finding lump sums of cash meant selling assets. So if your estate was valued at £100,000 then the duty would have been £6,500, which in today's money is in excess of £800,000!'

Miles was fascinated by this and wondered what, if any, financial planning went into tax avoidance.

Lucy continued. 'It only needed three generations to die within a short period to face three valuations and calls for death duties to put a family into unmanageable debt. In many cases, the large country houses were either demolished or reduced in size and value to minimise further duties. What is heartbreaking is that many beautiful country houses were bought by speculators who sold the land then demolished the house, selling off the architectural salvage for vast fortunes.'

'So why was this house of interest to you?'

'Two things. In 1923 two wings of the house were demolished to reduce it to the size it is now to de-value it considerably. But apart from the demolition work, what interested me was that all the historic timber panelling from the 1530s was ripped out and sold to an architect in America!'

'Bloody hell. Surely the house is a listed building?' Miles was genuinely horrified.

'Listed Buildings protection didn't come into force until the late 1940s, and that was more a survey of bomb damage and to prevent unnecessary demolition to claim compensation, than the protection of historical buildings. We lost a lot of our heritage buildings in the years between the economic depressions in the 1920s and 1930s, and the end of the Second World War. That was the subject of my dissertation.' Lucy stopped just before launching into one of her favourite soapbox topics.

'Oh bugger, I promised no lectures. Sorry, but you did ask! I'll go and check on Bunny and then doss in the room I usually stay in. Will you be all right here?

'Yes. The armchair can't be any more uncomfortable than an economy aeroplane seat!'

Lucy refrained from commenting that she found it difficult to imagine him slumming it in economy class.

Before tiredness, red wine and warmth now radiating from the Aga sent Miles into a deep sleep, he again pondered on the wisdom of buying Somersham Court. He questioned his decision and considered it might have been an emotional reaction to Helen's death. He had lost interest and his "edge" in the cut and thrust of the money markets. No longer did he crave the adrenaline rush of a high-stakes deal being pushed through. Nothing mattered anymore.

It had been a discarded *Evening Standard* left on a seat on the Tube that changed everything. A small article by a London-based estate agent promoting the potential of Somersham Court caught his eye. He could not save Helen from the ravages of cancer, but maybe he could save this lovely house from the ravages of time.

Miles forced himself to think of something else; he had promised Helen he would look to the future and not dwell in the past, hankering after what might have been. His thoughts turned to Norfolk and his house, its history and why Sir Stanley Jacks had surrendered his newly built home.

Chapter Eight
February 1721

Sir Stanley Jacks was not a welcome visitor to Lord Edgerton's house because of his perpetual complaints about the loss of his Somersham Court, which were both exaggerated and devoid of any personal culpability. As a result, Edgerton had received several letters from the extended family demanding that the upstart Matthews' underhand deeds should not go unpunished. There was also a great deal of self-interest hidden in their support for Jacks, as the extended family had presumed the availability of hospitality within easy reach of Norwich. One of the many cousins did indeed point out that Norwich was England's second city and there were many merchants of wool and textile in its location. It had been this point that sowed the seed for the downfall of John Matthews in Lord Egerton's mind.

However, he was not going to impart the details to Jacks, for despite their blood kinship, Edgerton thought the man a complete buffoon who probably deserved everything that happened to him. To invest so heavily in a company that had no assets, no visible trading and only offered soaring share prices seemed ludicrous to the financially savvy Edgerton.

So whilst the fire roared in the elegant stone hearth in Lord Edgerton's parlour, Sir Stanley Jacks had made himself comfortable in his cousin by marriage's leather chair. His legs stretched out in front of it to ease the aches of a long ride. Jacks had ridden because his coach and horses would have been too recognisable on the local roads. He sipped from his glass of Madeira and seethed with bitterness and resentment.

'So what have you achieved since I left?' he demanded.

'The scene is set.' Edgerton too had a glass of rather fine Madeira in his hand, which he sipped from to give himself a little time to decide how much to divulge to his rather dim-witted relative.

'John Matthews is a sound man, both in moral behaviour and financial probity. So difficult to find a weak spot in the man himself. He maintains true to his low-born wife, he does not drink to excess, nor lust after young women and has no taste for gambling.'

'A priggish little peasant!' scoffed Jacks.

'We need to know the heart of the man, what is important to him. Unlikely to be making quick returns on risky investment money.' Lord Edgerton was watching Jacks' face closely. It showed very little sign of intelligence. He had not picked up on the jibe. It was then that Edgerton decided the plan was down to him, and him alone. He considered this an advantage as it meant he kept control of the situation, and his name and reputation safe.

'Indeed, but there is one weakness he is blind to: his eldest son, Thomas, and his advancement from yeoman farmer status to landed gentry. A feckless young man, not without charm and intelligence, but spoilt by his nature and with a cruel, mean streak. He is a better quarry; bring down the son and the father will follow.'

'Quite so, quite so. Good plan.' Jacks nodded his head

vigorously to underline his agreement. Then, to demonstrate his understanding, he added another suggestion. 'Pity he hasn't got any daughters. There must be a handsome young buck with a title and no money who could be bribed to woo and despoil one or more of them!' Jacks thought this both a clever and funny thing to say.

'I will avoid the use of innocents to further your cause. It is the father and the son; no one else is to be involved.' There was a steely resolve in Edgerton's voice. He continued.

'Matthews values his standing in his community, he is acknowledged to be a fair and honest man in trade and a good landlord. He prides himself on these qualities. It is those very qualities we will destroy. We will let young Thomas fly high and then melt the wax in his wings.'

Jacks had understood his cousin's words until the last sentence. He was about to ask about the significance of wax, but Edgerton continued.

'You will need to excuse me, dear cousin, for an hour or so, as I have papers I must attend to before I return to London. We are to sit in parliament to debate The Quarantine Act and, given East Anglia's vulnerability from foreign sailors ashore and unchecked cargo, I must attend.

'Maybe you would like to accompany me tomorrow in my carriage? I can arrange for a groom to return your horse.'

'Kind of you, cousin, but I am due to return to Glemham Hall; it is where my carriage and manservant are at present. Dudley North is carrying out some extensive changes on the house and he has written to me of the new façade being built. His invitation to visit and admire the works came at a very convenient time.' Jacks had a smug tone to his voice, totally unaware that Dudley North was going to enjoy flaunting his wealth and new building works to a fool who gambled away his country house.

Jacks rose and went to leave the parlour. But as he opened the door, he turned. 'You will bring down that two-faced farmer and that pretentious whelp of his, won't you?'

Edgerton did not reply, he just smiled and nodded.

It gave him no pleasure to plot against the Matthews; he thought John a shrewd and capable man. As for Thomas, he knew that the next Lord Edgerton could be Thomas' bastard son. He really didn't care if the boy was healthy and lived to succeed him. He loathed his wife Adele and if someone was to satisfy her carnal needs on his behalf, he was grateful. However, knowing that the whole county was aware of his faithless wife and her beau, plotting his downfall provided a certain element of personal satisfaction.

But family honour took priority in his mind, his very devious and calculating mind. He also knew the very person to lay the trap for him. As he well knew, a trap is only as good as the position you put it in.

Edgerton took up paper and quill and set about writing to his friend, Thomas Herbert at Wilton House in Wiltshire. He opened his letter with solicitudes about Herbert's bereavement of his wife Barbara in August of the previous year. He then asked for his advice about the problems of trading with France, given the policies introduced by Colbert some forty years earlier which included the prohibition of French workmen emigrating. His reason for asking was as a favour for a good friend who had been asked to invest in a new venture that involved recruiting the skills of French carpetmakers. He was concerned that the difficulties had been underplayed and the investment was a risky one.

He also wrote to Cecile Le Fevre, engaging her to host a business meeting and soiree at Somersham Court. He outlined his need to have a meeting of potential investors in a private location and to impress them with fine wine and dining. He limited the details in the letter unless it should fall into unwelcome hands. He knew Cecile would read between the lines. He suggested that she should come to stay with him and his wife at her earliest convenience.

Like pieces in a chess game, Edgerton was laying out the players. They all had their part to play, but only he had the complete game plan. Or so he thought.

§

Cecile had received her letter summoning her to attend Lord Edgerton's country house on a specified date, which she did in the guise of a social visit, as people of their circle went about with regularity. She loathed and despised Lord Edgerton and his amoral and vacuous wife. But she was indebted to him and must do his bidding. No doubt she would be privy to the plans, possibly knowing her role in them by the end of the day.

It had been a long and tedious evening after a tiring journey to reach Edgerton's house, and Cecile was exhausted by the time she reached the bedroom allocated to her by Edgerton's housekeeper. Her head ached with the strain of the company. Keeping up light and polite social conversation was hard work, especially with his lordship's empty-headed wife.

Maud, her maid in public and her closest friend and confidante in private, had laid out her night attire on the bed. Cecile sank down gratefully into a padded nursery chair provided for the purposes of dressing. Maud carefully removed the wig of blonde, elaborately styled hair to reveal a mass of completely white tresses pinned tight against Cecile's skull. Gently she removed the pins and then, with a silver-backed brush, teased out the knots, long strokes turning the hidden tresses into a cascade of snow-white, wavy hair.

The rhythmic brushing started to loosen the tension in Cecile's neck and shoulders, and her headache began to subside. She extracted a folded letter from deep within the folds of her mantua and threw it onto the dressing table with disgust.

'I am yet again expected to be a part of Edgerton's plots. I cannot continue, Maud; I am in danger of losing my soul to this man's ambitions. I should have known that I am not *invited* to stay but *summoned.*' Maud just kept brushing in silence. She then helped Cecile out of her heavy mantua and undergarments, then put on the night attire that had been warming by the meagre fire.

'Don't leave me, Maud, stay a while. I need you.' The confident façade of the society hostess was lost and instead, now peering out from the bed was the frightened face of her childhood.

Maud slipped her shoes off and changed from being a maid to become Cecile's comforter. Still dressed, she slipped under the bed clothes and lay beside the petite woman who was starting to sob gently.

'There, there, *ma petite soeur.*' Maud gathered up the

disconsolate bundle in her arms as Cecile rolled into the crook of Maud's arm. She started to sing very quietly, an old French Huguenot lullaby, in her rich contralto voice. She kept repeating it until Cecile fell asleep. Reluctant to leave the warmth of the bed and the comfort their bodies gave, she thought about the strange story of their lives together.

She recalled it had been on her eighth birthday when she had risen a little earlier than usual to see if there was something special for her breakfast. She had just reached the bottom of the stairs when she thought she heard a mewing sound. Her heart raced, for it must be a kitten for her birthday. Luckily it had been a mild night for late November which had been fortunate. She opened the front door and saw a bundle of dirty rags in the corner of the doorway. She would have thrown them back into the street if she had not felt the weight of the object inside. It was a tiny baby, barely alive and dangerously cold. Possibly the unwanted by-product of prostitution or an unwise servant's liaison. Whatever the circumstances, the baby had been left to die.

'*Maman, Maman, vien vite voir* ça!' Maud thrust the bundle into her mother's hands which were covered with flour from kneading dough.

'Maud, how many times have I told you? Speak English. We must speak English all the time, even in the house and shop. We are considered strangers in this country and though we are many in Spitalfields, we must adapt.' Agnes Devaux was annoyed at being interrupted from her morning routine. *The bread will not bake itself,* she thought. She unwrapped the bundle and nearly dropped it in shock.

'*Mon dieu, c'est un nouveau-né.*' She too reverted to her

Huguenot origins in her anxiety. The baby moved slightly and made a gentle whimpering sound. Upon closer inspection, Agnes could see it was a little girl in desperate need of a wet nurse.

'*Trouvez la maison de Albert du Rieux, sa femme a eu un mort-né récemment.*'

Maud stared at her. Why was she speaking French when she had told her not to?

'Go, go, you stupid girl, we must not lose time.' Agnes had realised her outburst in French was the reason Maud was standing motionless and wide-eyed.

The shop door banged closed behind her. Agnes took a blanket from under a workbench, removed the filthy rags and then carefully wrapped the baby in the warmer and cleaner covering. Holding the tiny body close to her, she tried to rub some warmth into it.

Her husband, Pierre Devaux, had escaped persecution in France with his young wife in the 1680s, and they had come to live amongst the silk manufacturing community in Spitalfields, then an area outside the City of London under the control of the powerful guilds. His particular skill was with lustring, which was a form of taffeta that had become very popular amongst society ladies and Agnes was also a skilled dressmaker. Maud was their only child, who they loved dearly. Unfortunately, she had shown no potential to learn their skills and continue the business they had worked so hard to build up. But Maud was tall and strong for her age and would no doubt find someone to marry her, if only for her physical strength and gentle disposition; it certainly would not be for her looks.

Maud was beside herself with joy. God had sent her a little sister to love and look after. She begged that the tiny baby could stay with them. Agnes and her husband Pierre were unsure if they should, but they were kind souls and so did. It was St Cecile's feast day, so as Huguenots and committed Christians, the couple were ready to believe the baby had been a gift from God and named her Cecile.

Maud became besotted with the baby and mothered the child, earning her the nickname *Petite Maman.*

Now, Cecile became restless in her sleep, probably because she was too warm. Maud moved away from her though decided to stay for a little longer just in case Cecile's restlessness was the result of a recurring nightmare from which she suffered. An involuntary shiver went through Maud's body. She could not stop herself from thinking of the events of thirteen years ago when Cecile was barely into puberty.

How their lives had changed.

Maud blamed herself. One Saturday, she had been fretting about a kitten they had taken in to replace the old mouser that had been the shop deterrent against mice. The rodents nibbled corners off the bolts of cloth and left their droppings on work surfaces where fine silks were unrolled for cutting. It was late on a Saturday and every woman knew the narrow, dark side alleys were not safe for them. Drunken apprentice boys terrorised the streets at the best of times, but the new Act of Union in 1707 gave them an excuse to drink to excess. Cecile had been determined to find the kitten on Maud's behalf but instead found three boys who would not take no for an answer. The three of them took it in turns to rape the girl with the golden hair and tiny frame. Maud found her half-dead for the second time in her life and nursed her back to health.

Maud's gentle and loving nursing might have saved her, but the internal damage meant Cecile would never have children.

Her golden curls had turned white with the trauma.

English society believed Cecile to be the wealthy widow of a minor French aristocrat. She had all the correct mannerisms and social skills. She was very well-read and clever, with the ability to flirt with husbands without annoying wives. Many well-meaning acquaintances had tried to marry her off to suitable suitors, but she side-stepped their advances with charm. The only man Cecile was bound to obey was Edgerton. She never knew how he found out about her true background and now used his knowledge to command her. Edgerton engaged her to gather intelligence from commercial rivals at social gatherings.

Chapter Nine

February 2021

Bunny only really felt warm and safe in the kitchen. Her ancient armchair by the Aga was bolstered by lots of old cushions many of which were rather threadbare and had lost a lot of feathers over the years. She no longer lit the fire in the small sitting room where the modern TV lived, she had preferred the old one, but her daughter, Lottie, had bought the new one as a Christmas present and triumphantly took the old one away. The remote control was too complicated and referred to things she had no interest in or desire to be familiar with.

When James had been there, they watched a lot of television together, especially old films, missing great chunks of the plot by exclaiming to each other, "Look at that hat, I had one just like it", or "That blighter is wearing the wrong tunic jacket, that's not right for a Guard's officer" and other such "helpful" observations. Somehow sitting alone watching ridiculous programmes on mainstream television about people behaving in an unseemly manner was not entertainment to them. She soon lost interest in dramas as they were always about unpleasant people doing nasty things to others. Bunny was no prude, but the grunting and squealing in the sex scenes made her uncomfortable. She missed her youth and beauty, but most of all, she missed James. The last two weeks had been hell on earth for her. Lucy had taken her to see him in the hospital and he had begged her to take him home. The doctors had advised against it. So she left him there despite his protestations. She never heard his voice again, because four hours later a delayed massive haemorrhage in the brain ended his life in the blink of an eye. The guilt lay heavily on her, if only she had insisted, then James would have died at home, in the house he had been born in. She was convinced that she had let him down in his final hours.

Her reflective mood took her back to her childhood in the 1950s when society was so different, especially the expectations and aspirations of young girls. As a child, she had once made the mistake of saying to her nanny that she wanted to be a boy. Her brothers had been in the Cubs and had been learning how to light fires in the woods, while that same week the Brownies were taught how to darn socks using a darning mushroom. She was furious and had banged her little fists on the Scout hut demanding to be let in and allowed to join. Her punishment was to write in her best copperplate handwriting twenty lines:

Be a good girl, lead a good life, meet a good man, make a good wife.

Lottie had stayed for several days after her father's death, Bunny felt even further guilt, when she was relieved that her daughter returned to Tenterden. Especially after Colin outlined *their* plans for Bunny's future, not that her wishes seemed to be considered. She had promised Colin that she would not do anything or sign anything until she had discussed it with him first. Rather child-like, Bunny kept her fingers crossed behind her back; she had no intentions of complying, leaving Bunny to grieve for her darling James in private.

She had spent the night wrapped in James' favourite Harris Tweed jacket with its patches and threadbare lining. All her life she had been looked after by men. Her father doted on her as he had two strapping sons to pass his estate and title on to. It was her role to be "pink and fluffy", Daddy's little girl. She was not educated as well as her brothers, but the books in the library had been her solace and source of learning.

Darling James. He had mentally wrapped her in cotton wool and sheltered her from the unpleasantness of modern life because she was a woman. But now a steely determination came over. She pulled the jacket around her ever tighter. Colin will not win. She would make him suffer for his actions.

The following morning before she could make any phone calls, Denzil the vicar called in to discuss the funeral arrangements.

'James will have the same funeral as I'll have when I die; it was all arranged years ago when we chose our favourite readings and hymns. And of course, we will both be buried in our family corner of the graveyard. So there isn't much to discuss. I gave the details to the funeral directors.' Bunny was unusually curt.

Now, Denzil politely refrained from pointing out that neither of them had attended church for some time despite the proximity of the church to the old manor house.

Bunny did not like the new vicar; he was just a bit too happy-clappy for her taste. James had thought that a vicar who didn't like cricket and was evangelically anti-smoking, never mind being a vegetarian, was not a suitable person for rural living. The only redeeming aspect was the vicar's wife who was utterly charming. She could herd cats without them noticing and made the most heavenly cakes. Most parishioners thought she would have made a much better member of the clergy than her husband.

'Thank you, it was kind of you to call.' Bunny closed the door, muttering the suggestion that the vicar did not call again.

She phoned her solicitor next, only to be told he was very busy, and could she call back later.

'No. Tell him Letitia Boughton-Hay needs to speak to him urgently.'

There was a click followed by ghastly automated music. -Bunny recognised it as a metallic-sounding version of Vivaldi's *Spring*. She tutted with derision.

'My condolences on the loss of your husband, Letitia. How can I help?' Gordon Brownloe's baritone voice purred over the phone.

'I want to revoke my lasting power of attorney with immediate effect. I know you need it in writing and no, I haven't gone soft in the head. I then want to make a new will as soon as possible.'

The solicitor was taken aback; this was not the fluffy old lady he was used to. 'May I ask why?'

'Yes, you may. But I will not discuss it over the phone. I will say, however, that I know Colin Barton is not a fit and proper person to look after my affairs honestly and that my daughter, Charlotte, is such a milksop she could not stop his abuse of power.'

'Do you have any idea how you would like to revise your

will?

'Of course I do; it will be quite straightforward. But there must be no delay. As soon as James' probate is complete, Colin and Lottie intend to put me in a nursing home and let me rot, using the LPA. No time to lose.' Bunny felt awful being so dismissive of her daughter, whom she did love, but could see that her kind and generous nature had been warped by her ghastly husband.

Gordon Brownloe had a full diary that afternoon and there was little chance of rescheduling his other clients without serious consequences. However, his curiosity and deference to the now imperious Letitia got the better of him and he made a space in his diary as soon as possible. He assured her that the revoking of the power of attorney would be attended to immediately and that her new will could be drafted as soon as they had discussed the matter in his office.

Bunny's next call was to her kindly neighbour, Claire, who had offered transport when needed. Bunny explained she had to get to the solicitor's office the next day.

'Oh yes, please, I have an appointment with our solicitors, you know, legal stuff to sort out. It's trust business. I don't really understand any of it so just sign where Gordon tells me to!' Bunny glossed over the details expertly. Then she added,

'Claire dear, you must swear to secrecy. I need Gordon's advice about my financial position and assets. I want to move into one of those nice, new warden-assisted apartments they are building near Lenham. I know I should involve Lottie and I would love to have her visit them with me, but that Colin…' Bunny had no need to finish the sentence as Claire knew exactly what she was thinking.

'Do you want me to come in with you, in case you need someone to explain the details?' Claire was somewhat horrified to hear that her elderly friend was just signing anything put in front of her. Yet Claire always had a suspicion Bunny was a lot sharper than she let on.

'No, thank you, dear. Gordon and his father before him, have always had the Boughton-Hay's best interests at heart.'

'OK. I'll pick you up at 9:45 a.m. Would you mind if we called into the garden centre on the way back? I need some salt for the water softener. Maybe we could have a coffee and a cake, my treat.'

'Sounds lovely, dear. Could we call into the food hall nearby; I fancy something nice for my dinner.'

The following morning, they drove into Ashford as arranged. Right on time, Bunny was ushered into Gordon Brownloe's large office.

'Well, are you going to share this cunning plot you have dreamed up?' His face barely concealed his amusement as Bunny's lawyer indicated she sit in the plush leather chair opposite.

'I have not dreamed up anything. I am here to make the disposal of my estate crystal clear.' Bunny's voice was strong and determined.

Gordon was the senior partner of the practice, following his father and grandfather before him. He did not enjoy family legislation, but sometimes the eccentric whims of the elderly upper class gave him a little comic relief from the conveyancing and planning issues with which he routinely dealt. Gordon had been aware of the Honourable Letitia Broughton-Hay and her husband since his days he had been an articled clerk which was now over thirty years ago.

'You know that I only have one child, Charlotte. A dear, sweet child, but not the sharpest knife in the drawer. James and I made the mistake of not giving her education more attention; we assumed she would marry well and breed yet another generation of Pony Club children. She is married to an odious little cockroach called Colin Barton.'

Gordon had not met the cockroach but could imagine what she meant.

'He knows the price of everything and the value of nothing. For years he has been watching house values, keenly trying to assess the potential sale price on my house.' Bunny paused for breath only to ask when the tea would be arriving.

Gordon buzzed an intercom and asked the fuzzy voice at the other end to rustle up some tea and biscuits for his client. He took up his fountain pen and a legal notepad and wrote the time and date at the top, adding his client's name.

'Why don't you tell me exactly what you want, then we can get it all typed up in legal jargon that is tighter than…'

'… A duck's arse!' chipped in Bunny, who loved naughty phraseology. Gordon smiled at her.

Bunny started the conversation by explaining that she wanted to revise her will in light of James' recent death.

'Now firstly, I will deal with the contents. I want to make a list of all my dear friends who have been such darlings to James and me. I am going to specify a memento for each, something they have admired or I think they would cherish.'

'A Letter of Wishes is what we would call that. I need their names and addresses and the associated bequests.' Gordon scribbled on the pad as she spoke.

'I want Lucy Moncrief to have all the paintings in the house, except the ghastly family portraits in the dining room, they can go to Lottie. Not that Lottie will want them; they won't fit in with their executive new home with all its shiny chrome and endless shades of grey.'

'Are you sure? That is a large bequest to Lucy and could be quite valuable, shouldn't you have them valued and catalogued first?'

'I just want you to draw up a new will for me, not make decisions for me.' Bunny knew he meant well, so went on to explain her decision.

'Many of the paintings in the house are copies and only worth a few hundred pounds each. How do you think James and I managed to survive? On a government pension?' She laughed harshly.

'We had an arrangement that when we needed extra money, a copy was made to fool Colin, telling him that the original had been away for cleaning when it was really being sold! Lucy knows they are copies but loves the paintings regardless.' Bunny didn't feel her actions had to be justified to the solicitor, nor did the details of her arrangement with Lucy.

'The best of the antiques are to be sold and the proceeds divided equally between the PDSA and RSPCA. I will identify the artefacts and make a list.'

Gordon groaned inwardly. He considered charities a total nightmare to deal with during probate.

'The house and remaining furnishings are to be sold and the proceeds left in trust to Lottie and her children. Do you have any trustees in mind?'

'Yes. You and one of the partners, maybe the tea lady! I don't mind, as long as everything is watertight and safe from Colin. The main thing is that someone looks out for Lottie's best interests after I have died. I hope it will give her financial independence and the courage to forge a new life without him.'

'I doubt we can make leaving a husband a condition of a trust. But I understand the prime purpose of the trust. Talking of tea ladies, here we are.'

The door opened and a young woman with a fearsome amount of make-up and false eyelashes, which looked like giant spiders, brought in a tray with tea and biscuits. She glared at Gordon and smiled, unconvincingly, at Bunny and left the room.

'There is also the matter of the funeral arrangements; they can be specified in the will to avoid any confusion.'

'Confusion? There won't be any. No doubt dear Colin would have me put out with the black bins on Thursdays! I am to be buried alongside James in St Nicholas' churchyard. Simple service followed by tea and cakes at the vicarage. The lovely ladies who do flowers and cleaning and suchlike for the church have volunteered to provide great quantities of tea, cake and scones.' Bunny became tearful but did not want to be seen to be emotional. One of the younger ladies, who had been part of the group that provided a similar send-off for James, had assured her that they would do the same for her.

'I have one simple question, Gordon: can Lottie's husband challenge the will I have just described?'

'No, especially as he has no financial dependency on you. You have made bequests to friends and family; there is nothing to challenge. He cannot challenge the will simply because he's piqued at being left out.'

'What about me not being in sound mind or demented?'

'I'm not sure you mean demented, but in my opinion, your new instructions have been lucid and not influenced by a third party or a mental medical issue.' Gordon knew she could behave like a complete fruit loop sometimes, but he had always suspected that there was more to this lady than she ever let on.

Just before Gordon escorted her to the waiting room to await collection by Claire, he assured her. 'I'll get straight onto it. It would be helpful if you didn't die before we have completed James' probate, otherwise it will get very complicated!' He put a gentle hand on her shoulder and grinned at her.

'What do you mean? Why isn't it complete?'

'Very close now, just waiting for transfer of ownership of the house, land and assets into your name. We cannot legislate for third parties being tardy in responding to our transfers.' Gordon felt uncomfortable that his merry quip had been taken so seriously, as the Bunny he knew so well, would have seen the funny side.

§

Bunny was truly grateful for the lift home, even if the garden centre was rather crowded. Money was such a nuisance to her; there was never enough to cover the ever-increasing costs. It was only when James' grasp on reality had started to slip that she had got to grips with their finances. It had been a steep learning curve and she had fought off Colin's insistence on her signing a lasting power of attorney. She had contemplated asking Lucy, being the only person she trusted to look after Lottie's interests.

When she got home, Bunny stoked the Aga before taking sheets of paper from the library and, settling in her favourite armchair in the kitchen, started to make a list of the people who had shown kindness to her in the past and especially recently. She fell asleep trying to decide which of two Meissen pottery figurines to give to the lady in the post office, entirely unaware there was a £3,000 difference in their value.

The following day, she got a lift to the doctors' surgery, having made a bit of a fuss about getting a face-to-face appointment. Whilst others in the area had to wait for five weeks just to get a telephone appointment, Bunny had been considered a special case, given her age and recent bereavement. Not that any of the surgery's staff would ever admit to a patient getting preferential treatment.

'Good morning,' Bunny spoke brightly to yet another GP she had never seen before. He looked too young to be qualified.

'How are you today, Mrs Boughton-Hay?'

'I'm sleeping at all the wrong times of the day. I fall asleep in my armchair then wake about 2:30 a.m. and go off to bed. But I can't get back to sleep until first light, then I sleep past eleven o'clock. Sometimes I doze off for half an hour then wake up feeling so tired.' Though Bunny was describing the erratic sleep pattern she had had for years, it had never bothered her before now.

'I missed an appointment with the solicitor regarding

James' probate because I had dozed off in my chair. I just want to know how I can regain a normal sleep pattern.'

'Are you eating properly?'

Bunny was completely fazed by his question. He sounded like her dear old nanny checking that she had cleaned her teeth correctly. Pizza had become her guilty secret since Lucy and Miles' last visit after James' hospitalisation. *What wonderfully clever people those Italians are*, she had thought, *such delicious food. Just pop it into the Aga and then cut it up and eat with one's fingers. Minimum preparation and clearing up.*

'Oh yes, I eat well. And before you ask, my bowels are working fine too.' Bunny volunteered the information to the GP.

'Have you had anything to help with your sleep before?'

'Yes. They were very helpful in re-establishing a proper sleep pattern. It was a long time ago, though.' She lied through her teeth.

'Well, I'll give you a prescription for a mild sleeping medication which you should take twenty minutes before you are ready for bed. I'll phone you in a week's time to check on you.

'Be very careful not to take too many. If you take one before you go to bed, put the container away so that you don't take another one by mistake.'

Bunny smiled sweetly at the young man while thinking, *patronising prat.*

Afterwards, she picked up a copy of *FreeAds* in the small village shop. She wanted to find storage units for hire and some transportation for her treasures away from prying and acquisitive eyes.

Rather than going back into the empty house, she wandered off to the village hall. It was the Friends of the Church coffee morning, a good place for a free coffee, lots of cake and the opportunity of a lift home. So, she put on her dizzy duck persona and went to join them.

Chapter Ten

March 2021

Miles wanted to finish the restoration of Somersham Court but didn't know if he wanted to live there. He envisaged Lucy in his life, but in what capacity he wasn't sure. Did he feel he had the emotional stamina to cope with her? All he did know was he needed to find some meaningful work to occupy his mind. Meanwhile, work continued on the house and the grounds.

It was a beautiful morning; the sun was shining there was a gentle south-westerly wind. Davy and Ivor had already started work by the time Miles arrived at the edge of the woodland. The old stile had been demolished and they were hacking back the undergrowth, when Davy's efforts became concentrated on the area to the left.

'Hey, Mr Mortimer, come and look at this; it looks like the base for a gate or pillar, or some'mat like that.' Indeed, there was a large stone base with fragments of brick courses covered in moss and brambles. Davy started clearing, throwing the bricks to one side.

''Ere, look at this.' It was a large fragment of a much paler stone with what looked like part of a pattern on it.

'Looks like part of a pier cap with what might be a scallop shell carved out.' Ivor was not one for conversation but knew stonework. He looked at it carefully and turned it around in his hands, then grunted in agreement with himself.

Miles grabbed a spare bill hook and started to hack away at the undergrowth to his right. There, he found a similar stone base about ten strides to the right of the uncovered one.

'I don't think it would have been a gate because the gap is too wide. Besides, why would they have double gates from a meadow into a wood?' Miles was not expecting an answer, and certainly not from Ivor who could have been truly considered as the strong and silent type.

'Maybe it was just a fancy way of marking the entrance to the wood.' Miles was trying to imagine what landscaping features might have been in place three hundred years earlier. However, he did think his assessment had validity because the woodland entrance would have been clearly visible from the house.

'Let's assume it is an ornamental entrance rather than a gateway, clear back six feet and see if there is any evidence of brickwork,' Miles suggested.

Ivan grunted, removed his rather grubby green beanie hat, scratched his bald patch and then replaced the hat.

'Are you suggesting we clear a gap that wide right through the wood?' Davy strode from one point to the other and then reversed the process, thinking. 'It must be nigh on ten yards wide. It won't be an easy or quick job clearing a driveway. We understood you just wanted to clear the footpath to make it passable.' Davy was concerned about this incomer with more money than sense.

'I know, I had just wanted to establish what had been here before it became so overgrown. But if there was a driveway here, then the path can be cleared in line with its edge.' Miles was thinking it would be wonderful to reinstate the pillars and entrance and have the driveway restored but realised it would be a lot of money spent at this point.

'OK then, you're the boss.' Davy thought the man a fool, and, as he knew, fools were easily parted from their money. He was not going to turn work down, as long as it didn't interfere with his shooting.

So for the next hour or more, the three men worked on clearing the undergrowth and cutting down spindly trees. Miles was right, it appeared to be an entrance to a carriageway rather than a path and was angled slightly south rather than straight across. His back ached, his arms were covered in scrapes and tears from the brambles and he was exhausted. Yet his pride would not let him admit it. Mercifully, Miles was saved by modern technology.

'Hi, Leonie, nice to hear from you. What's new?' Miles nearly dropped the phone with shock when she announced that she was on the A12 heading north coming to visit him. The idea of Leonie leaving London was hard to imagine. Then dread filled his mind. What had gone wrong? Who had died? Had Wall Street crashed? Whatever it was, it was going to be serious.

He gave her directions from the point her sat nav would give up. Miles looked at his watch and thought he had time to make himself more presentable and get onto Google Earth to see if there were any aerial clues about the possible carriageway. He apologised to Davy and Ivor for having to leave and set off for the house.

'He's a strange one. Bet that call was arranged because he was knackered.' Ivan's dour, cynical outlook of incomers was legendary.

'Not sure, but he looked genuinely surprised by his call. But at least we can get on without him in the way,' replied Davy.

'If we rebuild the pillars, I wonder if he'll be wanting mobile phones rampant as pier caps.' Ivor chuckled at his own joke.

§

'Is this really you?' Leonie waved a beautifully manicured hand airily around the drawing room.

'It's very elegant, and I am sure the soft blues, greys and lemon colours were *de rigueur* in the early eighteenth century, but really, Miles?' He did not want to agree with her, but she was right, he did not feel comfortable in this pastel world. He made a mental note to himself: *bugger authenticity*. Instead, he would revert to his favourite relaxing colours and big, squashy leather settees.

'Let's cut the social niceties. You didn't drive up here to give me a second opinion on early Georgian décor. Let's start with the punchline.' He smiled encouragingly at her and refilled their coffee cups.

'Alex wants a baby. Is that to the point enough?'

'Blimey, not sure what to say to that.' Miles really didn't.

'And she wants you to be the father.'

Miles, who was midway through swallowing a rather large mouthful of coffee, coughed and spluttered, causing his drink to dribble out of the corners of his mouth.

'What! You cannot be serious, as John McEnroe would

say.' He was a little embarrassed by his explosive reaction and tried to lighten the moment with weak humour.

Leonie went on to explain in rather too much detail for Miles' liking how Alex wanted the whole thing: marriage, a baby and to move to the countryside. Leonie described how the "would be nice" had now become imperative, almost an obsession. She explained that Alex had sought a private medical opinion and that she was fit and able to conceive and carry to full term. Now Alex had issued an ultimatum: Leonie either came round to her way of thinking, or it was over.

'Well, that's not a good idea, trying to emotionally blackmail you into it. After eight years of living together, I would have thought Alex knew that would make you run for the hills.'

'Well, it made me run to Norfolk. How desperate is that!'

'Let's leave emotions out of this for now and approach it analytically. After all, it is what we do best! Forget that we have been friends as well as colleagues for over six years.

'Firstly, has your relationship with Alex possibly run its course?'

Leonie protested that she loved her partner and did not want her to leave. She also pointed out that unravelling their joint finances would take some doing and she would rather not be saddled with the eye-watering mortgage payments on their little mews house.

'Do you want children?' Miles noticed she hesitated, as though debating whether to be truthful or not.

She decided to be honest and said that, up to then, it had never crossed her mind, so never considered it. But on balance, she knew that she was selfish and enjoyed all the benefits of two good incomes and no children, living in London. Then after further thought she added she did not like children much and resented the mess, the noise and the commitment.

'What's your problem with marriage?'

'You don't need to be married to have a child. My parents didn't seem to think it was necessary and I survived.' Leonie's body language gave a different answer, the defiant shrug of the shoulders and jerky head movement betraying her.

'Neither of us is religious, so all that living-in-sin nonsense is irrelevant. Besides, not sure the CofE God ever really signed up to same-sex marriage. Anyway, weddings just seem to be an excuse for an overpriced party these days,' she continued.

'Why do you think Alex feels that you have to change to meet her needs?' As much as Miles liked Alex, who always seemed so amenable and supportive to Leonie, he couldn't really imagine her demanding anything, let alone declaring ultimatums.

Leonie ignored the question; the answer was obvious, the relentless march of time reducing the chances of a successful pregnancy.

'And what's this nonsense about me fathering the child?'

'Oh, that's simple. We don't want to adopt. God knows what mental and physical problems the baby might have. After all, the parents might have been drug addicts and the baby affected in the womb. It might have a sub-normal IQ. I couldn't cope with that. Anyway, Alex wants to carry the baby herself. There are some rather dodgy sperm donors around, and the idea of lots of unidentified semi-siblings knocking around is too risky in later life.'

If Leonie had just stopped for one second to look at Miles' face, which was now rigid with shock, she would have ended her speech there but ploughed on, unaware of his reaction.

'We know you're intelligent, calm-natured, resourceful, hardworking and, for a man, not unpleasant to look at! Don't worry, it would be done in a scientific way in a clinic, no one is asking you...'

'Stop right there.' Miles had jumped to his feet and went over to the window so that Leonie could not see his face. 'Never in a month of Sundays would I ever consider it. It's nothing personal against you and Alex.' Miles' voice had a slight tremor to it, but he went on looking out of the window as he offered his explanation.

'I did want a family with Helen. In fact, we both wanted children and had felt the time was right. We would have moved out of London, possibly to Kent; we had it all planned out. So, when she announced she was pregnant, we were the happiest people on Earth. Our world collapsed two months later when she was diagnosed with leukaemia, found during some pre-natal tests. The foetus didn't stand a chance. Nor did Helen.'

Leonie remained silent, so Miles continued.

'Can you imagine what it would feel like seeing my child running around with you two, not being able to call them son or daughter, even resenting them for not being Helen's lost child? I couldn't do it. How could you be so naïve to even ask me?' Miles' voice was now choked with emotion.

Leonie sprang to her feet and went over to him and, with the intimacy of friendship, slipped her arm around his waist and put her head on his shoulder. She spoke gently, telling him she was so sorry for her thoughtlessness.

Then the silence of the room was shattered.

'Hi, look what I have found…' Lucy's excited voice stopped immediately at the sight of Miles with a stunningly beautiful woman standing very close to him with her arm around his waist.

Miles spun round, livid. 'What the fuck do you think you're doing, barging into my house uninvited! What the hell is so important that you couldn't phone first or even knock on the fucking front door, after all, that is why there is one, to keep unwanted visitors out.'

Lucy was frozen to the spot. It had never crossed her mind that he would have company. Or that he would not be pleased to see her, let alone swear at her with such force.

'I came to tell you there's an auction coming up and there's a painting that might match the ones you and I have. I thought you might like to come with me to see it.'

'No, I'll tell you what you and Adrian really thought: let's get old Moneybags Mortimer to the auction and get him to buy it at any price. I'm sure you two have already checked it out.' Despite Miles' uncharacteristic outburst of anger, he was interested in the auction, but furious at Lucy's presumptive behaviour.

'I'll leave the details here.' She pointed to a small half-moon table by the door. 'Sorry to have disturbed you.' The shock of his reaction was obvious in her voice. She made a hasty retreat via the kitchen.

'So that must be the infamous Lucy you talk about so much. I think you were rather harsh with her. I believe it's traditional for country bumpkins to march in and out of each other's houses with impunity!' Leonie's attempt to lighten the situation fell flat.

'Go after her and sort yourselves out, as I ought to make tracks back to London anyway,' said Leonie.

'No, please stay, at least for some lunch and let me show you around.' Miles doubted Leonie would want to stay any longer. She had come and asked her question and though prepared for him to decline, had not expected quite such a verbally emotional refusal. She was embarrassed and angry with Alex for putting her in the position of jeopardising her long-standing private and professional relationship with Miles.

'Maybe Alex could have a change of career and work with children,' suggested Miles. 'After all, if she spends a lot of time with them, she might go off the idea rapidly. I know of one couple whose daughter did work experience in a primary school for one week and when she came home on the Friday afternoon, announced to her parents that they had better not look forward to having grandchildren!' Miles was well aware that he had overreacted to both Leonie's suggestion and Lucy's sudden interruption like the demon queen. He did not want Leonie to leave on a low note.

So reluctantly, Miles waved goodbye to Leonie as her Mercedes sports car's high-powered engine growled its way down the drive, accompanied by a shower of little stones flung up by the low-profile tyres. He was still furious with Leonie for all the crass and stupid things to ask of him, but she must have been under great pressure to ask. He was also livid with Lucy, crashing into the house unannounced. It had strangely troubled him that she had seen Leonie with him.

'Bloody women, they're more trouble than I need, like you great pile of geriatric bricks!' he shouted pointlessly at the house.

He was angry with himself for losing his temper and for Lucy provoking him. Fergus had got up off his pristine new dog bed and stretched his long, furry, juvenile legs. He stared the deerhound stare, the one they use when they are willing you to obey them. Miles knew only too well what he wanted: to run with the greyhounds in the meadow. Fergus instinctively knew humans were woefully inadequate at understanding dog body language, so to offer help, he stood by the door and prodded it with his long, aristocratic nose.

'You're right, I should follow her.' Fergus bound off across the gardens to look for his canine friends, bouncing along like a newborn lamb in spring.

Lambs might have started to appear in the fields, but that didn't mean it was a warm day. Miles doubled back to unhook his long, waxed jacket off the coat rack and wrapped a long woollen scarf round his neck. At least the wind had died down and it was now just the natural chill of spring. The trees in the woodland were just beginning to take on the faint green hue of new leaves; the willows down by the stream and water meadow were showing the new growth of their summer leaves.

He had been right; she had headed for the bench down in the water meadow area by the stream, which was already showing signs of its winter flow. Miles stopped to reconsider his actions. Should he return to the house and wait for the calm after the storm?

Fergus had unwittingly made the decision for him. Lucy

had drawn up her legs and was not so much as sitting on the bench but curled up in a defensive ball with her arms wrapped round her shins. The young dog was so delighted to find her that manners and reservations were thrown aside as he jumped up on the bench. He tried to stand on her and lick her face, his body quivering with canine excitement.

'Get off, you stupid mutt!' But Lucy could not help but laugh at his antics, making it hard to maintain an angry state. She was apprehensive about Miles' presence; she willed him not to continue the harsh words he'd spoken earlier.

'Could we talk to each other rather than shouting?'

Lucy's shoulders twitched in a random sort of way, it was hard for Miles to know if this was agreement or not. He persevered, nonetheless.

'I will not apologise for having money. I have worked hard for it and no one has suffered as a consequence. You are right; it probably could be considered obscene wealth when compared to other professions who work long, hard hours just to survive.'

Lucy did not move.

'You are right, it allows me to buy my way out of difficulties, indulge myself in expensive projects and even help other people. But to you, I only know what money can buy.

Lucy uncurled herself and put her feet on the ground but remained silent.

'I know money can't buy love, happiness, contentment nor make people like me or respect me. However, there is no joy in being treated like a walking wallet!' Lucy's head jerked round.

'I never said that!'

As she spoke, she looked up and Miles could see her eyes were reddened by tears.

'What do you want from me?' Miles just stopped himself from quipping "apart from money". He sat beside her.

'I don't know anything about you.' Lucy shivered.

Miles noticed and was about to offer her his coat but changed his mind. Instead, he stretched out his arm, the jacket held open and indicated she should share. He held his breath, awaiting a verbal onslaught. But she slid across the bench and leaned against him as he wrapped the coat around her. It was this gesture, the kindness and physical contact that broke the impasse between them.

'Money, or lack of it, has been at the root of everything that's hurt me. I've never had sufficient money to feel secure, content or even in control of my life. I'm jealous of you and the freedoms it gives you.'

Miles nearly broke the moment by speaking but stopped himself just in time.

'Money defined my future before I was born. My mother's family were all farmers, asset-rich maybe, but cash-poor. My father's family, not that I met them, were impoverished minor Italian aristocracy, desperate for my father to marry into money to repair the roof of their disintegrating palazzo in Tuscany.'

'How did they meet?' Miles noticed how she no longer referred to her mother as Mama.

'There was an American artist called Daniel Graves who founded an art school in the late 1990s. She visited the Florence Academy of Art during a trip there where she met him and fell in love with…'

'Oh, my god, is he your father?' Miles interrupted.

'No, let me finish. She fell in love with Florence, the romance of the city, its climate, culture and people. She applied for an art scholarship to attend a course there. When she came back to England, she badgered her parents, worked in crappy agricultural jobs, anything to make money. It was the only thing she needed to follow her heart to Florence. She got there, then lost her virginity and her heart to a young Italian, only to face his utter rejection. There are no photos of him, she must have destroyed them all, but there is a painting of hers of a group sitting out on a terrazza at a table eating olives and drinking wine, the Tuscan countryside in the background. I think he is one of them.'

'Let me guess, there is a young man who is tall, slim and good-looking. He has thick, wavy black hair and a bit of a Roman nose!' Miles butted in.

'As a child, I decided that he was like that and created a complete myth around him; a tragic Florentine nobleman who had died young in an accident and left my mother a poor widow. At least part of it was right: he left her and she was poor.'

'Many children make up stories to make themselves more interesting.'

'She spent the rest of her life trying to make ends meet by painting commissions and doing part-time jobs, all punctuated by passionate love affairs that never lasted, usually because her lovers went back to their wives.'

'How is money to be blamed for that?'

'She loved us but was thoroughly impractical. It was always

feast or famine for us. If she was paid for a commission, it was feasting time, lots of treats and trips out. But even then, she wasn't practical. She once bought me a beautiful party dress, all pink and flouncy, yet I had holes in my shoes! When the summer agricultural jobs and the tourist season waitressing jobs dried up, it was back to endless final demands and cheap, nasty food.' Then Lucy's voice tensed.

'Then she met Denis Moncrief.'

Miles could feel her body stiffen like a board beneath his jacket, she was no longer relaxed. He felt it was time to stop there; "Denis" was obviously the trigger word and she needed more time to get past it.

'Hey, look at the time, Fergus hasn't had his dinner, and the boys must be getting cold. Let's get back to the house, the kitchen should be nice and warm with the Aga running.' He stood up and the jacket slid off her shoulders. He quickly took it off and wrapped it round her.

They walked up the meadow towards the house. Miles reflected that restoring centuries of physical neglect of an old house was a piece of cake compared to trying to repair life's emotional damage done to a human being. He felt inadequate to do both and he feared there was a lot more hurt and grief in Lucy's life and it obviously started with Denis. Every fibre in his body screamed, "Don't get involved!"

'Come in and tell me about the auction.' They had come into the house via the kitchen. Ozzy and Marble waited politely whilst Miles wiped their wet paws on an old towel. Fergus wriggled about, making it as difficult as possible. Lucy spoke first.

'I really didn't think I needed to make an appointment

to visit. If I had known you were entertaining, I wouldn't have disturbed you. I needed the floor plans to refer to after a typically irritating phone call from Sean. Bloody man seems to think he knows it all.'

Miles just stared at her. Was that meant to be an apology? If so, it was pitifully weak. The phrase pot and kettle popped into his mind. No wonder Sean and Lucy clashed; both as opinionated as each other. But if he was a betting man, his money would be on Lucy winning every time.

'To save you the question, the woman was Leonie Kimathi. She's an investment researcher. I used to work with her.'

'She is very beautiful.' Lucy desperately wanted to ask why Leonie had wrapped herself around Miles.

'Yes, exceedingly so, and terrifyingly clever. But despite that, she doesn't have all the answers to what life throws at her. Her partner, Alex, wants to have a family but she isn't convinced. They must sort it out between themselves without involving me.' There was a finality to his statement. Miles wanted the topic of conversation to change, so he said, 'Let's recap about these oil paintings. What do we know? What do we think and what is just wild guesswork?' Miles was more than happy to talk about the paintings as they gave him a welcome distraction from Leonie's awful proposal.

'So we think the paintings are in a set. Possibly of five because of the "V".'

Lucy nodded her head in agreement.

Miles continued. 'We're sure they start with the view across the formal garden and then there's the one of the woodland path, with the two men and the packhorse. We have those two already and I doubt if there is one that precedes the view from the house. But there might be one of the meadow in between the garden and the wood.' Lucy nodded again, then chipped in.

'They're the same size and painted by the same artist, both on wooden board, which is odd because the fashion had turned to painting on stretched canvas by the early 1720s.' Lucy thought about this for a moment, then suddenly remembered something Adrian had mentioned.

'Did I tell you that Adrian thinks it might be possible he can prove that the paintings are painted on a single, larger board that was cut up for the purpose?'

'How?'

'On the reverse are sketching lines of a draft composition. Possibly a horse or pony, given the broad sweep of some of the lines.' Lucy had seen the marks. Though similar in style and material, none of the lines on the two paintings connected to make any sense with only two of them.

'What are the odds of a third picture coming up for auction within a few months of each other?' Miles' mathematical mind was trying to balance coincidence with logic. He picked up the auction catalogue and looked at the very small photograph of Lot 383. He wasn't convinced, but still he was drawn towards it. It was a meadow landscape with a pathway going off at an angle towards a woodland. He felt a tingling of excitement.

'OK, let's go. However, you failed to mention the auction is in Lewes in East Sussex! That's a very early start. Let's hope the A12 is clear and no more idiots start climbing the wires on the Dartford Crossing!' Miles hesitated.

'Before you go home, I wondered if you would care to,

I mean, join me…' Miles was in two minds as to whether to ask the question, but he took a deep breath and said, 'It's my birthday soon, would you like to join me for dinner? I thought The Old Manor restaurant could be good. It's got good reviews and it's old so you would like that.'

Lucy stared at him before giving a rather enigmatic smile and nodded.

Chapter Eleven
April 1721

All was not well with the Matthews household. Thomas was unbearable with excitement; Constance was permanently weepy, and the tension caused Joseph to wet the bed several times, much to his grandmother's distress.

No one had considered what furnishings Somersham Court needed or should have, but without discussion, they were provided by Lord Edgerton; just enough furnishings to maintain status in the public rooms and functionality elsewhere. Carver was still the steward. He had been happy to change employer, as Sir Stanley Jacks was a mannerless buffoon. His first impressions of Thomas Matthews had been favourable, and he knew that his father was good for additional coin if necessary.

It was a strange little cavalcade that travelled that day to Somersham Court. Even Alice was downhearted, fearful of Constance being left alone with Thomas, no longer protected by the proximity of her husband's family. Little Joseph also did not want to be parted from his grandparents and the two kind maids.

When they arrived, John was astonished to see the promised furnishings; they were the same as when he had originally visited Sir Stanley Jacks. Edgerton must have bought them from him and stored them somewhere. But why was unclear, as his own house would have been fully furnished. John couldn't help but wonder the reason Edgerton would have done that. How could he have known that they would be needed so?

Alice promised to have some of their provisions sent across to them whilst Constance got her new domestic routines organised. Thomas was in seventh heaven, as a note from Edgerton had been delivered that morning instructing Thomas to arrange a dinner party to take place soon.

No one could have been more surprised, or relieved, when Thomas had told his father of Lord Edgerton's proposal to lease Somersham Court and install him and family at the house as a business associate. John's first reaction was that it was too good to be true, but John's lawyer, Michael la Trobe, had been through the agreements thoroughly and found nothing amiss with the lease apart from some rather harsh penalty clauses in extreme circumstances. John had also asked Michael to appraise the terms of the business agreement between Edgerton and Thomas. This had been done without Thomas' knowledge or consent; so too the copy of the agreement made by the lawyer's clerk. John was unnerved by Michael's words of warning that the agreement was rather one-sided, much in favour of Edgerton and could leave Thomas vulnerable to litigation should there be unforeseen problems. But Thomas had signed and Michael could only advise on the contents not make changes.

The weeks had flown by as Thomas took up residence. Before the move, Lord Edgerton became a frequent visitor at Manor Farm and spent some considerable time discussing the processes and politics of the import/export business on which he wanted intelligence. Edgerton was pleasantly surprised at how quick a learner Thomas was, proving a lot more astute than he could have imagined. The only fault Edgerton could find was Thomas' humour, which bordered on the base and bawdy. This would not be suitable in the fashionable salons. But as this was not going to be a long-term business relationship, he dismissed his concerns.

Constance had become increasingly more depressed and introverted the closer the time came to move. Joseph was not happy either; he saw his mother's distress and he feared being isolated from his grandparents who seemed to protect him and his mother from his father's cruel behaviour. A resentful cook-cum-housekeeper had been hired by Lady Adele Edgerton to keep house: the grim-faced Mrs Phillips, who out of earshot was rather aptly nicknamed Mrs Bottle, as she was rather partial to the leftover contents of wine bottles and those opened "accidentally on purpose". A local girl had been brought in as a kitchen maid and general skivvy. Lady Edgerton was appalled that Constance did not have a lady's maid, and despite Constance's protestations that she was perfectly capable of dressing herself, Mary arrived on Lady Edgerton's recommendation. Thomas told Constance not to make a fuss and to be grateful for the advice of a "real" lady who knew how to conduct herself in social circles. Even innocent Constance couldn't miss the irony of his statement.

Several days after Thomas and his family left Old Manor Farm, Alice insisted John took to Somersham Court a flitch of dry cured bacon from their Tamworth pigs, bred and kept for that purpose. There were other provisions as well, but so closely wrapped in baskets he hadn't been sure of their contents. Still, Alice had told him they were to be delivered.

The empty baskets now rattled alongside him in the pony cart on his return journey. The reception he had received from Thomas had been lukewarm, but Constance had been pitifully grateful for a friendly face and different conversation. Mrs Phillips had been less than pleased by the gift of provisions, as it implied she did not do her job properly. The delicious jams and pickles were pushed to the back of the pantry's shelves until she could pass them off as her own efforts.

The visit had left John in a contemplative mood and the rhythm of the pony's harness and hooves lulled him into introspection. He feared he was losing his way in life. He knew he did not feel comfortable in the confines of Somersham Court and yet he had become estranged from his simpler life based on the cycle of the seasons at Old Manor Farm. John was also aware that Thomas now had a patron who had managed to spark some drive and purpose in him, which John as his father had failed to do. Never had John seen Thomas go about his schooling with such diligence and enthusiasm that Thomas now applied to his reading of *The Merchant's Magazine* and the *Course of the Exchange* and other business publications. The large writing desk in the airy parlour of Somersham Court was covered in reports of shipping lists, detailing the imports and exports alongside scribbled notes in Thomas' hand. What really surprised him was to see copies of *The Ipswich Journal* which had only been launched in the August of that year. Despite the weekly periodical's name, it offered national and international news and the circulation had a limited subscription to only a few hundred influential people. The person who gave Thomas access to their copies obviously sat at the high table of East Anglian commerce. John was concerned that Thomas was out of his depth and he did not trust the motives of Lord Edgerton, especially as John was aware Lord Edgerton's heir could be possibly his bastard grandson thanks to Thomas' dalliance with the fickle and faithless Lady Edgerton.

John was aware that Thomas' mood could not have been more different to his, as his son strutted around, elated that specially selected business notables were to dine at Somersham Court. He boasted to his father that he was to welcome a society hostess by the name of Madame Cecile Le Fevre, who would bring a small army of additional servants, including a cook. Thomas explained in no uncertain terms that neither he nor his wife was expected to do or provide anything, only to follow Madame Cecile's instructions. John was relieved that Constance was not expected to organise such an event. Though appreciative of Edgerton's generosity, it should have made John very proud that his son was moving in such social and commercial circles, but John felt a strange niggling in the back of his mind that it was all too good to be true.

After his father had departed, Thomas wandered into the drawing room and admired the newly hung painting over the fireplace, a family portrait that gave him a sense of "arrival" in society. He was unaware that he would be mocked behind his back because the painting was not by any recognised or fashionable artist. However, it was the smaller painting on the opposite wall that he held dear, of a fine-looking lemon and white greyhound with his son, Joseph, standing to one side, the child's hand resting gently on the dog's neck. A gilt plaque proudly announced the painting was called *Somersham Boy,* which was potentially misleading as it was the hound's name and not a reference to Thomas Matthews' son. The painting was one of quality, even Thomas could recognise that, which was why he asked the apprentice Edward Versey to stay on to paint his horse after Clive Millar had moved on to his newest patron.

As John drove the pony cart home, he was aware of a sense of foreboding. He could not immediately think what had put his senses on alert to this extent. His heart sank at the visible decline in Constance and Joseph's confidence and they seemed to cling to each other both mentally and physically in their gilded cage. Meanwhile, Thomas was thriving; the lease had been paid, so too the rent paid in gold was in his now depleted money chest.

Then it hit him: the furniture was the same furnishings he had seen when he had visited Sir Stanley Jacks to make the offer for Somersham Court. John had bought the house with vacant possession; there wasn't anything left when he took his family to visit the first time. Despite furniture not being foremost in his mind when he had been with Sir Stanley, he still had a vivid recollection of the brocade-covered chair where the pompous oaf had sat. Now it was all back, even in the same place.

'How did the furniture get back there?' He spoke out loud; the rhetorical question went unanswered.

He brought the pony to a standstill, as though the enormity of the question was so great he could not drive and think at the same time. He asked himself what the link was between Jacks and Edgerton. All the landed gentry in East Anglia were known to each other, most of them related by marriage, as hapless daughters were married off into other families to retain or gain lands. The only conclusion that made any sense was that Jacks had sold the furniture to Edgerton. But why?

He was still thinking about the concerns when he arrived home to find Alice, who was at the back of the farmhouse, in the area where the domestic work of the household was carried out. Once, these rooms had stood separate, but as the main building had expanded over the years, were now attached around a small courtyard.

She was mildly irritated by Daisy, one of the young girls from the village, who seemed to be incapable of remembering that the buttery was where the liquids and fruit were kept, and the larder was where the meat and fowl were kept. She had just found a jug of milk in the pantry where only bread and dry provisions should be. She had been about to find Daisy but stopped when she heard the sound of shod hooves coming past the windows and going to the stables. She had not expected to see Daniel in the back courtyard.

'Heavens above, son, you look fair worn out. And your clothes are soiled.' Alice was shocked at the state of her youngest son, who rather than his twenty-four years, looked more like a schoolboy who had been fighting behind the schoolhouse.

'Spent several hours at the Edwards' farm. Their cussed old horse knocked me flying off my feet.' Daniel grimaced at the thought of the younger children trying not to giggle at the sight of the landlord's son landing face-down in the farmyard muck and mud.

'Why were you there?' Alice asked half-heartedly, her mind still on the family's provisions and storage.

'Farmer Edwards is still plagued by that injury to his shoulder he received during harvest last year. He has limited use in his right arm some days. I visited him on another matter but saw him struggling to put his horse to the harrow.' Daniel avoided mentioning to his mother that he missed the physical side of farm work, the sight of the surrounding countryside and the sounds of a horse in harness working with the seagulls wheeling above his head. But most of all he craved the smell of newly worked earth and the sweat of an honest animal working.

'Do you mean our little Molly's father?' Alice's attention was now on Daniel, for she had a fondness for the girl who worked in the kitchen along with Daisy. 'Surely she has two brothers who should be working with their father?'

'Aye, but they are but twelve and fourteen; they are good willing lads but lack the physical strength of a grown man for the heavy field work. I will sort it out, as Edwards is a good tenant and a knowledgeable countryman.

'Now, I must wash and change, for I know you would not have me in the parlour like this. May I talk with you afterwards?' Then as an afterthought, he said, 'Where is father?' Daniel had wanted to speak to Alice alone.

'Only he knows that, for he did not think to tell me! He is out abroad, no doubt with business on his mind, for that seems his only interest.' Alice had not noticed the trap had come into the yard or that John was quietly rubbing down the animal whilst it munched gratefully on a manger of hay.

'Go, go and tidy yourself. I will wait in the parlour. Don't tarry, I have plenty to occupy me and have no time to waste.' Alice was curious about what her son wanted to say.

Daniel came back down a short while later a lot less dishevelled. He loved the intimacy of the parlour, a smaller room away from the large central hall which was the heart of the house, its occupants and their business. He felt both nervous and excited. He sat himself in the other chair by the fireplace.

'I want to marry.' Daniel, as always, came straight to the point. 'Thomas and Constance are now at Somersham Court. I would live here with my wife. She can assist you whilst learning your skills of house management and especially to learn your fine baking and brewing.' He grinned at Alice. Like most men, he thought a few flattering words would win the day.

Alice did not reply.

'You will be here to guide her through pregnancy and childbirth.'

Still, Alice did not respond.

'She is of an amiable nature; she is healthy and has healthy brothers and sisters also.' Daniel was now unnerved by his mother's silence. Had he misjudged his moment? He could not read her thoughts from her expression.

'Daniel, are you describing a woman you would give your heart and life to or a prize sow? Alice glared at him and continued. 'Though a practical approach is to be lauded, this young girl is a human being with thoughts, hopes and aspirations of her own. I have heard you speak of a mare with greater affection and respect.'

Daniel just stared at her. Surely his mother should be pleased that he wasn't in mind to marry a pointless woman like Constance. He had stated what he wanted, what he needed: a pleasant and compliant life companion to keep a good house and produce healthy children.

'Does this girl have a name? Whose daughter is she?'

'Ellen Holsey, she is the daughter of Alfred Holsey, a master mason of Swaffham. Her mother passed some years ago. She has a younger sister nearly old enough to take on the duties and responsibilities of keeping house for their father.'

Alice had always admired her pragmatic and logical son, but his words were a sad indictment of men's attitudes to her sex.

'She has a good nature; I have seen her with nieces and nephews.' Daniel, unaware of his mother's reaction, continued.

'She has pretty russet-coloured hair and freckles across the top of her nose.'

At last, thought Alice, *he is actually thinking of her as a person rather than describing her with the merits of a prize animal. But then, of course he is besotted with her and thinks I would be more impressed by listing her good points first.*

'Does she find any merit in you?' Alice was amused to see her favourite son blush.

'I believe she thinks me steady and sober in nature and not unpleasant in countenance and, most important of all, is that I will honour my marriage vows,' Daniel replied solemnly.

'If she is of such an amiable disposition and imbued with so many points of recommendation, then she will be made welcome here. However, you do not have to convince only me; you must persuade Ellen and her father that your proposal is welcome.' Alice had spoken with a light tone, but it came as no surprise when Daniel's face fell as he had not even considered the possibility that Ellen's father would not give his permission. Alice knew her son to be serious-minded, but she hoped he would develop a sense of humour, which to her way of thinking was a necessity in marriage.

'Daniel, I only want you to consider this, for I would not want to give offence to Ellen nor her father. Consider your words carefully before you speak to him. As Ellen is motherless, I would consider it a privilege if she were to be married from our house, which is only a short walk to the church. I would prepare her in readiness for the day and put on a good wedding breakfast.'

Alice did not know her son as well as she had thought, unaware that he had already talked to Ellen about marrying from Old Manor Farm and that they both hoped fervently that Alice would volunteer. Ellen's father was infamous for the tightness of his purse strings.

'Am I to be consulted on this matter?' John opened the parlour door wide, making both Daniel and Alice start as they had been unaware of his presence just outside the door. John had, to his shame, listened to their conversation and his pride as head of the family was offended that his wife and son should be discussing and agreeing matters without his consultation.

'Do you object?' Alice asked curtly.

'No. But, Daniel, you should have come to me first.'

'Why?' Daniel knew his father was right.

'Because it affects us all. A marriage means a new person living here. Such matters should not be taken lightly.'

Alice dropped her gaze to the ground and left the room; Daniel at least offered John a mumbled excuse before following her. Both mother and son exchanged looks, thinking the same thing. John's demand for consultation on major family matters was hypocritical, for he hadn't felt the need to consult his family when he had made his decision to buy Somersham Court.

CHAPTER TWELVE
April 2021

Miles, delighted to have all the dogs together, was concerned because now he could not leave the premises for any length of time. Fergus' house training was good but not perfect, with occasional accidents. He knew the solution: he needed more help besides the two stalwart ladies who came in to clean on Thursdays, their tuts and clucks of annoyance could be heard when forced to clear up the large amounts of dog hair and muddy footprints. There were the gardens to consider too; everything had been laid to lawn over the years for easier maintenance. Whilst Miles did not want the intricate pattern gardens that needed tending by an army of gardeners, he did think that some colour and form in the borders would soften the starkness of the layout.

Now, stretched out on a settee, Miles did rather find the idea of domestic staff rather scary, with all the employment laws in force and the risk of costly tribunals and suchlike if things went awry. What if he hired some complete rip-off merchants and got stuck with them? Though he did not subscribe to the treatment of servants of centuries ago, they could at least be dismissed with impunity.

It was five o'clock. Marble was watching him like a hawk as it was the dogs' dinner time and he was waiting for Miles to move. Fergus was lying upside-down on a rather gaudy-looking throw on another settee. Miles chuckled to himself. He was obviously beginning to become "Normal as Norfolk" given a telephone conversation a few days earlier. Fergus needed socialisation classes as he had to learn to mix with other dogs of all different shapes and sizes. Miles had spoken to a rather intimidating-sounding lady in Beccles who gave him a list of things to bring with him. A favourite toy was the first hurdle as Fergus loved them all equally, throwing them around the house, leaving them on staircases and even leaving them outside to get soggy in the rain. Miles decided on "Floppy Fox". He had also been instructed to bring his dog's bed. Now that was an even bigger decision because there were dog beds in various rooms of the house, all mostly ignored. Fergus' favourite place and position was lying on one of the settees, upside-down with legs stretched out as though in full gallop, showing his juvenile "crown jewels" for all to see. Miles quickly took a photo of Fergus in his recumbent position and sent it from his mobile phone to the dog trainer, explaining that the dog's favourite bed was too big to get in the car! It was meant to be a joke. Big mistake. A frosty reply pinged back, suggesting just a blanket for the dog to lie on.

When he turned up for the class he was amazed at the variety of breeds and sizes. Fergus towered over them and of all the puppies present, Fergus decided a tiny Chihuahua no bigger than his head was now his new best friend.

Later that same evening, he phoned Leonie. He told her that he had to find a new purpose in life and would she be interested in looking at some fledgling business ideas sometime.

She was not surprised. 'What sort of thing have you in

mind?' asked Leonie.

Miles explained about Lucy's old ducks and how they had been asset-rich but cash-poor; how they had struggled because they did not know about wealth management. Miles put forward an idea as to how such people could be given access to courses and websites, or even counsellors to advise them of their options.

'I think Age Concern and the Citizen's Advice Bureau and suchlike have rather beaten you to that gig, Miles!' Leonie did not mean to mock Miles, but there was an element of smugness in her voice as she had the previous year repeatedly challenged him as to what he was going to do out in the wilds of Norfolk.

They kicked some ideas around for a while, but Miles knew in his heart he was clutching at straws. Leonie then laughed triumphantly.

'Marry Lucy, make lots of babies and live happily ever after in your country estate.' Then she made her excuses and rang off.

Miles stood staring at the phone. What had made Leonie say something as stupid as that? Alex had obviously warped her mind with baby talk.

Leonie's flippant comment about Lucy had appeal but was not the solution. He needed to be comfortable with what the modern world referred to as the work-life balance. He bent over to collect up the newspapers and supplements scattered around, including the one that featured management vacancies. Then something caught his eye. It was an advert for a consultant wanted by a software house on the outskirts of Cambridge specialising in money-trading systems. He tore it out, but then all the good reasons for not applying flooded his brain. Did he want to go back into an office environment again? What about the dogs? Cambridge was over sixty miles away. Did he need the money? Despite his reservations, Miles decided to phone the following morning to ask for more information.

The next morning, he initially had a favourable preliminary conversation with someone from the software company, until he learned that they wanted someone to be more of a peripatetic project manager rather than a true business consultant. So Miles dismissed the idea. He decided to have a chat with his mother about domestic help. His mother, Sally, was a sensible and pragmatic woman. She suggested a look at *The Lady* magazine's website might prove a good starting point for finding a solution to domestic and canine needs. This was a whole new world to Miles who found the advertisement for a "Dynamic domestic couple" offering their services, interesting. However, he immediately regretted phoning them. His relief was palpable when they announced that the position was not what they were looking for; his house and estate were too small and did not include much entertaining. He was however much taken with the "Experienced gardener, loves dogs, and wife does domestic duties". Much to his relief, they were local and were keen to come for an interview; so keen, they visited the next morning.

Miles took to them instantly, Betty and Dick Brown. They were "on notice" as their employers had died and the estate was being auctioned off by probate requirements. They had not been given the opportunity to buy their tied cottage; they admitted that they couldn't afford it anyway because of incomers with bigger budgets wanting its beautiful location. Dick had been a jack-of-all-trades on the estate whose passion was vegetable growing. Betty had worked in the house in a domestic capacity but expressed a concern that she hadn't been an actual housekeeper, which Miles instantly dismissed as a problem.

He explained that their accommodation would be the old coach house; he thought it sounded slightly more attractive than calling it "the old stables". The outbuildings had been the first thing he had restored so that he had somewhere to live himself until the problems of the main house had been addressed. He told them that he would like to engage them, subject to references. With a deadpan expression, Dick assured him that there was no need for a reference as he knew a couple of chaps who worked for Sean the builder and played lawn bowls at Badingham. He confirmed they had vouched that Miles was a fair-minded chap and would make a good employer. Miles was speechless.

Betty, seeing the look on Miles' face, interrupted her husband to say that they had written references from their current employer which should prove satisfactory. There was only one hitch in hiring this couple: Betty always referred to her husband as "my Dick" which sparked off a suppressed schoolboy sniggering in his head. But a small matter. It was agreed that Betty and "her Dick" would return in a few days' time to discuss details of their roles and get to know Somersham Court.

Miles had barely cleared away the tea tray following their visit when the landline rang. It was Dick Brown. He wanted to know if the old kitchen garden was to be restored and if he could keep a few Bantams. Miles expressed his concerns that the dogs might play havoc with the little chickens. However, they did agree that a house like Somersham Court should have an enclosed vegetable garden with fruit trees and chickens strutting and clucking as they foraged.

Dick rang off a very happy man.

Fergus had been fed and now stretched his legs in the garden whilst Miles sat at the wooden garden table watching the sunset. He thought of Lucy's first visit and the beaming smile she gave him when she found the dog treats for Ozzy and Marble.

There was still a chill in the night air, so Miles called Fergus in and returned to the sitting room with a large glass of red wine. Once the fire had been lit, he found himself yet again mulling over the last ten months and in every memory, there was Lucy.

He thought of her charging around the countryside in her ancient car, trying to right the wrongs of the world. He likened her to someone trying to save World War I casualties armed with just a bottle of aspirin and a box of plasters: totally ineffective but done with great enthusiasm and a heart full of love. He got up and wandered over to the windows to admire the sunset across the meadow. He hoped she was looking at the same sunset but across the Kent Weald.

§

The following morning, Miles was busy, his tasks including booking a table for two at The Old Manor restaurant. He was not one for making a fuss about birthdays and though he did not relish getting another year older, he was looking forward to dining there. He was intrigued to see inside after having seen it only fleetingly from the car on his first visit to Adrian. He was about to send Lucy a text about the booking when his phone started ringing. It was Lucy.

'You must be psychic; I was about to message you,' quipped Miles.

'Hi, I really need a favour. Can you help?' There was considerable urgency to her voice.

'Depends on the favour!'

'Adrian isn't here; I haven't seen him for days and his phone is switched off. I've got to go down to Devon to see a prospective client and I want to call in on Bunny on the way home.

'Could Ozzy and Marble come to stay for a couple of days? I can't leave them here, what with Adrian off on one of his jaunts. God knows when he'll return, he is being even more secretive than usual.'

'Of course, drop them off on your way. Fergus would love to have some company; as Skye isn't coming for another couple of weeks.'

She thanked him profusely and said she'd see him later in the day.

Miles realised he hadn't asked her to bring dog food with her, so he went down to the kitchen and, from one of the storage rooms which Lucy called the buttery, he took another raw dog food package out of the freezer.

He put the kettle on to make a pot of coffee as he thought she might like one before her drive. It didn't seem long before Fergus' barking announced the arrival of the Morris Minor and the disembarkation of two over-excited greyhounds.

Lucy stood on the doorstep, with arms full of dog beds, blankets, soft toys and a plastic bag that appeared to be dripping blood on the stone steps.

'Sorry it's dripping. I'd already defrosted it.' She made no move to come in.

'Would you like a coffee before you go?'

'No thanks, I must get going. I am really nervous about the meeting; it is a really interesting restoration project and it pays well.'

Miles took advantage of her arms being full and took her gently by the shoulders. 'Calm down, you need to concentrate on the driving.' Then to Lucy's surprise and his own, he gently kissed her on the cheek. 'The boys will be fine with me. Let me know when you arrive and how it goes tomorrow.'

She shoved all the dog bedding into his arms and with a cheeky grin, kissed him on the cheek and assured him she would.

§

The little Morris Minor bounced its way over the bumpy road up to Boughton House. Lucy's heart sank when she saw Colin and Lottie's Volvo already parked there. She wandered around to the side door, but before she could knock, the door opened and a belligerent Colin barred her way.

'I see it didn't take long before the vultures arrived then.' His pudgy face was contorted with malice.

The first thought that went through Lucy's mind was that he was referring to himself. The thought was quickly followed by the desire to punch the little shit in the face. She ignored him and called out for Bunny, but there was no reply or, if there was, she didn't hear one.

'Get back into that ridiculous car of yours and return to yokel land. Lottie is looking after her mother and I'm in charge of what needs doing.' As if that wasn't rude enough, he continued, 'So you can take your envious eyes off my family's antiques and stop trying to worm yourself into Bunny's will.'

Now that really was the pot calling the kettle black, thought Lucy, the idea so preposterous she nearly laughed. 'I would like to see Bunny. Now that is not too much to ask?' She fought hard to keep her temper under control.

'She is not available to see anyone. Leave now or I will call the police.'

Lucy stepped back in astonishment and found the door firmly shut in her face.

She drove about half a mile down the road and pulled into the car park of a small pub and having skipped breakfast, was hungry. She rang Miles and explained what had happened. He was horrified and angry.

Unbeknown to Colin, Bunny had heard the exchange and his imperious statements. She was livid with the way Colin had spoken to Lucy. Colin would rue the day he had spoken to her like that.

Colin and Lottie had already taken it upon themselves to visit several care homes within easy reach of their home in Tenterden. They had discussed the idea of building an annexe onto their house using money from the sale of the big house and using a lasting power of attorney to control the proceeds. They considered the annexe option would take too long, also planning permission and then the physical building would mean months of care home costs, but neither of them was prepared to commit to the physical care of Bunny should her capabilities diminish in time.

Chapter Thirteen

May 1721

Carver had finished supervising the unloading of the delivery for the cellars. His main concern was that the wines had time to settle, especially the port, and keeping them out of the clutches of Mrs Phillips, the housekeeper. Everything was going according to plan, which always worried him as it made him think he had overlooked something. Or was it someone?

Carver used the back stairs to get to the room that had been allocated as a temporary studio for Clive Millar and his apprentice. It was one of the smaller bedrooms on the first floor, on the north side of the house, chosen for the clarity of its light. Carver was aware Millar had moved onto pastures new and left young Ned Versey to finish off.

Carver knocked on the door before opening it. 'Good day to you, Ned.' Ned looked up and was grateful to see it was Carver and not Thomas Matthews.

'I'll be needing these two paintings for the drawing room before next week's dinner party Master Thomas is holding. Can you ensure they are ready to hang by then?'

Ned looked startled. The paintings had been prematurely hung in the drawing room for John Matthews' visit because Thomas had wanted to boast and impress; pointless, as his father had barely noticed them and certainly not observed that they were unfinished and without varnish.

'I have only just put the last layer of varnish on the family painting. It should be dry enough by then but must be handled carefully. But the hound needs at least one or more coats of varnish and there are some little touch-ups needed. So I would need the painting returned for completion.'

Carver nodded in agreement but doubted that it would be returned to the studio for a second time once Thomas had had them back in pride of place.

He walked over and looked carefully at the portrait of the greyhound. 'Did you paint this, Ned, or did Millar?'

Ned hesitated. He had painted it but, as an apprentice, he could not put his signature on the canvas and it would probably be signed by Millar.

'Aye, I did, but it is accredited to Master Millar.'

'Well, that is nonsense. It is by far the better painting.' Carver picked it up, much to Ned's consternation, and carried it over towards the window. 'I am no artist, nor knowledgeable in these matters, but the detail of the coat, the definition of muscle. And the animal's eyes are as real as the living creature.'

Ned wasn't going to argue with him because he knew Carver's assessment was true. He kept quiet.

'When does your apprenticeship end?'

'I am not sure. I have had five birthdays in his employ; I must be close to the end. I seem to remember that when I attain the age of majority, I am free of indenture.'

'Well, it's about time you found out and signed your own work.' Carver put the painting back on the easel, much to Ned's relief.

Later that day, Constance did not hear the coach wheels

crunch across the gravel and pull up outside the main entrance to Somersham Court, nor watch two liveried servants jump down and, with practised ease, one went to hold the lead horses' heads whilst the other let down the step and opened the coach door. The first sight of the occupant was a pale grey, gloved hand on the forearm of the footman. There followed a petite woman, barely visible in a travelling cloak wrapped around her. She stopped and looked up at the house and was disappointed; not as grandiose as she was led to believe. Her footman scampered up the steps to call for the steward. The length of time she was left standing at the main entrance did not impress her. She tapped her foot on the stone tiles in impatience.

An unwanted fleeting thought flashed through her mind, but it stayed long enough to remind her that it was exactly twenty-nine years to the day that she had been found wrapped in rags, discarded on stone tiles at the entrance to a weaver's workshop. No name, no family and no life expectation.

The door opened, and she was bidden to enter, taking a careful and critical note of the entrance hall and the rather disappointing staircase, not one that could be used for a dramatic entrance.

'Madame Cecile le Fevre,' announced Carver.

Constance was taken aback when Thomas had demanded she prepare herself for a visitor later that day, without giving any details. Now she found herself feeling flustered and unprepared as she stood by her husband. They were mesmerised by the diminutive figure who, upon having her cloak removed, revealed a pale bluish-grey silk dress. The silver threads that formed the extravagant patterns of fruit and leaves were caught by the shafts of light from the nearby window. The heavy train of her mantua had been looped up and so skilfully cut that only the right side of the material showed. Wealth and elegance radiated from the top of her curly blonde hair barely contained in a small linen cap, right down to the carved wooden heels of her damask-covered heeled shoes.

Constance gasped. She felt colourless and drab, not for the first time, in her brown woollen dress by comparison. Thomas' reaction to this beautiful socialite was a primitive stirring that fortunately was unseen due to the generous amount of material in his satin breeches.

All three acknowledged each other with a polite bob of their heads.

'Madame Le Fevre, welcome to Somersham Court. Lord Edgerton wrote of your visit and its purpose. Come in, can I offer you refreshment after your travels?' Thomas executed a perfect courtly bow.

Constance was transfixed, she had never seen such a perfect, dazzling woman before.

Cecile walked towards her with her delicate little hand extended. '*Bonjour*, Madame Matthews, delighted to make your acquaintance.' Cecile had to stifle a giggle as Constance performed a clumsy curtsy.

Constance had no way of knowing just how fake Madame Le Fevre was. She was entranced by her charm, the clothes and the strange accent. What would she have thought if the truth was known to her?

Cecile Le Fevre was not so much a fake as created by a carefully woven mix of fact and fiction. What society was told and accepted was that she was a French widow with private income. Indeed, she had been loved and raised by a Huguenot family in Canterbury, which gave her knowledge of commerce and the power of money. The ruse was put in place because a widow could legally own property, manage their estate and have no male to determine the future. There was no husband, nor ever likely to be. She was naturally bi-lingual, but it suited her to be thought of as having a restricted comprehension of English. She had discovered that people chatter more freely amongst themselves if they consider the foreigner unlikely to understand.

During the next hour, Cecile explained exactly how the party was going to be carried out. There was a natural authority in her voice that meant nothing was challenged by the master and mistress of the house. The reality of it was that they were both relieved, for various reasons. Thomas did not have to pay and Constance did not have to organise nor host the event. What could have been simpler for them?

'I see you do not have a musical instrument in your drawing room.' Cecile's eyes had noted a good many things about the quality and taste of the furnishings. Edgerton had told her that the furniture had been provided by him and was part of the tenancy agreement. She noted the predictable painting over the fireplace, a somewhat unremarkable painting of the Matthews family with their rented house in the background. Cecile found the pretensions of the wealthy tradespeople rather predictable. She would not have seen the irony in that given her start in life.

'Do you have a musical instrument anywhere? Harpsichord or spinet, Madame Matthews?'

Constance flushed and stumbled over her words of apology, but before she could finish, Cecile interrupted.

'A petite bent-side spinet would look very pretty by that wall. I have one in my London residence. I could arrange for a similar one to be delivered. Maybe, Madame, you would like to keep the instrument here and learn to play a little Purcell or Bach to your visitors?'

Constance was dumbfounded by the suggestion and Thomas was about to reject the idea out of hand until he realised that Cecile might offer to teach her and would have to make multiple visits to instruct.

'Madame Le Fevre, what a charming idea and be assured Constance will be a willing pupil.' What sounded like a compliment to his wife, she considered it more of a threat if she failed to learn.

Constance finally found the courage to speak and questioned what attire she should wear. She was very much aware of the quality of their visitor's apparel and that her own wardrobe consisted of rather unremarkable mantuas now going out of fashion. Cecile dismissed her concerns with a wave of her tiny hand and assured her that her maid, Maud, would attend to her and make everything *"tres joli"*.

§

The following week, Cecile Le Fevre fulfilled her promise.

The whole house was a hive of activity. Strangers moving about everywhere. Constance had endured the attentions of Madame Le Fevre's maid, her hair being teased into curls and fashionably dressed, topped off with a lacy cap. A beautiful dress of the palest green lay on the bed with an exquisitely embroidered stomacher.

'Mother, look, come and look.' A very excited Joseph had climbed onto the window seat and had his face pressed to the window. There were two large, horse-drawn carts full of boxes and panniers. The first cart had a fierce-looking and downright disgruntled middle-aged woman sitting up beside the driver. The two men sitting in the following cart did not look much happier.

'Come here, Joseph.' Constance put her arms out to invite him to sit on her knee, a gesture much frowned upon as he was now considered too old to be held and mothered in such a way. He was not aware of this and so climbed happily onto her lap.

'Today is very important to your father. So both of us must do exactly as he asks of us. It would not favour us should we anger him.'

Lord Edgerton's cook was taking her displeasure out on the young footmen who had come with her and was thoroughly disrespectful to the Somersham Court staff as she belittled their efforts. Everyone curbed their opinions and the preparations went ahead as meticulously planned by Cecile Le Fevre.

However, it did amuse her to see that Lord Edgerton had loaned only his second-best silver and plates for the event. But she also knew that what she saw was a statement of taste, an indication of comfortable wealth and, most important of all, a household of some considerable status. *All of it a total sham,* she thought, *the house is leased, the furniture on loan and the façade of successful trade just there for a day.* Though she had neither liking nor regard for Thomas Matthews, she did have a concern that Constance and Joseph may get drawn into one of Edgerton's machinations. Her loathing of men and their power games only fuelled her ruthlessness, but her heart was not so hardened against women and children, who were often collateral damage in these ruthless times.

The remit Edgerton had given her was to organise a dinner party of quality but not too ostentatious; targeted invitations to men of trade, not the key players in Norwich but those hungry for money-making schemes who would elevate their status and coffers, strangely enough, men whose wives were of lowly social significance to avoid exposing Constance as a daughter of yeoman stock. All this she could do with ease and someone else's money.

A talented puppeteer of people.

The guests arrived just after noon. They were greeted by Thomas who was the epitome of the perfect host. Even Constance rose to the occasion, her nerve emboldened by the simple but beautifully made formal dress in delicate green that brought out the colour of her eyes and complimented her pale, smooth skin. Two gentlemen factory owners came unaccompanied; an elderly investor brought his daughter and a merchant of woollen goods brought his new and much younger bride who was almost paralysed by nerves.

The seating arrangements were that the gentlemen sat together at one end of the large dining table, whilst the ladies sat at the other. With Cecile's light and rather naughty descriptions of life at court, the lady guests were soon put at ease and the conversation flowed easily. Constance even joined in a conversation about sketching and painting. Meanwhile, at the other end of the table, the men started talking about horses, dogs and hunting. Thomas spoke loudly and clearly of how he wanted to build a Beagle pack but there were difficulties matching the hounds to have both good scenting and speed over rough ground. He also waxed lyrical about Somersham Boy and his prowess on the coursing grounds.

'Why do men give their horses such silly names?' Cecile asked the ladies close by, who gave gentle giggles in response.

'Lord Edgerton has lovely horses and calls them after jewels because he says they are precious to him,' Constance chimed in.

The food and service were excellent. The first course of soup and fish was followed by the fricassees and ragout. Each course was put on the table by the footmen and the soiled plates removed and replaced by clean ones kept by the fire to warm. There must have been nigh on twenty dishes put on the table which allowed everyone to help themselves. The footmen managed to control their mirth when Thomas' lack of expertise in carving the massive joint put before him caused meat juices to splash everywhere. Constance visibly stiffened in her seat but relaxed when Thomas made a jest of his clumsiness.

The table was cleared for the last time for the dessert of fruits, nuts and syllabubs. The ladies had hardly had time to finish before Thomas stood up and suggested that they might like to retire to the drawing room where green tea was being provided. They did with some considerable relief as the topics and language of the men had become somewhat bawdy.

'Well, gentlemen, now to business. I have some fine port to be served; let's see if we can match its quality with our plans.'

One of the gentlemen guests started up a conversation that turned into a heated debate about the acts going through parliament to curtail the activities of the board of the South Sea Company.

'Outrageous what those coves got up to! Served them right to have their authorities revoked and prevent them from making free with the assets,' shouted another, whose half-chewed mouthful of fruit nearly ended up spat across the table.

'Not too bad for some, eh, Thomas? If Sir Stanley Jacks hadn't invested so heavily, your father would not have bought this place for a knock-down price,' retorted another.

'My father paid a fair price and settled the outstanding debts associated with it,' Thomas replied in a prim tone of voice. He continued. 'We are here to discuss the creation of a syndicate, not to gossip like idle wives.'

'What about the Game Act? When is that made legal? At least then we can shoot the thieving bastards taking game off our lands.'

The food and wine had loosened tongues, just as Edgerton had wanted.

Thomas outlined the opportunities for investment from Holland. Their so-called Golden Age of trading was diminishing but not before a privileged few had made a great deal of money. This money was now ripe for investment, if not in Holland, then why not in England? This caught the men's attention, and so too the idea of a syndicate, setting up a factory in Norfolk to manufacture using new woollen carpet techniques and looms.

Now the men around the table were in their element; wool, loams, carpets, sales and profits were the mainstay of the conversation and each showed a willingness to take up a percentage of the enterprise and its initial costs divided into shares; a syndicate using a large majority of Dutch investment money, using skilled workers enticed from France on the promise of high wages.

The lively discussions were accompanied by the clink of decanters refilling glasses. Enthusiasm was tempered by caution, but the thought of greater wealth and status in the commercial world spurred them on.

Thomas had unwittingly set the bait in the trap which was being set for him.

§

Once all the guests had gone, Thomas strutted around the house like a cockerel surveying its roost. He leant against the wall opposite the new family painting. He was dissatisfied with it. It did not adequately portray him as a man of means, with a son to follow him in his footsteps, Joseph sitting upon Constance's lap like that. It made the child look like a weak mother's boy who couldn't even stand up to have his portrait painted. Joseph was far too old now to be cosseted and treated like a baby. It had to be changed. Thomas sent for Ned.

Ned was given strict instructions to change the painting; remove the child from Constance's lap and have the boy standing proudly next to his father. Ned wanted to protest, for it was not his painting to alter, but he did not dare disagree with Thomas. So the painting was returned to the workroom where Ned started making the changes. But he was still uneasy as to what Clive Millar would say if he ever found out.

Chapter Fourteen

April 2021

The A12 had never been a favourite of Keith's. The rhythmic repetitive *thud, thud* of the concrete breaks in the prefabricated road surface were annoying, especially when trying to doze. He shifted in his seat, more to change the points of pressure rather than any real discomfort. His car was not as young as it used to be, nor was he, for that matter. But like him, it was mechanically sound, reliable and with plenty of mileage left.

He glanced over at his newly appointed partner. This was their first field outing since making Jack a junior partner. Whilst their professional backgrounds were similar, their spheres of knowledge were very different. Keith's forte was tactics and the psychology of the criminal mind, whilst Jack could make modern technology jump through hoops. Their skill sets complemented each other. On less important levels there were areas of irritation; there was only a limited amount of time Keith could stand the car radio blaring out the hits of the '80s and '90s. He preferred to travel in silence.

'You OK driving? Do you need a break?' he asked.

'I'm fine, but it might be an idea to fill up soon, this old banger of yours is quite a thirsty girl!' Jack was being deliberately irritating because he considered the nine-year-old Volvo XC60 automatic boring to drive.

'OK, stop at the next service station. One more smartarse

comment about my car and you can walk the rest of the way! Keith's face was smiling but his eyes were not.

'Anyway, the last thing we need is to be driving a flash, expensive car that attracts attention from thieving little shits, especially with all the equipment in the back. So if you want to drive a flash "look at me" car, do it in your own time. And stop bashing Bertha.'

After they had filled the car's capacious fuel tank and had a moan about the cost of petrol, used the facilities and stocked up on plastic-wrapped sandwiches and bottles of water, they got back onto the A12, heading for the Suffolk/Norfolk border.

They had just negotiated a large roundabout south of Ipswich It was only after they had peeled off north towards Woodbridge that Keith spoke.

'Shall we just run over the sequence of events again?'

Jack didn't reply, but Keith could feel his inexperienced impatience. After all, they had discussed this several times back at the office.

'We know where both properties are. The bungalow is the first target, isolated and the surrounding area is unchanged from the last two versions of Google Earth. Unfortunately, I couldn't get a good visual on it as *street view* only goes as far as the start of the track. The house is our secondary target. Again, *street view* was not particularly helpful, but the auctioneer's details do give us a floor plan. There is a footpath that goes quite close to the house on the south side, so we should consider potential hikers complete with Ordinance Survey map trundling past. Our primary goal is to find the painting. Failing that, install surveillance equipment to monitor conversations that might reveal its whereabouts.' He turned his head to check that Jack was listening and not zoning him out. Keith continued.

'Bungalow first, as the most likely place to find it. There are two occupants, Adrian and his sister. There is no evidence the sister is involved but can't rule it out. Should be straightforward as he appears to have done a bunk and the sister often visits the rich boyfriend in the big house. There could be dogs or poultry that might make raise an alarm.'

'How do you want to handle that?'

'To the north of the property, there is a Forestry Commission plantation with well-established tracks and paths. It meets up with a road running parallel to the east. I suggest that we park up on that road, put on hard hats and hi-vis vests and walk down the edge of the trees to see what stirs when we approach.'

Jack groaned; he was a city boy and saw no pleasure in creeping around in the dark, damp countryside.

'Somersham Court is a different matter. The rich boyfriend is Miles Mortimer, unlikely to be involved as his interests are more on the sister than fine art. The sister seems to come and go ad hoc.'

Jack sniggered. 'Never had a girl who can come ad hoc!'

'There's a housekeeper and gardener that live in the small coach house building near the main gate.' Keith decided to ignore Jack's smutty juvenile humour.

'Any dogs?'

'Yes, four.'

'Fucking hell, what are they, Malinois?'

'Deerhounds and greyhounds. More likely to lick you to

death than bite you. But they bark loudly.' Keith was not happy about their instructions to place surveillance equipment in the big house, for the chances of it being empty of humans and dogs at the same time were very slim. So it might have to be "phone engineers" checking "broadband connections"; a high-risk ruse, but telling their client Mr Smith they had failed was a much higher risk.

Keith had booked three nights in a rural pub that offered bed and breakfast. It wasn't the peak holiday season so they could find alternative accommodation if they had to stay on. He had booked them in as "father and son", explaining to the owner that they were there to do a bit of fishing to get away from work. He threw into the conversation that they were hoping to visit Costessey and Billingford, which were good fishing lakes not far away. The landlady confirmed she was happy to take a cash booking as requested, especially in the low season.

They would need a return trip to recover equipment once the surveillance was complete, but that couldn't be scheduled now.

The car's wheels crunched over the pea shingle in The White Hart pub car park, and Jack reversed the car so that the boot was firmly up against the back wall, an instinctive precaution to prevent the tailgate from being opened. Keith had seen the pictures of the pub online, but they did not do it justice, the early evening sun now making the honey-coloured bricks positively glow.

Keith and Jack took their bags up to the room, a twin-bedded one with an *en-suite*. Jack chose the bed nearest the window, while Keith didn't give a damn which one he used.

They left some toiletries in the bathroom, several fishing magazines on the two beds and printouts from the websites of the nearby fishing lakes.

The temptation to go into the bar and just relax with a couple of pints of the local bitter was strong, but work came first.

They drove along the road that ran parallel to the no-through road to the bungalow and parked up by the woodland close by. Though the sun was now low, the light was sufficient to see where to walk yet not for them to be too easily identifiable.

Then they put on hard hats and safety goggles and carried red and white, candy-striped poles. They walked down the side of the treeline, stopping at regular intervals, as though assessing the density of the trees, meanwhile keeping a very close watch for any movement in the bungalow. No lights came on, no dogs barked, no cars parked in the driveway.

They stashed their brightly coloured jackets, hard hats and safety glasses in the undergrowth, easily retrievable. Keith sent a text to say that they were now in position and about to affect entry to the property. A reply appeared on his screen:

MR SMITH
Switch body cams on now.

Keith, with years of expertise, made short work of the back door lock, and they went inside. Having established the layout, the studio was the centre of their attention. Quickly, quietly and methodically, they searched the studio, taking care not to disturb anything, or fail to replace it correctly in its original position. Various small movement-activated cameras were placed to transmit any activity. Jack investigated the fridge and reported there was no fresh food or milk. No one had been there for days.

Another text appeared:

> **MR SMITH**
> Nothing? Leave cameras. Get out now.

Before Keith could acknowledge the instructions, another text came in:

> **MR SMITH**
> If painting not recovered elsewhere.
> Torch the place after retrieving cameras.

After one more look around to see if they could have missed a hiding place and to check that nothing had been disturbed, they retraced their footsteps down the side of the wood. No one asked them what they were doing because there was no one around to ask, the luminous letters on their backs which spelt out SURVEY were redundant.

They retreated to the pub and enjoyed several pints of bitter that washed down a mammoth slice of chicken and leek pie with piles of steamed vegetables. Afterwards, Jack went to the room early to watch football on the TV while Keith walked round the village, hoping to aid the digestion of the rich, buttery pastry sitting like a brick in his stomach. He needed to think. He never signed up for torching people's homes; he was a surveillance specialist, not a thug. *Maybe it's time to retire*, he thought. *Somewhere round here would be nice.*

He also mused on his decision to make Jack a junior partner; maybe give it a bit of time and then sell the business to him. Keith was unimpressed by the type of clients Jack had brought in. He had to admit they paid well and promptly, but they were not on the side of the angels. He might have been thrown out of the force for being a "bent copper", but there was a limit to how far he could and would bend. Yet there was nothing else in his life. The life of a police officer was not compatible with family life. The wife he adored was now adored by a different husband; the children at whose births he had cried with joy, barely gave him the time of day. There was only work in his life, now too tired and cynical to even attempt a new relationship and too scared of failing someone again.

Chapter Fifteen
May 2021

Miles was enjoying a much-needed quiet evening to himself. His parents had been to visit and had stayed overnight the previous evening. As much as he loved them, the gulf between them caused by Helen's death and Miles' successful career and aspirations had widened. He had hoped they would be impressed with the progress of the restoration work. They said all the right things, smiled and patted him on the back at the appropriate points, but he knew they were not really interested. He did, however, know they loved him and were very proud of his academic achievements. But now their faces were bland, nothing like the day he graduated from Cambridge when their pride shone like lighthouses on full beam. He thought they felt more at home with his sister, Pip, in her large, semi-detached in Braintree, enjoying a trip to Bluewater.

Miles fixed his attention on the eighteenth-century family in the painting, now cleaned, restored and hanging over the fireplace. He speculated how the subjects had got on with their parents. He wondered if the landowning classes even cared about such niceties; money went from generation to generation and everyone knew their place in the social hierarchy. No one stepped out of line.

His contemplative mood was interrupted by his phone

ringing. He picked it up only to reject the call but then saw it was Lucy.

'Hi, stranger. Not heard from you for a while. All good?'

'No. I don't know where Adrian is, or what he's up to.'

'Lucy, he's a grown man, he doesn't need a nanny!' No sooner than Miles had said the words than he regretted being so short.

'Miles, I'm serious, I just know he's in trouble.'

'How come?' Miles agreed with her but didn't want to make matters worse. Yet he had never been convinced about the telepathic powers of twins.

'He isn't here. As you know, I've been back to Devon for a second meeting for that restoration project and I've just returned. But the boys are missing. It is very unlikely he would have them with him unless there was an emergency.' Her voice was tight and staccato.

'Stop there. The dogs are here, so stop fretting.' It sounded like a sob of relief on the other end. Miles wondered if Adrian knew his place in the pecking order of his sister's heart.

'Thank God. But why?'

Miles explained that a few days earlier, Adrian had phoned him and asked for a couple of favours. Adrian had wanted to know if he would look after the dogs and then give him a lift to the station as he had to get to London to meet a prospective client.

'So he came over in the Land Rover, dropped the dogs off and then left the vehicle by the stables. I drove him to the station. He had a rucksack and a large portfolio case with him; probably had paintings in it.' What Miles did not mention to Lucy was that he did not see Adrian cross the bridge for trains going south.

'Are you there?' Miles asked, as the line had gone silent.

'Someone has been in the house. I can't explain it, I just know they have.'

Miles was about to tell her to stop being such a drama queen when a nagging doubt entered his mind. 'Are you really that worried?'

'Yes.'

'Grab a bag and a toothbrush and come over here.' Desperately trying not to sound melodramatic, he suggested she come via a route that would expose anyone trying to follow her.

Needless to say, Lucy received a rapturous reception from Ozzy and Marble. She dropped an overnight bag by the door, together with a small parcel wrapped in felt that he assumed to be a small painting. Miles was genuinely concerned when he saw Lucy's pale and drawn face.

'I like the new throws. Are they to add colour or to keep dog hairs off the sofas?'

He knew she was trying to lighten the mood. 'A bit of both really. Ozzy and Marble have commandeered the dog beds behind me, so Skye and Fergus have developed a taste for lounging around on the sofas.' Just as he said that Skye settled herself on one of them as an impromptu demonstration. Miles suggested Lucy went up and had a long, hot soak in the bath to relax, followed by some "doorstop" cold beef sandwiches and a bottle of really good red wine.

Miles had nearly finished his first glass when Lucy appeared in the doorway to the drawing room. The colour had returned to her face; her hair was a mass of dark curls tightened by the steam of the bath. But what rendered Miles speechless was the fact she wore his dressing gown wrapped tightly around her, and for a split second he speculated what, if anything, was under his robe. He was so envious of that dressing gown, with its inanimate arms around her.

'Hope you don't mind, but I didn't think I should appear in just a nightshirt.' Not waiting for an answer, she saw the sandwiches and was already halfway through one in the time it took Miles to pour her a glass of wine.

Miles, as always, was amazed by Lucy's ability to eat anything in considerable quantity without worrying about calories. Every woman he knew seemed obsessed with the nutritional values of everything, but not Lucy. She loved food and food loved her enough not to hang about on her hips or thighs.

'Sorry if I interrupted your evening, but I've brought something for you.' She nodded towards the parcel she had put on the spare sofa.

Miles explained that there was nothing much to interrupt; he had only been reading the Sunday papers and musing on what sort of family life the portrait people had had.

'It was an unhappy marriage.' Lucy pushed his feet out of the way so she could sit on the sofa next to him. He could smell the fresh soap and sense the damp warmth of her body next to him. She seemed oblivious to the effect she was creating as she launched into an assessment of the painting over the fireplace.

'Look at the composition. Although the house is in the background, it's also centre stage. I reckon they were "new money", and the house is the symbol of their wealth. The wife is pushed aside to the right, isolated, especially when considering there was originally a small child on her lap. More than likely, it had died before the painting was complete; probably a boy, which means she failed the family. The group to the left of the husband, son and a favourite dog, are dominant. The wife is just a baby-making machine, expected to replace the loss of a child with another one. There is no love or sense of family in this picture.'

'Wow, that's me told! Are you sure?'

'The one thing you learn about art history is that paintings are one of the biggest manipulators of the truth. They are riddled with political messages, metaphors, negative PR, everything except the truth!' Lucy turned to look at Miles and laughed.

'You look disappointed. Simple example: Richard III's reputation was muddied by the Tudors referring to him as a hunchback to distract from their part in his downfall. He had scoliosis, which meant his back was bent not humped. Paintings were altered to show an exaggerated difference in the height of his shoulders; rewriting history by pictorial propaganda.' Then Lucy remembered Miles' scornful words of a few months earlier about her lecturing him.

'Lecture over; only to be continued by request.' Lucy stretched out her arm and gave him a playful pat on his thigh.

He decided to change the subject. He wanted to ask what she had brought him. He was pretty sure it was the painting that he had bought at auction, now cleaned and varnished. He wanted to see the finished result as the painting had been in a poor state when they got it, but he decided it could wait.

'What is going on with Adrian?'

'I feel a fraud now, all warm and safe here with you. But I was truly scared; there was something wrong about the house. I can't explain it, other than I felt I wasn't alone, as though it had been searched. Nothing was out of place but somehow not in its right place.' Lucy twisted round to watch Miles' face, expecting him to laugh.

He didn't.

'What alerted you to the fact it'd been searched?'

'You'll laugh, but the place didn't smell right! Oh, there was the usual smell of linseed oil and turpentine in the studio, and the kitchen was bland, as Adrian only microwaved dinners when I'm away.' Lucy hesitated before she spoke again. 'There was a smell of men.'

Miles couldn't help but laugh.

Her reaction was to sit bolt upright and glare at him.

'So what do men smell of then?'

'Everyone has a skin smell of their own, depends on their diet, soap, deodorant and suchlike. Adrian always smells of his favourite cologne which has a light citrus smell. And of course, Ozzy and Marble have their own unique greyhound smell. But this was different. There was a masculine smell, not sweaty but a form of body odour.' Lucy could not suppress the involuntary shiver that went down her spine. Miles reached out and took her hand and held it gently, he did not know what to say that would either comfort her or allay her fears.

They sat in silence for a while then Miles suddenly spoke. He had meant to ask about the painting, but out of nowhere in his mind, he blurted out.

'Tell me about Denis.'

He felt her stiffen, but she did not move.

'Why do you want to know?

'Because there is bad history there and I wondered if it might be relevant to Adrian's disappearance.' Miles knew the excuse for asking was weak, but he couldn't retract his question now.

'Very unlikely.' There followed a deathly silence. Then in a low, calm voice, Lucy began.

'I was away at university in my final year studying art history when Mama phoned in high excitement to tell me that she had taken in a lodger for six months and had given him my room as it was the biggest available. Mama prattled on about how attractive he was, how clever, how charming and so on. My immediate reaction was that the reality was probably that she had bagged herself some boring, old, crusty academic whose rent was going to get the bills paid for the next six months.'

'Bit mean, turfing you out of your room.'

'What I didn't know was that she had told anyone who'd listen that Denis was her toy boy lover!'

'Was he?'

'God knows, I doubt it. Denis liked them young and firm!' Lucy continued.

'OK, edited highlights only. Denis became my lover; the first big love of my life. I adored him. But he treated me appallingly and robbed me of my self-confidence and worth. The only refuge I had was my studies. I became obsessed with him, however. He would talk about us setting up a summer school for art on the Gower Peninsula, renovating an old Welsh long-house and running art courses and history seminars. I was so excited about the prospect I couldn't wait to go to the Gower and visit the places Denis spoke about. I thought I would do a little market research whilst I was there and ask in various villages about any local art schools.' Lucy took a large swig of wine before she could continue.

'I was directed to one. At the end of this track was a beautifully restored Welsh long-house. I spoke to the charming woman there and made enquiries about summer painting holidays. She was a tall, striking-looking woman with long, steel-grey hair worn in a single plait. She gave me a brochure and price list. Her recommendation was a course on coastal watercolours run by her husband, Denis. It was his handsome, debauched face that smiled out at me from the brochure.'

'Bloody hell, what on earth did you say?' Miles was appalled that anyone could be so duplicitous.

'I didn't say anything; I fainted.' She turned to look at Miles' face and was touched by his reaction.

'When I came round, the charming lady was most solicitous and took me inside, offered me a glass of water and then changed her mind and brought a couple of glasses of brandy.

'Apparently, I wasn't the first and she doubted I would be the last. She very sweetly told me I was the most attractive. I rather tartly suggested that was probably what she said to all the girls.' Lucy took a large swig of wine and continued.

'I drove like a maniac back to Norfolk and confronted him. We had a row to end all rows and I drove off. Halfway back to university, I felt I should apologise for my angry words and mend bridges. It was one of his many manipulative ways: he made me feel guilty even when he was in the wrong. Such was my obsession with him that I would have pleaded guilty to anything if I thought he would take me back into his arms and love me. Anyway, it was late at night by the time I got home, so I crept back into the house and sneaked up the stairs into his bedroom.'

'Oh no, don't tell me he was in bed with your mother!' Miles blurted out.

'No, Adrian, and they were physically active!'

§

Miles lay in bed but he could not sleep. His mind just kept running Lucy's words through his head on a permanent loop. How could any man behave like that? How could Lucy have been such an innocent that she allowed herself to be taken in by him? What made it even more painful for him was the idea that he might not have heard the worst of it.

His thoughts were interrupted when he thought he heard a floorboard creak, but it was his bedroom door being pushed, now ajar.

'Are you awake? I can't sleep.' Lucy's voice was so soft and subdued; Miles did not know what to say. He propped himself up to see Lucy standing in the doorway; the light from the corridor held her in silhouette. There was a piece of paper, a letter, which had been folded in three, dangling from her left hand.

'Bunny is dead!' She walked towards his bed and sat lightly on it. She offered the letter to him, which he took even though there was insufficient light for him to read it. 'The letter is from her solicitor. The funeral is being arranged and

I will be told when it is to be held. He wants to speak to me. Apparently, I was supposed to phone him days ago, but I only picked up the post earlier this evening before I came here.'

Miles could not think of anything to say that wouldn't sound like a platitude, so chose silence. He held his hand out to her. She took it; hers was freezing cold.

'But it's worse than that. Apparently, she made all the arrangements, got her will up to date, even left strict instructions about the funeral and then…' Lucy's sobs stopped her words until she managed to continue. 'She committed suicide!'

Without speaking, he lifted the corner of his duvet and Lucy slid in beside him. She felt stone-cold. He held her in his arms, not sure if the shivering was from cold or grief. She relaxed a little and curled up against him, her arm across his chest. He started to stroke her hair gently. It wasn't long before the gentle sobs stopped and her breathing changed to a gentler rhythm.

He spoke softly. 'Bunny's suicide is not a rejection of you nor anyone else. I have no idea what religious convictions she had but, given her wonderful, quirky way of looking at life, it probably meant she believed in an afterlife and has gone looking for James in the Elysian Fields.'

Lucy's arm tightened across his chest and her body moved closer to him.

'I am not Denis, nor your brother, not even your mother; I would never knowingly hurt you. I wish I had never asked now, but it does explain a lot of things.' He leant over and kissed her on the forehead. She made a strange little muffled sound. Eventually he fell asleep, but not before he had concluded that he must be the dullest and least sexually attractive man on the planet because when a beautiful woman had climbed into bed with him, she just wanted to sleep.

§

When he awoke, he was alone. He lay in bed wondering how the previous night's events, or even lack of them, was going to affect his relationship with Lucy. He found his dressing gown discarded on the other side of the bed and, was about to hang it up, when instead he buried his face in its folds, hoping to catch her scent. He quickly showered and dressed, and then went downstairs, where he found Lucy in the kitchen.

'Hi, there you are. Hope you don't mind but I've made some coffee for myself. There's plenty more in the pot. I haven't let the dogs out. I would have given them their breakfast but wasn't sure of the quantities for Skye and Fergus.' Lucy looked bright and breezy and totally unfazed by the previous evening.

'Great, thanks. Yes, I'll feed them all now.'

Lucy just gave him a big smile in acknowledgement and went upstairs to arrange the three small paintings along the back of a sofa.

Miles soon joined her with four happy dogs and a large mug of coffee. Glancing at the paintings, a light-bulb moment struck him.

'They're telling a story. The first focuses on the gate out of the garden; the second is not about the meadow but the entrance through the woodland and the third one, now it's been cleaned, shows a journey through the wood. Is that a horse and rider on the path?'

'Exactly what I thought. Because when I was cleaning the picture, the detail became clearer. It's more like a packhorse with something slung across its back, rather than a packed and balanced load. Also, there are two men, one leading and one with his hand on whatever is being carried.

'More than that, if you look very carefully at the first one, everything points to the gate: the stag is looking at it and if you follow the eyeline of the birds, they all meet at the gate. These are all techniques to draw the audience's eye to the focal point.'

'Like the vanishing point?' Miles had heard the term but wasn't too sure if it was the same thing.

'No, the vanishing point has to do with perspective. I did first look at that as a possibility, but it isn't that; it's the focal points in each of the pictures that are key.'

'Stan is all wrong!' Miles jumped up and pointed at the first painting, then grabbed it and went over to the window. 'Look, Stan is facing the wrong way.'

'I am right, definitely a pointer. By the way, why Stan?'

Miles made a rather embarrassed, dismissive gesture with his hand.

'So the focal points are the gate, woodland entrance and the packhorse, which is nearly out of the woods.' Lucy was convinced.

'Where are they going?' mused Miles.

'And what is the significance of that loaded pony? Also, the light is odd, not like sunlight.'

'It's the Roman numerals that still don't make any sense to me, other than there might be five.' Miles looked to Lucy for an answer.

'Possibly, but I was trying to think why anyone would commission five paintings of such bland subjects.' Lucy knew that eighteenth-century painters did not waste time and materials painting for pleasure, so there had to be a very good reason for these commissions. But what was it?' Lucy did not expect an answer from Miles.

Miles finished his coffee and was in two minds whether to refer to the previous night's visit to his room. He thought better of mentioning it, but he did want to know about Bunny's funeral.

'Would you like me to come with you to the funeral, whenever it is?'

'Oh, yes please. I didn't like to ask, but I don't think I could face it alone. If only I knew where Adrian was and that he is OK.'

Chapter Sixteen

July 1721

Constance felt so small and vulnerable in the marital bed, in her mind she tried to shrink herself into nothing and nobody. She prayed fervently to God to let her husband drink himself into a stupor and fall asleep in the parlour. She then prayed even more devoutly, asking for God's forgiveness for failing in her wifely duties and for being so elated that Thomas was going to be away for several weeks.

Her young son was also restless; he felt his mother's anxiety and could not sleep. Joseph had just entered her bedroom, hoping to sleep in the warmth and comfort of his mother's bed, when the door was violently kicked open.

'Get back to bed, you snivelling little runt!' Thomas barked at his trembling son. 'Your mother is going to have a real man in her bed tonight.' His handsome face twisted into a drunken leer as he shouted at his wife. 'Take him away, then return without delay. You have wifely duties to perform tonight.' His laugh was deliberately harsh and cruel, knowing the effect it would have on Constance.

Thomas prowled round the room, discarding his outer garments on the floor, looking for the little ornate decanter of port he knew Constance kept somewhere in the bedroom. He gave up, fell back onto the bed and made himself comfortable in the small, warm patch Constance had left behind.

The door opened slowly and quietly, she daring to hope the drink had overpowered Thomas and that he would be unconscious.

'Come in, dear wife, you will be delighted to know I am ready to take you now.' Not that he was in any fit state to, but Thomas' cruel satisfaction was to watch Constance start to tremble, unable to hide the look of fear on her gentle face.

'Get in.'

Constance slid into the bed beside him.

'You'll be needing this.' He triumphantly held the little pot of goose grease usually hidden on her side of the bed.

'Let me help you and your dry, unwelcoming cunny.' He reached under the bedclothes and lifted her nightshift. She froze, but he easily parted her thighs and then, without the use of the grease, he brutally forced the first three fingers of his left hand into her. She screamed with shock and pain.

Thomas was soon bored and sleep overcame him. Some considerable time later, Constance slipped out of the room and went to her son. She fell asleep in the child's bed, the boy in her arms.

Daniel and Carver were downstairs making sure that all the luggage and paperwork were in order. They heard the shouting and Constance's scream. Daniel was about to rush upstairs when Carver put a restraining hand on his arm.

'What goes on between husband and wife is no concern of ours.'

Daniel was shocked by Carver's comment. Carver was not a squeamish man, for he had witnessed the brutality of war upon women during the first Jacobite rebellion in Scotland. However, he had grown fond of the kind and gentle

Constance and believed that despite their marital status, no man should take a woman against her will. He could well imagine what sort of pain Thomas would inflict on his wife for his own gratification.

They were not the only ones who had heard the scream, Ned Versey had been working late on the large canvas. Millar had left Ned to finish refining the faces and folds in the fabric of their clothes. He was grateful as Ned loved the intricacies of this kind of artwork, whereas painting trees, clouds and houses did not interest him so much. But Millar had taught him the shortcuts and quick fixes to get these less interesting features of a painting finished, before moving on to the next commission of new sets of family portraits.

Though not a servant, Ned was not expected to use the main staircase, so he crept down the back stairs and without the benefit of the light of a candle, he used the darkness and shadows to his advantage. He was in full sight of the landing and the main sweeping staircase that ended in the hallway. He never questioned himself why he needed to know what was happening, but Constance was in danger. Not that he could protect her.

He was nearly discovered when he saw Thomas erupt from the bedroom. The light of a candle showed his face twisted in incandescent rage as he staggered along the corridor to Joseph's room. He was shouting drunken obscenities about his wife. In no time at all, the sounds got more fearsome as he re-emerged from the dark, candle holder in one hand, dragging his wife behind him by a large handful of her hair. Joseph was clinging onto his mother's nightshift and crying. His father cursed him and tried to kick him away, but the distraught boy clung on.

This was too much for Daniel. He started up the staircase, shouting at his brother, hoping to modify his behaviour and language. Thomas was on the landing now where everyone could see the extent of the situation. Constance sobbed quietly and tried to reassure the boy whose wailing was getting louder. The two younger men on the stairs could not fail to notice the blood on her nightshirt.

Thomas put the candle holder on a side table. 'Daniel, stay there, this is nothing to do with you. I'm master in my own house.'

Daniel instantly thought that his brother was master of nothing, least of all the house.

'Thomas, you need to…' Daniel just stopped himself in time from voicing that point. '…rest as we have an early start and it is a long and tiring journey ahead of us.' The last thing Daniel needed was complications before the journey to Great Yarmouth to meet with the ship to take them to Holland. He now regretted that he had agreed to join his brother on the trip to Holland.

Then, without warning, Joseph launched himself at his father, unaware of the irony of his little head hitting Thomas' genitalia full-on. Thomas doubled over in pain and staggered back towards the head of the stairs, whilst Joseph's little fists pummelled the brocade waistcoat, demanding in a furious, high-pitched voice that his father should leave his mother alone.

'Well, well, our little piss-a-bed is giving me orders now!' Thomas thought this very funny but was also rather pleased that his son had found some fighting instinct in himself.

Thomas stepped back and looked long and hard into the child's eyes. He was taken aback by the look of pure hatred and hostility he saw there. Thomas made an exaggerated mock bow to the boy and turned his back on him, seeming to appear to have lost interest in the situation. But instead of walking away, he turned on Joseph and hit him so hard that the boy was bowled over like a skittle.

Constance didn't so much as scream but let out a blood-curdling cry and charged at Thomas. Although only a slight woman, her unexpected physical assault knocked him off balance and he staggered back further, except his final step was not on the floorboards of the landing but to the empty space above the last step of the stairs. The tumbling body of the bully was watched by all in silent horror.

Daniel quickly checked his brother, then rushed up the stairs and consoled his sister-in-law with the fact Thomas had only been knocked out and nothing seemingly broken. He advised her to take Joseph back to bed, lock the door and stay there until he and Thomas left for the post coach in the early morning.

The mother and son took their battered bodies and hearts to bed.

Whilst Daniel was with Constance and Joseph, Carver had taken a close look at Thomas. There were no external signs of injury and so concluded concussion was probably the reason for his inert body. His mind raced; survival ran deep and strong in a McGregor, as did the ability to spot a golden opportunity. He looked down at the drunken bully of an Englishman and valued his life little against his own survival, not for the first time. All Carver could think of was being free of the shackles of his Jacobean masters, who blackmailed him into working for Lord Edgerton, a well-known member of Whig society and supporter of the Hanoverian king. He had sold information to anyone who would pay because Carver didn't give a damn who was King; he wanted a new life and to be free of any allegiance to anyone. If he could assume Thomas Matthews' identity and get to the continent, especially with gold in his pocket, then onto the Americas for freedom.

Swiftly and without mercy, he took hold of Thomas' head and with a quick, practised movement, broke Thomas' neck. Ned heard the sickening sound hidden in the shadows, too scared to move. He clapped his hand over his mouth to stop any sound of shock from escaping.

Daniel returned and Carver shook his head solemnly. 'His neck is broken. He's dead.'

'Mother of God! What do we do now?'

Carver took hold of Daniel's arm and pulled him away from his brother's corpse. 'We need to move him in case Constance and Joseph should return.'

They dragged Thomas' body into the parlour. Daniel stared at the lifeless body that had only minutes earlier had been so frighteningly alive. Carver broke the silence.

'There is a choice to be made. He is your brother and you must do what you consider to be right.' Carver had no intention of letting Daniel do anything other than what he wanted, but he knew the younger brother well enough to be aware of a stubborn streak that needed to be steered rather than instructed.

Daniel remained silent, so Carver continued. 'By law, we

should inform the magistrate immediately and explain the situation; how his death was pure misfortune with no malice aforethought.'

Daniel nodded, in agreement, but was still too stunned to speak.

'However, we need to consider who the local magistrate is. I believe there is little liking between him and your family, though I could be mistaken. It would mean taking the risk that he might hold Constance responsible for a violent act, resulting in death and have her detained in Norwich Gaol whilst he investigates further.'

'Oh God, no, that cannot happen.' The very thought of it had shaken Daniel out of his stupor.

'So what alternative is there?' Carver knew Daniel did not have one, and with perfect timing, he came to Daniel's help.

'I must speak plainly and honestly to you as an equal, not as a steward bidden to obey without question. What I am about to propose demands trust on both sides; we will be covering up a crime but for the greater good.' Daniel did not object, so Carver continued.

'Thomas is due to leave early for Holland with you tomorrow morning, therefore his absence is not going to be noticed for weeks. The body needs to be hidden safely, maybe to be discovered at a later date. I fear Constance and her son would not withstand close scrutiny about tonight's events.' Carver had Daniel's attention and poured two large glasses of brandy; he picked one up and handed it to his silent companion.

'If I was to assume Thomas' identity, for we are of a similar age, build and colouring, I could accompany you on your journey, then we part company abroad and you report your brother missing abroad and return to let your family grieve in peace.'

'But what do we do with Thomas' body? It cannot be put into non-consecrated ground or left for wild animals to rip him to pieces!'

It was these words that galvanised Carver's plan into action. 'He *will* be buried in consecrated ground. Old Annie Morton was buried today in the churchyard. The spoil on her grave will not have settled and be easy to remove. We can bury him in the same grave.' Carver resisted commenting that he didn't think Annie would mind sharing her eternal bed with a lusty young man.

'I apologise for my boldness; it is a ridiculous idea and I should not have suggested such a blasphemous one.' He knew full well that neither of them had any great belief or liking for church but were sensible to the traditions of the religion they were brought up in.

The silence was only broken by the sound of a loud swallowing and the draining of Daniel's glass. Daniel was not squeamish and it did sound feasible, but there wasn't much time before dawn. His main concern was how much trust he could put in Carver. Would he play the role of his brother convincingly on the journey? And, more importantly, would he truly disappear once abroad?

'Where will you go in Holland?'

'I would either travel south towards France, or east towards Germany, to join groups of Protestant refugees heading to the ports to travel onward to America. A new name and a new life.'

Daniel's mind was swimming with images of Constance and Joseph being subjected to harsh questioning from the authorities. Also, his father's potential reaction to the death of his favourite son being exposed as a thug and a bully in public. Both these thoughts made his decision for him.

'I have to place my trust in you, Carver. And you will have to trust me.'

§

Ned could not hear the conversation in the parlour. He was cold and suffering from shock, both making him shiver uncontrollably. He feared his teeth would start chattering and give away his presence.

He had guessed that Thomas was cruel and violent towards Constance but witnessing the physical assault on her was beyond Ned's compassionate-minded comprehension. In a perverse way, he was proud of little Joesph for trying to defend his mother against the violence, though the consequences had been dire. The one thing he should have been most repulsed by was witnessing Carver expertly breaking Thomas' neck, but his hatred for Thomas left no room for horror.

He was relieved the odious man could not harm anyone again. These two perpetrators could make a pact of silence between them, but if they knew there had been a witness, what then?

Ned thought of hiding in his room, but instinctively he wanted out of the house and retreated to the stable block where he felt safe amongst the horses and the soothing sounds of their sleep. He was halfway across the yard when he realised that the stable boy would be in the hayloft above the stalls; he made his way into the large room used for storing the hard feed and harnesses. Thrown in a corner along with other discarded things, such as empty hessian feed sacks, was the saddle whose tree had been damaged. Thomas had bought a young, rather spirited horse that had been easily spooked. He had ridden the animal hard; it had been tired when he made it try to jump a large hedge and ditch. There was not enough power in its young, exhausted legs to clear the hedge, nor had the horse the experience to keep its legs beneath him. It crashed through the top of the hedge and somersaulted, its weight breaking the tree in the saddle when it landed. Thomas had been thrown clear, and whilst the animal lay winded on the ground, he had taken his riding crop and thrashed it.

Ned remembered the stable boy had been in tears as he tended to the terrified animal. The horse was then sent away.

He curled up in the sacks and put his head on the seat of the saddle. Then the door was flung open and two men came in and lit up a candle.

'We can't carry him that far; he's too heavy.'

Ned recognised Carver's voice.

'There is a pack-saddle somewhere in here; we could use the pony to get him to the graveyard.'

Through the hessian layers covering him, Ned could see the candlelight moving around. He held his breath.

'Leave it, we just need a bridle and a couple of spades to shift the soil from Annie's grave.' Carver was impatient and becoming irritated by the noise Somersham Boy was making in his kennel.

'I'll let that blasted hound out, then maybe he'll hold his

noise,' suggested Daniel.

Indeed, the dog did cease his barking soon after, as it was killed. What Ned could not see was that the edge of a spade brought down on the back of the dog's neck had silenced it forever. Now both master and hound were loaded onto the back of the pony, both lives cut short swiftly by having their necks broken. They would soon be interred in consecrated ground for eternity, along with old Annie Morton.

Chapter Seventeen
July 2021

"Death's Door" was wide open, both heavy, oak, iron-studded doors, to allow the pallbearers to carry the late Letitia Boughton-Hay's coffin to her family's ancestral plots in the corner of the graveyard to lie beside her beloved husband, James.

As Miles watched as her coffin was solemnly carried past him, he could not help recalling with some irony that it had been less than a year since Lucy had introduced her friend Bunny and had explained the strange nickname of the impressive front door. But now, only too soon, there was the visual truth of it.

Lucy's eyes were boring into the back of Bunny's loathsome son-in-law's head, not just because she thought he was an odious little man, but because it stopped her from looking at the wicker-woven coffin. Lucy tried hard not to conjure up the image of the fragile, lifeless shell of her "Dizzy Duck" lying inert in the coffin. Instead, she concentrated on the thought of her dear friend being buried in a picnic basket, going off to join James and their long-departed friends. She imagined there were plates with cups and saucers in leather-restraining straps inside the lid. Would there be little pieces of toast with smoked salmon to sustain her on her journey into Valhalla, or wherever death took the good, the kind and the gentle? More than that, was there a corkscrew amongst her "grave goods" for Bunny to open a good bottle of her favourite red wine she insisted on calling Ribena? Lucy was unaware that her suppressed giggles, even though a coping mechanism, were causing her shoulders to judder.

Miles interpreted her shaking shoulders as barely controlled grief. He put his hand out and found hers, carefully taking it in his, half expecting her to pull away in one of her somewhat annoying displays of independence.

Lucy was aware of her hand being engulfed in Miles' warm hand with his fingers firmly wrapped around hers. It felt so good; not just the physical connection, but there was a current of warmth flowing up her arm, washing through her whole body sensing a real emotional connection. She gently squeezed his hand in thanks; he acknowledged her acceptance with a gentle squeeze in return.

The service was simple as Bunny had specified to their local vicar on several occasions. Luckily, there had been no interference from the daughter and son-in-law, who despite specifically being told there were to be no flowers had laid a large, garish and somewhat vulgar wreath on the coffin. Lucy had cut some sprigs of herbs from her garden before leaving Suffolk that morning.

There were more mourners than would be expected for such an elderly lady. As is often the way with the very elderly, old friends have already died or are incapacitated and unable to attend; relatives who have expectations of the will might come or simply await a letter from the executors.

But the mourners at Bunny's funeral were local people of all ages and backgrounds who came to pay their respects to the eccentric from the "big house". Lucy looked at their genuinely grieving faces, a testament to Bunny, that despite her privileged titled background, she was liked and loved by so many people from all walks of life.

Lucy vaguely recognised Bunny's solicitor, but the majority of the attendees were unknown to her, residents from the local village, all happy to share their amusing tales of Bunny and James' strange hospitality and grocery requests. James wearing country outfits that made him look like Gussie Fink-Nottle out of a P.G. Wodehouse novel and Bunny's insistence on driving at break-neck speed around the Kentish lanes in an ancient Mini Cooper. She appeared to think the white lines up the middle of the road were there to be used like guidelines on a sewing pattern and kept the front wheels astride them!

The laughter ceased and a reverent silence took over as the mourners gathered round the grave as the service started and the coffin was lowered into the ground.

The first handful of soil splashed down on the coffin, partially covering the brass name plaque, and then others followed suit. Lucy threw in her posy of herbs, carefully chosen for their meanings of yesteryear. Bunny would have recognised the "tussie-mussie" and loved the short-stemmed bunch tied together with raffia: rosemary for remembrance, fennel for praise, thyme for courage, lavender for devotion and parsley for gratitude. More by chance than accurate throwing, the posy landed right in the middle of the coffin. For some reason this annoyed Colin. He could not contain himself and destroyed the solemnity of the moment by shouting, 'Letitia did not want flowers, or what looks like bouquet garni! Trust you, Lucy, to think you know better.'

An audible gasp came from everyone.

Before everyone dispersed, the vicar announced that his wife had laid out afternoon tea at the vicarage and everyone was invited. Miles wondered what life must be like for a vicar's wife, rustling up endless sausage rolls and ham sandwiches. He need not have worried; the spread was provided by the M&S food hall only a few miles away and prepaid for by Bunny.

'I want to know about the will.' Colin detained the solicitor by putting an impatient hand on the gentleman's arm. Everyone within earshot either stopped or slowed down to hear what was to come next.

'Mr Barton, this is neither the time nor the place to discuss Mrs Boughton-Hay's personal financial matters. I can assure you that everything is being executed according to Mrs Boughton-Hay's very precise instructions. You should, however, note that probate will be delayed until the completion of Mr Boughton-Hay's probate is signed off, as the two wills are interdependent. You will be notified as and when necessary.' Gordon Brownloe was not impressed by Mr Colin Barton.

'What about the contents of the house? There are valuable paintings and furniture. God knows who has spare keys. Anyone could just help themselves.' Colin stared pointedly at Lucy.

Unbeknown to Colin, Bunny, prior to her death, had already considered this situation and, with the assistance of Gordon Brownloe, had planned the distribution of her estate with precision. The house had been prepared for probate whilst she was still alive. Her cunning plan had taken several drafts and some of the ideas modified before being carried out. Bunny prepared a list of paintings and artworks that were for Lucy and had them crated up and put into secure storage in Ashford. A good selection of antique furniture was also listed and sent to a specialist auction house in Surrey and was sold for the proceeds to be divided between two animal welfare charities. A sum of money was given to the Friends of St Nicholas for the upkeep of the local church where she and James would end their days together. The final *coup de grâce* was that the proceeds from the sale of Boughton Hall would be put into a discretionary trust for the benefit of her daughter only.

'I need access. I've got to arrange for a house valuation and get the place on the market. It's my wife's inheritance, after all.' Colin was floundering as he was not in control of the conversation.

'I will repeat once again; this is neither the time nor the place to discuss this. Nothing is to be done until probate is granted, which could be delayed because of complications with her late husband's probate currently being settled.'

Colin turned on his heel and as he stomped past Lucy, he paused.

'Don't think I'm letting you get your grubby little hands on their paintings.' He stormed off and rather rudely indicated to his wife to follow him. She offered a weak smile to Lucy and mouthed what looked like "sorry".

'Don't worry, Lucy, your paintings are safe; Bunny explained everything.' Gordon smiled encouragingly at her, entirely unaware of the effect of his words.

Miles led Lucy to a bench by an old yew tree and sat beside

her. He looked at the amazing view across the Weald of Kent and tried to identify the hills and ridges on the horizon.

Lucy broke the silence. 'I want to go home now.'

'What did that chap mean about your paintings being safe?'

'Please, not now.' Lucy turned her head and Miles could see so much pain and sadness in her eyes it startled him.

'Tell me, there is no one else here; they have gone to partake of tea at the vicarage.' Miles adopted a silly high-pitched voice, hoping to make her laugh.

Lucy burst into tears.

'OK, from the start. Take your time.' Miles put his arm around her shoulder and felt her relax a little.

Lucy turned to look at him. 'Well, as you know I first met Bunny and James when I was writing my dissertation about the effect of death duties on country houses and estates.

'We devised a scheme whereby they could realise some money from their assets without having to explain themselves to Colin.'

Lucy went on to explain that she would take a painting of theirs back to Suffolk and Adrian would act as a broker by finding a private buyer and then taking a commission for facilitating the sale.

'There's nothing wrong in that.'

'But before sending it to the new owner, Adrian would make a copy, then make it look cleaner but not brand new. I would take the copy back for them to hang on the wall as a replacement. If anyone asked, it had been away for restoration and cleaning.'

'So it was replaced with a forgery?'

'Don't be stupid, it wasn't a forgery, it was a copy. Adrian put his name and date on the reverse of the canvas to ensure that.'

Miles felt reassured.

'So it was agreed that when they died, the copies would be left to me so they wouldn't enter the public domain.'

'Well, interesting, but it doesn't sound illegal. If the copies are only used as copies and can't be sold, then why are you so concerned?

Miles noticed tears had started to roll down Lucy's cheeks but assumed it was just the sadness of the day. But what he heard next horrified him.

'Adrian is in trouble; I just know it. I think he's been using his copyist skills for illegal purposes. I have been so distracted by the work at Somersham Court that I've not really taken much notice of what he's been doing. But I have noticed he's become more secretive and uncommunicative. I think it is all wrapped up in this London contact he knows, a Mr Smith. Maybe that is his name but sounds rather dodgy to me.'

'Shit, that sounds serious.' Miles' mind was racing. If Adrian was a forger and successfully counterfeiting paintings, he imagined seeing the headlines: *Cambridge fellow caught up in art forgery racket*. That would put paid to his visiting fellowship before it began.

CHAPTER EIGHTEEN

September 1721

The wind was a moderate south-westerly and the cargo ship was making good progress across the North Sea. Daniel never realised just how noisy a sailing ship could be, the water thudding against the wooden hull and crashing over the bulwarks onto the deck; the timbers creaked and groaned as the waves twisted and slapped against the thick planks of the hull; the wind in the rigging had ropes squeaking with strain and wooden pulleys clattered against each other. Then there were the shouts and calls of the crew as they adjusted the sails and altered course to make the maximum use of the wind and its direction. Daniel wasn't exactly motion sick but found it easier to maintain a calm stomach by watching the horizon, barely distinguishable from the sky as the blue-grey haze of both seemed to run into each other.

Daniel was beginning to feel the enormity of the previous couple of days. He might not have liked his older brother and found his cruel and spiteful nature repugnant; he was still blood and kin. He thought of his father's despair when he finds out that his eldest and favoured son was missing, presumed dead. His mother would mourn the loss too; she was no stranger to grief. Thomas wasn't her firstborn; Daniel remembered his eldest brother and sister, both taken in the vicious winter of 1709; such pointless, cruel deaths. His eldest brother, Henry, had been determined to help his father look for stray sheep to bring into the barn to protect them from the plummeting temperatures. Martha, his much-loved older sister, insisted on going with them; she had been distraught with worry about her pet ewe, Blackie. Against Alice's better judgement and protestations, John set out with his two eldest children and managed to round up the majority of the sheep and get them under cover, but Blackie was still missing. Martha had gone back to look for her. John and Henry found her collapsed with the cold and carried her home. Martha succumbed to hyperthermia within days, and so too Henry a week later. *How could I be the only one left*, thought Daniel. What would Henry have done in the circumstances? Would Martha have had a calming influence on Thomas?

Daniel's mood darkened. He caught sight of Carver coming up onto the quarter deck gesticulating at him to go below. He picked his way carefully across the main deck towards the poop deck, under which was the access to the limited number of cabins in the stern next to the captain's quarters. Just as he went undercover, he heard the six bells of the fore-watch being rung.

Carver grabbed hold of his arm and pulled him into the meagre-sized cabin they shared. Daniel thought he heard Carver say something about counterfeit but assumed he had misheard. Once in the cabin, Carver sat on the bunk and looked very serious.

'Daniel, what exactly did Thomas say he was to do when he got to Amsterdam?'

'I cannot tell you anymore that I already have, which is he was to present himself to an eminent trader whose name and address are on the letter of introduction. They were to discuss a business proposal on behalf of a syndicate and then he was to return to England and report to Lord Edgerton.'

The cramped, airless little cabin was already beginning to make Daniel queasy.

'I have opened the letters,' Carver remarked rather blandly.

'What would possess you to do that? They will know they have been tampered with!' Daniel was horrified.

Carver assured him they had been re-sealed and the recipient would be none the wiser. He refrained from admitting that he had been paid for doing this for years, undetected in each household he had worked in.

'The letters are honest and straightforward. The trader is one of the most respectable burghers of Amsterdam.' But Carver, who listened at doors, quizzed servants and read documents carelessly left lying around, knew that Thomas was being set up. As to why, he had deduced several good reasons.

'So what are your concerns?'

'Apart from being eleven days late.' Carver stopped himself grinning.

Daniel reacted with a quizzical shrug, thought about it and then replied, 'I will not be late. When Thomas asked, I said I must leave England by the 25th of September to be on time for my appointments at the Korenbeurs on the Damrak Canal. I am due there on the 11th of October. I see no problem with that.' Daniel was baffled.

'Thomas obviously did not know about the differences between the Julian calendar in England and the Gregorian calendar in Holland.' This time Carver allowed himself to laugh out loud.

Daniel then worked out the reason, but his reaction was one of near panic. 'The ridiculous fool did not take account of the date changes. The arrogant idiot would have turned up many days late, thus offending the Dutch and bringing Edgerton's business into disrepute, before he even presented the proposal.'

'Oh, it would have been worse than that, especially after he had handed over the gold.'

'How?'

'Merchants do not appreciate being paid in coins that have been tampered with.' Carver leant back onto the bunk and studied Daniel's face closely to judge his reaction. He was relieved to see the shock and lack of comprehension, which confirmed Daniel was not party to the doctored coins.

Slowly Carver pulled out from under his topcoat lying on the bunk, a collection of gold guineas and half-guineas and invited Daniel to inspect them closely. Daniel looked at them and shook his head uncomprehending.

'Pick them up one by one; don't concentrate on their look but feel their weight against each other. The difference is but small.'

Daniel picked up the guinea coins first, turning them in his fingers, weighing them in his palm. Carver watched carefully as Daniel started sorting out the genuine coins by weight. He threw a handful of guineas and half-guineas back onto Carver's bunk.

'These don't feel right, they're lighter. What is wrong with them?'

'They have been counterfeited. What they have done is

take two genuine guinea coins and filed them down wafer-thin discs one showing the heads and the other the tails details. They are then soldered onto a copper disc to give them the size of a genuine guinea. The edges are then gilded to cover the false centre disc. Pure gold is heavier than copper, hence the weight difference.' Carver could see Daniel was struggling to comprehend the consequences of this discovery, so Carver knew he had to spell it out.

'Thomas would have presented the gold in good faith. The Dutchmen would have automatically weighed it because they didn't get to be one of the largest global trading empires by taking everyone on trust. The tampering would have been discovered immediately and Thomas thrown in jail. Simple as that.'

'But why?' Daniel's voice was weak with shock.

'Because Lord Edgerton did not appreciate Thomas tupping his wife on a regular basis, nor did he appreciate how much his eldest son looks like Thomas. On top of that, he was coerced into bringing your family down by his cousin, by marriage, Sir Stanley Jacks, who did not appreciate being called out as a financially irresponsible buffoon, which he is.'

There were so many emotions running rife in Daniel now; his feckless brother could have brought ruin upon the whole family, yet still, he would have been an innocent victim of an evil man whose power and status would never be queried.

'How do you know all this?'

'A good steward knows everything. In most households, all servants are invisible, just part of the fixtures and fittings. Private matters are discussed at the dinner table; ladies' maids talk amongst themselves, and servants talk to visiting servants.

Nothing is secret and I make it my job to glean every drop of intelligence from within the house and the surrounding area. Always very helpful is a buxom and willing local barmaid, unless they are very ugly or poxed.'

'No doubt you were rewarded for your insider knowledge.' There was a bitter edge to Daniel's voice.

Carver ignored the barbed comment; his mind was focused on converting the situation into a workable plan. There were few amendments, but given the shocked state of Daniel's mind, he went through them step by step again.

They would disembark as expected and make their way to the recommended inn. The place had a good reputation for being clean and that it served food acceptable to most foreign palates. Daniel would then go into Amsterdam to meet his contacts at the right time, on the right day and conduct his business as though nothing was amiss. Carver, acting as Thomas, was to make sure enough people heard him complain loudly about how his younger brother, Daniel, had made a mess of the arrangements and how he was now eleven days late. Carver asked for writing paper and ink so that he could send a letter to Thomas' contacts, begging their pardon and to be given the opportunity to introduce himself on a later day. Whilst Daniel was in Amsterdam, Carver was to leave the inn and disappear, but not before tearing Thomas' distinctive waist jacket and ripping up the letters of introduction, leaving them to be found by a canal bank. A simple but effective plan, they thought.

When Daniel and Carver got off the ship, they felt decidedly unsteady on their feet and it took a few minutes for them to regain the feel of solid earth beneath them. The dockside was like any commercial port anywhere, a hive of activity with piles of cargo, including some round, yellow, hard cheeses stacked and confined in loading nets ready to export to different destinations. The noise of men working, shouting and cussing and the rank smell of the stale sea water used for washing out holds and storage areas, filled the air. Even the cobbled dockside and streets seemed familiar to Daniel and Carver; the only difference being that the voices were incomprehensible as the majority were speaking Dutch, with a mix of other sea-trading nations' languages.

The wooden clogs of the working men made a distinctive sound on the cobbles; the handcarts with their metal-rimmed wheels grinding and groaning under their loads, sounding more familiar. The warehouses and merchants' business premises bore the distinctive gables of Dutch architecture.

Between them, the two men carried the travelling trunk with their change of clothes, spare footwear and other necessities, including writing materials for letters and promissory notes. When they needed directions, they showed the address written on a scrap of paper to passers-by. Often, they were answered with a shrug or else directions delivered in rapid Dutch. Then a respectable-looking gentleman spoke to them in passible English and sent them off in the right direction. Neither Carver nor Daniel spoke to each other, both now feeling the pressure of the deception they were about to carry out.

The inn was run by a very large, muscular man called Johannes and his diminutive Dutch wife, Jinke. The landlord had in fact been born John Pascoe in the West Country and been many things in his life, including a prize fighter. No one sober or sensible picked a fight with him. Naturally, he spoke English and Dutch fluently and knew more German and French than he ever let on. Travellers felt safe staying under his roof, but John would still warn them of the dangers of wandering off into unknown areas. He would make of joke by saying that a thief, footpad and pickpocket didn't care what language you spoke.

'*Goedendag, heren, wat kan ik u geven?*' Johannes' voice boomed across the nearly empty room. No one looked up until they realised there had been no reply.

'My name is Daniel Matthews. Do you speak English?'

Laughter could be heard coming from the small group by the window.

'Indeed, I do, Master Matthews. Will you be wanting rooms for tonight or just good beer to wash the salt from your lips?'

'This is my older brother, Thomas, and we have come to Holland on business.'

'Well, that is nice for you and your brother, Thomas. But as I say, do you want rooms tonight? I only have one room but there is a truckle bed that can be used. Hot meals are available; my wife cooks well and the rooms are clean.'

'That is sufficient for our needs. And we don't anticipate staying here for long. I expect we will be asked to stay with business associates once we have made our presence known.' Carver did a wonderful imitation of Thomas' ill-mannered voice.

Johannes made a mental note to ensure payment in advance, the haughtier the customer, the less likely the bill would be settled.

Daniel sensed the wariness of the landlord. 'We will not know how long our stay will be until we have had our first meetings. Maybe, if we paid in advance, we could secure the room for four days and nights?'

Johannes grinned broadly and his opinion of Daniel rose. But he still didn't like the look of the surly brother.

'Jinke, komt deze heren naar hun kamer brengen.' A diminutive Dutch woman appeared and beckoned them to follow her.

Once in their room, they spoke very quietly because they were nervous about anyone listening in to their conversation. Carver took off his jacket and shirt to reveal the strips of linen wrapped around his torso which he carefully unwound. The linen strips contained a series of pockets sewn in and Edgerton's fake coins were hidden in the folds of the cloth. He had considered it more dangerous to be found in possession of tampered coins than the possibility of being robbed.

'We must dispose of these fakes without delay,' Carter announced. What he didn't share with Daniel was his intention to hide one in the stitching of his boot where the leather folded over. He thought some evidence of Lord Edgerton's duplicity may come in handy in the future. Carver was always alert to situations that might be played to his advantage; his survival was key to that.

Carver stayed behind at the inn whilst Daniel made his way into Amsterdam for his pre-arranged meeting. The previous day, they had spoken just loud enough to be heard, but not so loud their conversation could be considered staged.

Daniel explained his plans to Carver, including his stay overnight as a guest with his merchant contacts and how he expected to return to the inn within three days. Carver feigned petulance at being left alone at the inn, being less than complimentary about the area in which they were staying. Also, that he had to wait at the inn to receive a reply from Edgerton's contacts. What they were actually doing was giving Daniel a cast iron alibi for when "Thomas" disappeared. Carver played the part very well, but then he had had enough practise observing the real Thomas' speech and behaviour.

The plan was put into action. Daniel left to travel to the centre of Amsterdam to meet the grain merchants. There was much laughter amongst them when Daniel recounted how his brother had missed his appointment due to the calendar differences, but the merchants were impressed by whom Thomas had letters of introduction for. Daniel spent the night as a guest and enjoyed dining with his host's large family. The following morning, Daniel was present at the corn exchange where proposals for trading the next harvest's tonnage were made. All the time he was presenting a façade of confidence, his mind was in turmoil.

Carver prepared himself carefully once Daniel was out of sight and in good reliable company that the authorities could not question. He folded a plain waistcoat as tightly as possible into his satchel along with a pair of unremarkable shoes, his own clothes rather than Thomas' showy apparel. He left the rest of his belongings strewn around the room to indicate that he intended to return later in the day. He hung around at the inn, getting increasingly more querulous and objectionable, appearing to imbibe a large amount of the local gin while deftly pouring the lethal liquid down a large crack in the floorboards. Announcing he was leaving to find a bit of entertainment to liven up his wait for his brother to return, he left the inn with a staged stagger and slur to his speech, much to the innkeeper and his wife's relief and disinterest. When he failed to return for the evening meal, no one noticed or, if they did, didn't care. As far as John Pascoe was concerned, he had given the brothers fair warning of the potential perils and had taken four days bed and board in advance. Let the older brother fall foul of the darker side of the town.

Daniel was on the way back from the *Korenbeurs* Amsterdam City when the maid discovered that the elder brother had not returned to his room the previous night. At first, Johannes was not concerned; he imagined Thomas Matthews had fallen into a stupor in some poxed prostitute's bed and would not return until he had sobered up and found himself penniless. However, by late afternoon, even Johannes was getting concerned, so asked some local men to search the docks, canal banks and the well-known areas where an unwary traveller could be robbed.

It was as Johannes had predicted, but probably with a much worse outcome. A patch of distinctive material obviously ripped from the missing man's expensive waistcoat and a shoe with a recognisable buckle were found with scraps of torn paper close to the discarded and now empty money belt. The authorities were informed, statements made and Daniel was quizzed on his return to the port. The local magistrate was not about to make further investigations as it was fundamentally obvious that the Englishman had been robbed and his body thrown into the canal; just another stupid foreigner wandering around parts of coastal towns where the law-abiding locals never ventured.

Daniel's contacts had helped with the reporting of "Thomas'" disappearance, primarily with the language barrier, and were in accord with the Dutch authorities and they encouraged Daniel to return home to break the news to his family and Lord Edgerton. This was not a task Daniel looked forward; he a fundamentally honest man having to maintain such deception, especially to his nearest and dearest.

Meanwhile, Carver had sought out a local area where French and German Protestant refugees gravitated before seeking out new lives and religious freedoms in the Americas. He had come across a relatively young French woman struggling to push a handcart with her meagre possessions on, two small under-nourished children hanging on her skirts. He struck up a conversation with her. His French was understandable but his accent made her giggle. She was struggling not only with her handcart but a perilous future. Her husband had recently died of a fever, which luckily, she and the children had been spared from. Now, she was too scared to return to their former home where they had been persecuted for their beliefs her only choice was to continue on to the sea journey to the Americas, but as a vulnerable woman on her own. Carver did what he was best at, taking other people's difficulties and turning them to his advantage.

He suggested they travel as a family. He would adopt her husband's name and offer her the physical and psychological protection she needed. She would in return provide him with a new identity. He assured her he was not a wanted criminal, which in theory was true but far from the truth in reality.

What choice do I have? she thought.

So Carver once again transformed himself into a new person and set sail for his new life, having now acquired a wife and two children.

CHAPTER NINETEEN
September 2021

Mrs B, as she became known, was upstairs cleaning the bathrooms. She used an old horse grooming kit box for all her lotions, potions and sprays; everything had its place and everything was in its place. She did not like to see "things" as she called everyday cosmetic products cluttering up the surfaces, so Miles' badger hair shaving brush, its accompanying shaving soap pot and razor were put back in the cupboard where they belonged, not left lying around. Miles had wanted to mention that there was no need to leave each room as though it was a hotel room awaiting a new occupant. But she was a godsend, so her overzealous cleaning and tidying was forgiven. After all, there were worse sins.

Miles was in a rather good mood and was looking forward to telling Lucy about his interesting conversation with a former tutor at Cambridge. She had gone back to the bungalow at his suggestion to check that all was well, maybe collect more clothes and bring her paperwork over. He had offered her the use of one of the spare rooms as a study for her to work from. She had been reluctant to accept as it seemed further dependence on him, yet she did not want to be alone in her own home without Adrian.

Adrian was really worrying her now, as she still hadn't heard from him. She had tried phoning his friends but worried that she sounded like an angry parent whose child was out past curfew.

He heard the front door open and laughter. Lucy and Dick were carrying in a small filing cabinet; the drawers kept flying open because Lucy had lost the keys years ago.

'What on earth are you two doing?'

'Isn't it rather obvious?' Lucy's tart comment was accompanied by a big smile.

'Why didn't you use the porter's trolley in the shed?' Miles shook his head in disbelief at the impracticality of them, but it was nice to hear laughter in the hall, which continued up the stairs as this uncooperative metal box was trundled up the stairs. The staircase was well-proportioned, sweeping down into the hall in the bold style of its day. Yet he felt the lack of warmth and a general sense of gloom there; not even the big, bold display of flowers cut from the garden on the circular table broke the feeling.

Once Lucy had got herself settled in her new workplace, she joined Miles in the kitchen. 'You look very pleased with yourself.'

'I have every reason to be.' Miles went on to explain that his former tutor at Cambridge was approaching retirement and had made him a proposition. The economics faculty, next to Selwyn College, was looking for visiting fellows with experience in putting academic knowledge to good use in the commercial world. His tutor wanted to put his name forward.

'Cor, that sounds very posh and highbrow! Do they pay you or is it just for the kudos?'

'I'm going to visit him next week to discuss it in further detail, you mercenary piece of work!' Miles instantly regretted his merry quip, knowing how touchy Lucy was about money. But she didn't bat an eyelid, which he considered progress.

He reminded her that his birthday was in a few days' time and asked her again if she would like to go to the Old Manor restaurant for dinner.

'Looking forward to it. I've even brought a dress from home just for the occasion.'

'Have you thought any more about reporting Adrian's disappearance?'

Lucy knew he was right, it had to be done. She asked him to come with her to the police station as he had been the last one to see him.

He was going to suggest they went the next day, but worried she would change her mind again if they delayed.

'OK, we'll go now and get it over and done with.'

It was a quiet journey to Wymondham; neither Lucy nor Miles felt like talking. Lucy knew what she had to do and why, but her instinct told her that the police were the last people she wanted to involve.

It was as just as she imagined. They waited for some time until a rather bored-looking, uniformed constable ushered them through to an interview room.

Lucy calmly explained that Adrian had been missing for over a week and she had not heard from him. She had to admit that they didn't exactly live in each other's pockets despite living at the same address. Miles reported that the last time he had seen Adrian was when he asked for a lift to the station after leaving the Land Rover at his house. The constable clipped a photo of Adrian that Lucy had brought with her onto the file, assured them someone would look into it and would be in contact very soon.

Neither Lucy nor Miles were particularly inspired by the constable's lacklustre words.

§

The following day, Miles phoned Leonie to tell her about the invitation to be a visiting fellow at his old college at Cambridge. They talked about topics that might make for interesting and illuminating lectures. They both voiced their concerns about some of the minority mindsets that dominated and dictated how work should be perceived currently. Leonie let off steam about some young administrative assistant who couldn't get her head around the concept that she needed to book a day's leave to cover her absence, it being her birthday not a sufficient reason for bunking off work.

Whilst they were laughing about this, Miles suddenly felt uncomfortable sitting in the study, as though he was not alone. He interrupted Leonie who was telling him about other such ridiculous requests for time off.

'What's wrong, Miles?'

'Do you have the name of the company that does the regular sweeps of the offices for listening devices?'

'Why? I thought the only bugs anywhere near you were death-watch beetles!' quipped Leonie.

'Just text them to me please. Listen, Leonie, I must go. Give my love to Alex. We'll talk soon.' With that, he rang off and started to pace around the room. Miles was about to share his concerns with Lucy but decided to leave her working upstairs on some research project.

§

Somewhere in London, the voice-activated recording stopped but the alarm was already raised in Keith's office. He and Jack had had a minimum amount of time to hide the tiny devices in the study on the ground floor and the kitchen in the basement. The hawk-eyed housekeeper was determined to keep an eye on the phone engineers checking the broadband equipment but couldn't be in two rooms at once. It meant that the equipment would have to be retrieved from both properties.

The instruction to torch the bungalow did not sit well with him. Mr Smith was Jack's client and it was that Jack had volunteered to set the fire in the bungalow on his own.

§

Mrs B was brushing Skye's thick grey coat in the kitchen. Apart from keeping long dog hairs shedding to a minimum, she loved the gentle giant of a dog who stood so still whilst the brush detangled her coat.

'I was in the kitchen, Skye the old hound was inside. I was in the kitchen; Skye was being brushed.' Mrs B was half singing and humming a tune from the days when she had been a huge Pink Floyd fan, bending the words of *Seamus the Dog* to suit. When the phone rang, she waited for several rings to see if anyone else answered. She picked up the receiver just in time.

'Good afternoon,' she said in her best telephone voice.

'Lucy Moncrief?'

'No, Miss Moncrief is not here.'

'Well, where is she? When will she be back?'

Mrs B did not like the tone of his voice and decided she would not be helpful when the imperious voice further demanded,

'Who are you? What is your name?

'I am the housekeeper and there is no reason for you to know my name.'

'Well, what use are you to me then?

'I am sufficiently intelligent and literate enough to take a message.'

'Tell her Mr Smith phoned and that I am looking for her brother.' With that, the call disconnected.

She wrote a note, saying that a Mr Smith had called enquiring about Adrian, which she left on the big sideboard thinking, *I must remember to tell Lucy.*

She promptly forgot.

§

It was Miles' birthday. Having showered and changed, he was now ready to go out. Miles wandered into the hall and hoped that Lucy wasn't going to be one of those females who took forever to get ready. He should have known better. On cue, he saw the tall, slim woman in a dark emerald dress walk elegantly down the curving staircase, her hair neatly coiled up on her head and her subtle make-up that only an artist could have applied it so skilfully. His stomach churned; she was so beautiful.

Lucy stopped just before the bottom of the stairs, feeling unnerved. *Why is he staring at me?* Her first thought was that her dress was caught up in her knickers or she had on odd shoes. Her confidence was wafer-thin.

'Will I do?' She tried to keep the anxiety out of her voice.

'Lucy, you look stunning. That is a lovely emerald colour.' He turned sideways to offer his arm to escort her to the front door and outside to where a local taxi driver was waiting.

The Old Manor restaurant was not that far away. Miles had first passed it when he went to visit Adrian with the paintings Lucy had found. The restaurant had been closed because of COVID-19, but loyal local foodies had returned and it was once again a thriving concern.

'I hope you'll like this place,' Miles muttered, as their coats were whisked away.

'I know I will. And I promise, no history lectures!' Lucy grinned at him and then confessed.

'Actually, I know this house really well; I was at school with Rachel who lived here with her parents.' Once seated, she leaned close to him.

He could smell the hint of expensive perfume.

'She had a bit of a thing for Adrian; thought that if I was her best friend, she would get close to him. Wrong tree!'

At Miles' request, Lucy gave a short description of the house, briefly describing how it might have developed over the centuries to create its many different sections and levels. Miles' imagination was caught when he realised that where they were sitting might well have been where the open hearth had been in the hall before the upper floor had been added, along with chimneys. Still, the hall remained the heart of the house.

The food was wonderful; the lightly chilled champagne started the evening and accompanied the scallops and then they shared a Chateaubriand with a rich and velvety Côte de Nuits. Neither of them wanted a dessert, so nibbled instead at a cheese selection and grapes.

It seemed no time at all before the taxi returned for them.

Lucy switched on the drawing room lights, closed the shutters and drew the curtains whilst Miles poured two brandies. She smiled sweetly and thanked him profusely for a lovely evening then announced she was going to bed. She put her hands on his arms and kissed him on his left cheek.

For a split second, he was going to grab her, kiss her passionately and drag her onto a settee. Luckily, he stopped the thought just in time. Lucy would not appreciate the caveman approach to courtship. He just had to be patient.

His bed seemed cold and empty, but Miles had let Lucy decide. She had disappeared to her room. He switched off the bedside light, but the room did not go totally dark as the mobile phone he had put on charge gave off a green glow. Then he heard movement on the landing his door opened slowly. He could not believe his eyes.

'Would you like to unwrap your birthday present now?' Lucy stood in the doorway with what looked like just a large sheet of wrapping paper round her and a red ribbon round her neck.

Miles was just about to leap out of bed when he realised that his rampant penis was sufficient confirmation that he would very much like to unwrap his birthday present. Somehow, it lacked subtlety and would make him feel rather silly. The phrase "it's rude to point" shot through his mind.

'Yes please, very much so,' his voice almost cracking with emotion and shock.

Like the time before, she slipped into the bed beside him. Only this time, she wasn't crying and instead pressed her body against his. She placed a hand on his chest and slowly, with a feather-like touch, moved it down his body until she found exactly what she expected. The emotional memories of the past just melted away. Miles felt no guilt for making love to someone other than Helen and Lucy's fear of emotional abuse just evaporated as they expressed their love for each other in physical form.

Lucy was dozing off, completely sated with love; the wonderful sex, good food and wine all playing their part. Miles shifted himself so that he could look at her face. Her eyes were closed and a gentle smile softened her face like he had never seen before.

'Hey, you going to sleep?'

'Pink Zs can't be denied,' she said, then fell fast asleep.

Miles wrapped her in his arms, wondering about her comment before he was soon fast asleep too.

His mobile phone rang and he turned to look at it, as if scowling at it would stop its racket. The caller ID showed "Davy" and the time was 1:48 a.m. It rang off, then started again. Miles snatched it from the cradle.

'Mr Mortimer, please tell me Lucy and the dogs are with you!' Davy's broad Norfolk accent was wracked with worry.

'Of course they are. Are you pissed out of your brains, phoning at this bloody time of the night?'

'I had to know because the maid's house is on fire. I was so worried she might be in there.'

'Hang on a minute, are you saying there's a fire at Lucy's bungalow?'

'A right nasty one; looks like it started at the studio end. I have to talk to you, Mr Mortimer, private like.'

'We'll be there as soon as possible.' He rang off.

The glow of the fire and the pall of smoke rose in a plume into the night sky, illuminated by the multicoloured lights of the emergency services. Miles' car screeched to a halt at the start of the track, a police constable blocking his way. Lucy was nearly hysterical. Miles explained she was the co-owner of the property and was concerned that her twin brother might be in there. The constable used his crackling radio to ask for instructions. A disembodied voice told him to let them through but to park away from the bungalow and leave room for more fire brigade vehicles if necessary.

They walked towards the fire, Adrian's half thoroughly alight and the roof had caved in. A fireman came lumbering up to them, his ability to walk hindered by the layers of protective clothing and safety equipment. He identified himself as the senior person at the scene. He kept asking questions, but Lucy's answers were garbled so Miles intervened.

'I am sure as anyone can be that there was nobody in the property. Mr Albini has been away and Miss Moncrief has been staying we me.' He went on to explain that there were inflammables in that part of the property as Mr Albini was an art restorer and there were cleaning solvents, oil paints, canvases and suchlike.

He then had to repeat himself to the police sergeant who wrote it all down in his notebook. The fire was under control by now and the blackened roof trusses looked sinister as they pointed to the sky. Miles gave his details to the police and told them to come to Somersham Court when Lucy had had time to take in the disaster.

They were walking back towards the car when a dark figure appeared to jump out of the hedge. It was Davy who had been sitting on the stile, waiting for them to leave.

'My poor maid, are you… was…' Davy held out his huge powerful arms and enveloped her in them.

Miles was not impressed. 'No, he wasn't in there, he's missing, I don't know where he is.' She slowly pulled herself free of his embrace. 'Thanks for phoning us, Davy. But how come you were here at this hour to report it?' Her blunt question was a rather strange way of offering thanks.

'Well, I was "entertaining" somebody in the woods. She likes the *al fresco* hanky-panky.'

'So why the subterfuge then?'

'Er, her husband doesn't like *al fresco* hanky-panky and wouldn't appreciate his wife looking elsewhere!'

'Davy, you dirty little monkey! Who is she?' Lucy managed to smile at the thought.

'The reason I wanted to talk to you is because this was no accident. I saw a figure dressed in black leaving the property just before I could see the flames and heard breaking glass.'

'Have you told the police?'

'Christ, no, man, my outdoor playmate is the sergeant's wife!' Davy confessed. 'Can you imagine the havoc he could cause me? My shotgun and rifle licences would suddenly develop "problems" especially before large shooting competitions.'

'If you were doing it *al fresco*, how could you see what was happening at the bungalow?' Miles did not believe him.

'Simple. I was leaning back on the rucksack I use to carry the rug and drinks in and was taking my ease as she pleasured me. I could see over her head. Shall I draw you a picture?' Davy couldn't help smirk at the sight of Miles' puritanical look.

'No need, thank you.'

§

The following days were difficult. Lucy was shell-shocked and could not think straight. She kept muttering that she didn't understand why or how all this could happen in such a short space of time. Bunny's death and the unpleasant fall-out over her will, Adrian's disappearance and now her home burning down. All these horrors overshadowed the joy of spending the night in Miles' bed. It was all too much.

Miles had spoken to the fire brigade, the police and the insurance company; all very practical. Mrs B kept making tea and had rustled up a fresh batch of Lucy's favourite biscuits to try to tempt her to eat. She very proudly told Miles that carbohydrates were a natural sedative and that they were just as good as any doctor's pills. He didn't really agree with her, but he liked the sentiment and they were very good ginger biscuits.

Lucy wandered around the kitchen, absentmindedly opening and closing cupboard doors, taking out a mug then putting it back, lost in thought.

'Come sit yourself down, Miss Lucy.' Mrs B gently steered

her towards the large, scrubbed pine table. 'Try not to worry yourself; it won't change anything. He might have met some gorgeous young lady and is having a whirlwind romance, selfishly forgetting everyone else.'

'He's gay.' Lucy couldn't fail to smile at Mrs B's gaff.

'Oh, I'm sure he *is* a happy person.'

'No, I mean he's a homosexual; he doesn't like women in that sense.'

Mrs B sat down on the chair next to Lucy and gently took her hands into hers. 'Oh, you do have cool hands, no wonder your shortcrust pastry is better than mine.' Indeed, Mrs B's hands felt warm and reassuring to Lucy.

'Fretting won't help; it won't change whatever has or hasn't happened to your brother. He might walk through the door tomorrow and wonder what all the fuss is about.'

'Do you and Dick have children, Mrs B?'

'No, we were never blessed.'

'Well, if you had had a daughter, I would have liked to have been her.' Lucy started sobbing wholeheartedly; she could just about cope when everyone was being businesslike, but someone being kind made it all too much to bear.

§

The next morning, no one in the house had noticed the sound of a car coming to a stop on the gravel drive. The two occupants remained in the vehicle for a couple of minutes and exchanged glances.

'Well, this looks very nice, could be something of interest here.' Jeremy Tindall was a slightly built man with thinning, fair hair and intelligent pale blue eyes that didn't miss a thing. His companion was his career-minded constable, Janet Duncan. They were from a specialist Metropolitan Police unit.

They had travelled up from London as soon as the trigger on their computer system alerted them to the arson attack at the address of Adrian Albini, a person of interest in a global investigation into art theft and fraud. Though only a small cog in a very large wheel, the report of his disappearance and suspicious fire in his studio was sufficient reason to investigate his contacts. It also flagged up that his sister was under suspicion for duping old people out of expensive paintings, a complaint made by an irate relative.

Jeremy Tindall rang the doorbell and quickly followed it up by an emphatic bang on the front door. Mrs B was like a greyhound out of a starting gate, she liked to answer the front door in her role as housekeeper. It amused Miles and he was more than happy for her to enjoy her status.

'I would like to speak to Lucy Moncrief. Is she here?' said a strong male voice with a slight London accent.

'Mr Mortimer and Miss Moncrief are not receiving visitors today.'

Miles was in the drawing room and could hear this and had to stifle a laugh. From where did Mrs B get these phrases? She had obviously watched far too much *Downton Abbey*.

'They will see us; we are police officers.' With that, two warrant cards were presented for inspection.

'It's OK, Mrs B, we reported Adrian's disappearance to the police. It will be about that or the fire.

'Come in.' Miles beckoned them into the drawing room

and indicated for them to sit down.

They remained standing.

'My name is Detective Sergeant Jeremy Tindall of the Metropolitan Police Art and Antiques Unit and this is Detective Constable Janet Duncan.'

Lucy ignored their introduction and got straight to the point. 'Have you found him? Is he all right?' Lucy had only heard the word police and failed to take in the name of the specialist unit. 'Your constable the other day seemed so indifferent; I never expected to hear from you so quickly. Where is he? Is he in hospital? Why hasn't he been in contact?' Lucy was talking so quickly, her Norfolk accent sounded more like machine gun fire than conversation.

'I think you have mistaken our purpose. We are from London, the art and antiques unit, and we need to talk to you about your brother.'

It was obvious that the Detective Sergeant was not a dog lover and the dogs recognised that at once. Ozzy and Marble being rescue greyhounds sensed disapproval and immediately got up and disappeared down to their dog beds in the kitchen. The deerhounds took a totally different approach; this strange human needed further scrutiny and so both got up to investigate. This involved pointedly sniffing his crotch, which was conveniently head height for Fergus and Skye. The Detective Constable had to supress a giggle at her colleague's obvious discomfort.

Miles ordered the dogs out.

'Before we go any further, please explain why you want to speak to Adrian and why you have come to my house to find him.' Miles' voice had taken on a business-like tone.

The senior police officer gave a well-used overview of the unit; how art and antiques are vulnerable to crime and deception as investors and obsessive collectors will pay substantial sums of money without checking, or even ignoring weak provenance.

'Adrian Albini is a person of interest in a large-scale international investigation. Your report of him missing triggered a flag on our investigation, so too the report of the fire, especially the studio. It is imperative we follow it up.'

'Why would you be interested in Adrian? He's a copyist. He doesn't even have a valid passport, let alone be part of some global gang of thieves!' Lucy protested.

'You obviously don't know your brother as well as you think. He had a new British passport issued three months ago,' said the young policewoman.

'We are unable to give our reasons for wanting to talk to him, but we do believe you can give us some useful information. You called him a copyist; tell me more.' The Constable had her notebook in hand and was poised to write down anything they thought relevant.

'Well, he copies paintings rather than paints originals. I can't believe you haven't read our website before coming here.'

There was no response from the two police officers. Miles, who was sitting beside her, reached out and took her hand in his.

Lucy continued. 'For example, he painted a series of pictures for a new boutique hotel in the Cotswolds. Each room had a theme artist and they wanted two or three pictures. He was given a list of artists, mostly French impressionists. He showed the proprietors the *catalogue raisonné* for each of their chosen artists and let them decide which paintings the owners wanted copied. They were painted on modern canvas and stretchers, then he signed his name and dated the back. That cannot be considered fraudulent. For fuck's sake, he isn't Norfolk's answer to Wolfgang Beltracchi!' Lucy was getting angry because she considered they should be looking for Adrian to make sure he was safe, not bleating on about international art fraud which had nothing to do with her brother or her.

Miles was getting concerned. Though he believed Lucy was free from any suspicion, he was worried that her fiery temper and protectiveness of Adrian would cause her to speak out and regret her words, which could be twisted and misinterpreted.

'Lucy, I think it would be better if we let these police officers ask their questions and keep our answers as brief and succinct as possible.' He squeezed her hand, hoping that she wouldn't let rip at him, but she squeezed back in acknowledgment.

'Miss Moncrief, when did you last see your brother?'

Lucy tensed, wanting to berate this pale, insignificant-looking man for asking the same stupid question as the others.

'As I said in my statement at Wymondham Station, it was approximately…' Lucy repeated, in a clear and icy tone of voice, the exact same words she'd used in her statement at Wymondham Station, pointing out that the facts had not changed from the previous day.

'And you, Mr Mortimer?' the Constable asked.

Miles gave a precise description of Adrian's phone call asking for a lift to Ipswich station. Leaving the Land Rover at

Somersham Court and having an overnight bag and a good-sized wooden portfolio case with him when he dropped him off at Ipswich Station. He also said that he did not see Adrian cross over the platform bridge to the southbound platform as he needed to get out of the drop-off zone quickly.

Miles and Lucy watched as DS Tindall cast an experienced eye over the paintings hanging in the drawing room. He dismissed the large family painting for what it was, but his gaze lingered on the painting of Somersham Boy.

'One of your brother's copies?' He knew he was being provocative.

They ignored him and he didn't press for a reply.

'Now, Miss Moncrief, tell me about Letitia Boughton-Hay's paintings your brother faked.'

Lucy's nerves collapsed and she had tears rolling down her face. She remained silent.

'Detective Sergeant Tindall, I find your attitude and tone both insulting and unnecessarily offensive. I want you to leave my house now.' Miles stood up.

'However, I will answer your question so that there is no room for misinterpretation.' Miles gave a business-like description of the transactions, how the money was handled, the documentation completed and steps taken to ensure the copies could not be offered on the open market. He also pointed out that the complainant was probably Colin Barton, the vindictive, mercenary son-in-law who had made the libellous, false accusations against Lucy.

At that moment, the door opened and Mrs B arrived with a tray of tea and slices of homemade lemon drizzle cake. She put the tray on the low table in front of Lucy.

'Who are you?' DS Tindall asked, rather taken aback by the arrival of the tea tray.

'I am Mrs Betty Brown, housekeeper for Mr Mortimer. My Dick is the gardener here and we live in the Coach House. Who are you?'

'We are police officers interested in Mr Albini's disappearance.' DC Duncan was economical with the details.

'Who is Mr Albini?'

Lucy explained that it was her brother, Adrian.

'Oh, Miss Lucy, I am so sorry, I totally forgot what with the fire and all the commotion. There was a message for you yesterday. A gentleman called Mr Smith called, asking for your brother's whereabouts. I made a note of it and left it on the sideboard in the kitchen.'

'Mrs Brown, could you show me this note, please?' DC Duncan thought it was a good excuse for a quick look around and to ask more searching questions.

How mistaken she was. Mrs B had nothing detrimental to say about her employer; she had never met Adrian and confirmed there was no studio on the premises. When asked if she could use the toilet, Mrs B showed her the cloakroom door and effectively stood guard and then escorted the Constable back to the drawing room. Mrs B knew that in all good TV dramas, the junior officer asks to use the bathroom and then goes poking around in the house instead. She wasn't having that.

Lucy and Miles stood outside the main door and waited for the car and its occupants to leave the premises.

About a mile or so further down the road, the Sergeant pulled over into a gateway and stopped. 'Well, Janet, what do you think of that?'

'Gut feeling, he knows nothing and so, if she is involved, she hasn't shared it with him. Can't get over the existence of Mrs B and "her Dick". The mind boggles. Who the fuck has a housekeeper these days?' What she really thought was that Lucy was a lucky cow.

'You could be right. I don't think they can add anything. But if their Mr Smith is our Mr Smith, then they are paddling in dangerous waters. We'll keep a watching brief and come back to them if needs be.' He pulled out of the gateway and headed back towards the southbound A12.

'I did like the painting of the greyhound in the sitting room. I wonder who the artist was; it is a different one from the mediocre one of the house.'

Chapter Twenty

September 1721

There was a gentle knock on the door. Ned assumed it was one of the maids and shouted at them to wait. He opened the door expecting to see Kitty who had a habit of hanging around when he was working, but instead there stood Constance Matthews.

'Please accept my apology, Mistress Matthews, I would not have told you to wait had I known it was you. I meant no rudeness, I assure you.' Ned was thoroughly flustered.

'Ned, calm yourself, I took no offence. I just want to talk to you.' Constance was taken aback by the number of boxes Ned had been in the process of neatly packing with paints, brushes and a plethora of artist materials. She walked into the room, carefully gathering her skirts around her so as not to knock anything to the floor and looked out of the window. 'What a wonderful view of the meadow from here.'

'Yes, mistress. Please mind your dress, Master Millar is not a tidy person in his work.'

'Come down to the parlour; I wish to talk to you.' Constance gave what she thought to be a reassuring smile and left the room.

It was now Ned's turn to nervously knock on a far grander door than his. He entered at her invitation. She beckoned him to sit down on a chair near to her.

'Ned, can you explain to me your work relationship with Master Millar, as I am confused.' She smiled sweetly at him to try to put him at ease.

'I only enquire because I would talk to you about taking a further commission and I know not with whom I should make the arrangement.' She smiled and waited for Ned to reply.

'I was indentured when I was fifteen years old. It was all done proper like, my father has a good hand at writing and he reads well, but slowly. Master Millar paid his stamp duty as required. I was happy to be apprenticed, as sketching and painting have always brought great pleasure to me, even when I was younger. I visit my parents as and when I can, but always once a year on the anniversary of the signing as it coincides with my birthday. I have travelled to Lavenham five times now.'

'Surely that implies your apprenticeship is finished.' Constance knew more about the subject than Ned because of her father's apprentices. She shuddered involuntarily as she remembered the uncouth, foul-mouthed creatures.

'Well, Master Edward Versey, I shall offer you a commission to paint some small landscapes around Somersham Court. But on one condition: as you sketch and paint, I want you to teach Joseph the rudiments of your craft.'

He was already taken aback by the use of his full name, never mind the idea of earning his own money.

Constance was rather amused by Ned's reaction.

'Oh, Mistress Matthews, please do not think me ungrateful for your offer; I would be honoured to accept. However, I do not wish to inconvenience Master Millar nor incur his displeasure. I need to ensure that the apprenticeship is ended properly. Also, I must speak with my parents as they receive a large proportion of my wages, and they must be aware that I might struggle to send them more money once I have no regular wage.' Ned didn't believe that they would, but he didn't like loose ends, or to appear untrustworthy. On the other hand, he was being offered work in his own right.

'What would you have me teach Joseph?'

'A broad range of subjects; he has shown an interest in the countryside, nature and animals. But also, the discipline of lines and perspective that sketching buildings provides. He must not travel too far from the house; across the meadow and down to the stream or across to the woodland are both lovely vistas. Maybe the trees in the woodland. I thought the church on the other side of the woods would be a good subject, especially with all its different angled walls and pitches of the roof.'

Ned was taken aback by the sense of Constance's choices, and it would make a change from painting the predictable houses, horses and gundogs.

'An excellent choice, madam. Would you like me to paint the same vistas, or did you have something else in mind? I have a large board I could cut into four pieces to paint upon, creating smaller pictures that could be displayed in a group.' Ned did not mention that it had some draft work on it of the horse which Thomas had flogged. Ned was confident that a painting of a sold horse for a dead owner was never to be completed.

'Joseph is not feeling too well today and I do not want him sitting outside where he can get cold. However, he is most impatient to start with his sketching lessons.' Indeed, Joseph did look rather pale, but Ned thought that some fresh air would do him more good than being cosseted in the house.

'How about we sketch what we can see from the window?' Ned suggested to Joseph. This idea was met with smiles and nods of approval from the young boy. 'Why don't you help me gather the easels, pencils and paper, Master Joseph, from the studio?'

The child perked up and the idea distracted him from his dark thoughts.

'When you return, Ned, I have some news which might please you.' Constance was determined that there was not going to be an atmosphere of doom and gloom. After all, she relished the idea of at least two weeks without Thomas tormenting her.

Ned set up his and Joseph's easels to look out across the formal garden, towards the ornamental gate and over the meadow.

Safe in the knowledge that Thomas and Daniel had left for Holland, the two little greyhound girls, Leto and Metis, had been released from the kennel block and were happy to be living indoors being petted and fussed by both Constance and Joseph.

Once the easels had been set up and Joseph was wrapped up in a large overall, Constance decided to make her important statement.

'I should have shown you this letter yesterday, but I wanted to tell you myself. Well, Ned, you are no longer an apprentice, but a painter in your own right!' declared Constance with a note of triumph in her voice.

Ned did not respond as he wasn't sure what to say; to challenge her statement would be considered rude or argumentative.

'I have received a letter from your mother; she has confirmed that you have passed your twenty-first birthday and therefore are free of your indenture.' She waved the letter at him.

'So time to sign your own paintings, Ned, or should I say Master Versey?' She was laughing and her face lit up with the excitement of the discovery.

'You should go and celebrate with your parents, for they must have missed you sorely during the last five years.'

Ned thought that they would only miss the proportion of his wages he sent to them now will stop.

'Not that much, mistress, as I have a five-year-old little sister now.' Ned blushed to the roots of his hair as soon as the words left his head. He glanced over at Joseph who seemed oblivious to the conversation and certainly its innuendo.

§

The next day, Ned set out for Lavenham in Suffolk with his savings and the money Constance had given him for sketching lessons; the first money he had earned outright himself. Despite the sense of freedom from being Millar's apprentice, at the beck and call of a second-rate artist, Ned was apprehensive about his future at having to find new clients and, the worse part, ensuring they paid. Though he had no liking for Millar nor respect for his artwork, he did admire his stubborn persistence when it came to making clients pay.

He imagined having to stand up to the likes of Thomas Matthews when they would not settle their account. The thought sent shudders down his back. But he had been bound to return to Somersham Court to teach Joseph how to paint a series of landscapes and Constance had also commissioned him to paint her two small greyhounds. The idea made him smile; they were lovely dogs and Constance was honest. But these cheery thoughts did not stop the recollections of the events on the staircase; he really wanted to confide in someone to ease his burden. Yet he knew this would be disastrous for the people he most cared for.

On the journey home, Ned sat on the back of a half-empty farm cart with his legs dangling over the tailgate. His feet were sore from walking and the respite was welcome, so too was the sight of the landscape and familiar buildings as they approached Lavenham. At first, he decided to write an account of that night's events but then worried it might fall into the wrong hands. He looked up at the vast East Anglian sky and watched the clouds drifting past, wondering where they were going. Then the idea came to him: he could use the cover of teaching Joseph to create a set of pictures that gave clues pointing the way to Thomas' body.

The wheels of the cart were now on cobblestones. Coming into the village of Lavenham, he could see the enormous church of St Peter and St Paul, its large tower pointing up into the sky. Many of his mother's relatives were buried there, especially after the outbreak of smallpox in 1712-1713.

The cart pulled up just before the square and Ned jumped off, thanking the carter for the lift. There, at the top of the square near The Little Hall, stood his mother with young

Mary hanging onto her apron. Ned's heart lifted. What could be more precious than the love of a child for its mother? The innocent love in Joseph must be protected from past events.

§

Ned's departure from Somersham Court was not a day too soon, because Lord Edgerton paid a visit and his mood was not one to be trifled with.

'Good day, Mistress Matthews.' Edgerton strode into the drawing room and sat down unbidden. 'I will come straight to the point; have you heard from your husband recently?'

'No, my lord. But it is only a matter of days since his departure with his brother, Daniel.' Constance was all too aware of the social distance between this glowering member of the aristocracy and herself. But she felt good manners was the gift of all classes.

'What do you mean, woman?' His anger dismissed all such social niceties.

'Exactly what I said, my lord,' her politeness exaggerated to highlight his rudeness.

'To be in Amsterdam on the date I specified, he should have nigh on over two weeks ago to allow for travel and the calendar difference.' Edgerton could barely keep a civil tone and continued.

'Surely he must have known that Holland is on the new Gregorian calendar, unlike England. Dear God, the man must be a complete imbecile if he was not aware of that. I specifically stated the date was NC.' Edgerton got up and started striding up and down, unsure if his carefully choreographed plan was unravelling or had just been enhanced by Thomas' ignorance. His original plan had been for Thomas to present counterfeit gold coins to the eminent merchants in Amsterdam and then get arrested. However, he saw merit in exposing Thomas as incompetent. At least it made sense of the letter he had received from Amsterdam that morning reporting that Thomas Matthews had not presented his letter of introduction nor delivered the gold as expected. The sender wanted to know what they should do next.

'Can I offer you refreshment before you leave?' Constance held her voice calm and steady, but her nerves were jangling.

Lord Edgerton neither acknowledged the offer nor bade Constance good day but left as abruptly as he had arrived.

Chapter Twenty-One

September 1721

News soon reached Lord Edgerton that Daniel had returned to England and was back at his family home of Old Manor Farm. He lost no time in ordering a coach to be brought round and to be driven straight to the Matthews' house.

He did not wait to be granted entrance, just strode into the house and stood in the hall, shouting for Daniel. Everyone within earshot came rushing in thinking that some terrible accident had happened or other emergency. All they saw was a diminutive old man in expensive clothes and a large wig that obscured most of his facial features.

They knew exactly who he was.

'What gives you the right to barge your way into my home unannounced?' a very irate John Matthews demanded.

'Where is your son, Daniel? I must speak with him. But moreover, where is my gold? It must be returned because of your son Thomas' incompetence.' Edgerton was aware of his plot back-firing but thought there was a chance he could bully Matthews into making good on his perceived losses.

'I am here,' Daniel said. 'If you would care to sit down and lower your voice, I will tell you exactly what I know.'

The angry lord did not sit down, but Daniel did at the long dining table that ran the length of the hall. Daniel then quietly and calmly repeated the official line. His heart was racing and his stomach churning because it didn't matter how many times he recounted the tale, it did not get any easier.

Edgerton effectively called Daniel a liar and said that he and his brother had colluded to steal the gold and make up the story. Daniel wanted to scream at him that he knew that most of the coins were counterfeit and that it was a trap for Thomas to walk into; a trap Thomas would have been lucky to get out of Holland alive.

'Lord Edgerton, you declare your coin has gone missing. That is true; the officials in Amsterdam have recorded the loss as the result of a robbery and my brother presumed murdered during the theft. Surely, you cannot suggest that I have managed to fake the circumstances, or that the documentation provided by the judge under Roman-Dutch law is of no consequence?

'I must insist you leave now. You have entered my father's house in a hostile manner, you have made slanderous accusations against me and you have exceeded your authority.' Daniel then quickly added, 'You have taken no consideration for the fact this is a house in mourning and that our family is grieving and warrants no such foul behaviour.' Daniel walked over to the large oak door and indicated that Edgerton should leave immediately.

'You will regret your words and actions, Daniel Matthews, be assured of that.'

Daniel was assured that Lord Edgerton meant it and would waste no time to exact his revenge.

§

Constance sat in the shade of the garden wall watching Joseph draw the stag statue. His little face screwed up in concentration and barely noticeable was the tip of his tongue between his front teeth. Her heart ached with worry about his future and prayed that her little blond angel had not inherited his father's cruel and loveless heart. Constance heard a voice calling from the house and was astonished to see Cecile Le Fevre waving to her as she approached.

'*Ma cherie* Constance, I must speak urgently with you. Let us walk in the shady part of your beautiful garden or in the hay meadow through the gate.' Cecile went over to Joseph and dropped a gentle kiss on his curly blond hair and bade him stay to finish his picture.

The two women went through the wrought iron gate in the garden wall and were soon out of sight of the house.

'Constance, I come to you in friendship and as one woman to another in a world where men can dictate and destroy others' lives on a whim or a fancy. Please do not ask questions I am not at liberty to answer. All I can do is to offer some immediate advice.'

Constance was speechless.

Cecile continued and to press her point took Constance's hand in hers.

'You must leave here as soon as possible, with only your personal belongings. Since Daniel has reported that your husband has been killed and Lord Edgerton's gold disappeared, Edgerton plans to wreak revenge by humiliating and embarrassing anyone close to Thomas. He intends to have you evicted with the worst publicity he can create.'

'But how can he do that? The house belongs to my father-in-law.' Constance was not taking in the severity of the situation.

'Edgerton holds the lease and it is under that authority he acts.'

'Why are you telling me this? Surely, he is your benefactor and you work under his instruction. How do I know you are not part of this cruel charade?' The panic in her voice was now uncontrollable.

'You cannot know for sure, but can you afford to ignore that I might speak the truth?' Cecile turned to return to the garden entrance and quickly told Constance that if anyone should ask, tell them she came to arrange for the collection of her spinet.

Constance watched her leave, then bent down to admire the picture Joseph had drawn. 'How would you like to visit Grandmother and Grandfather Matthews? Maybe we could stay for a few days and you could draw some of the real animals rather than stone ones?' She gave her boy the biggest smile she could muster. Judging by the huge grin on his face and the speed at which he collected his drawing materials, she knew he would not make a fuss.

She set about packing their immediate belongings. She made no request from her maid, Mary, nor did she send for the trap to be made ready, as she was more than capable of harnessing a pony herself. Between the mother and young son, they carried the boxes downstairs and hid them in the parlour whilst Constance brought the pony and trap round.

'Mary, Mary, where are you?' The hard-voiced Mrs Phillips could be heard calling up the servants' staircase. The maid popped her head over the banister on the first floor. Before she could answer, Mrs Phillips barked out her orders.

'Find the mistress immediately; an urgent post has arrived for her.'

Constance could hear this exchange and once Joseph and the boxes were safely on the trap, she wandered in through the front door as calmly as she could manage, though sure they would hear her heart beating so loudly.

'Did someone call me? I was in the garden.' She walked through the hall into the drawing room and sat down, as though awaiting tea to be served any minute.

'Ah, there you are.'

Mrs Phillips' manner of address and attitude to Constance was usually abrupt, bordering on rude, but this level of off-handedness really unnerved her.

'This came by special post for you.'

'Thank you, I will take it to my room to read. If there is a reply to be sent, I will send for someone to take it. I will inform you when I want tea served.' With that, Constance left the room and made her escape with Joseph in the pony and trap.

It was a couple of miles down the road and well out of sight of the house before she slowed the pony down to a walk and handed the reins to Joseph. She opened the letter and realised she owed Cecile a debt of gratitude. Constance travelled on towards Old Manor Farm.

§

Meanwhile, Alice was feeling tired and drained. Not only was her eldest son missing somewhere in Holland, presumed dead, but it was the rumours that he had stolen money that cut her to the quick. She knew Thomas to be many unpleasant things, but being dishonest with money was not one of them.

She sat in front of the kitchen fire watching the smoke curl up the chimney and wrap itself around a large gammon joint, whilst the pot of stew simmered gently on the hanging trivet. It was very warm and smoky in the kitchen, which was why John had insisted on the creation of an outbuilding specifically for cooking purposes. But Alice liked the atmosphere, even though John complained about the smell of her hair at night-time, he never complained about the flavoursome bacon or the rich, warm stews put on the table at mealtimes.

She was more defeated than depressed, for had she not warned John of the consequences of overindulging Thomas and giving himself airs and graces above his station in life. As for getting on the wrong side of the likes of Sir Stanley Jacks and his cousin, Lord Edgerton, well, that was just plain foolhardy.

The sound of a pony's shod hooves and a trap's metal-rimmed wheels on the cobbled courtyard pulled her mind back into the present. Thinking it was either John or Daniel returning for their midday meal, she gave the stew one last stir and removed it to a trivet at the fire's edge to keep warm.

Alice came out of the kitchen door and saw it was Constance and Joseph getting down from the trap, upon which several travel boxes were precariously strapped.

'Joseph, be a good boy and look for your Uncle Daniel to help unload these boxes.' Alice wanted the boy out of earshot so she could quiz her daughter-in-law about her arrival.

'Mother, please don't turn us away; Joseph and I need

somewhere safe to live. We cannot stay at Somersham Court. I can explain, but I doubt you and John will credit the tale I have to recount. If nothing else, take your grandson in; he is an innocent in all this.' Constance's voice waivered, not with weakness or indecisiveness but with the heavy burden of such emotional strain.

'Hush, hush, child, this is your home now.' Alice patted her arm and motioned for the two travellers to warm up inside whilst she unhitched the pony and put him away in a stable, a flour sack across his damp back and a full manger of hay to console him after his heavy load.

A little later that evening, Joseph was asleep in his new bed and the family assembled in the main hall seated around the oak table whose size dominated the room. Constance by this time had calmed her nerves and felt more relaxed now her future looked assured.

'Constance, now we are all together, can you recount what occurred to you this very morning?' John asked in as gentle a tone as he could manage.

He was pleasantly surprised when Constance replied in a clear and confident voice, 'It was never my ambition nor desire to live in such a house as Somersham Court. It has become even less to my liking since Thomas left for Holland and what befell him there.' There was a pregnant pause at this point as they never discussed Thomas' disappearance amongst themselves.

Constance continued.

'Everything belongs to Lord Edgerton: the lease, the furniture, even Carver was his man.'

'Have you heard from Carver?' Daniel asked rather

abruptly.

'No, nor has anyone else. But I have received this letter.' Constance threw the single sheet of paper on the table which slid to a halt in front of John. She indicated he pick it up and read the contents, which he did.

'This is outrageous! How dare he behave in such a high-handed manner to my family when I own the house!' He slammed the paper down.

It was within Daniel's reach, so he picked it up and read the contents. It was only as to be expected from Edgerton. Written in brutal terms, devoid of any compassion for a potentially widowed woman with a small child, it spelled out clearly that she had three days to evacuate the house. On the third day, a clerk would be sent to check the inventory of contents against the list of goods supplied in Thomas' name and she would be liable for any items unaccounted for.

'Constance, what is left in the house that you own or need?'

She assured John very little, only various items such as her sewing box and other personal belongings she had had no room for in the boxes. She added that there were Thomas' personal effects also to remove but offered no suggestion as to where they were to be taken.

Daniel spoke out. 'Father, with your permission, I would like to return to Somersham Court tomorrow with one of the men from the farms to collect the remaining items, including Thomas' personal belongings.'

Before John could reply, Constance interrupted and insisted on accompanying him for she, and she alone, could identify her property. So it was agreed.

The following morning was thankfully dry and the little cavalcade set out determined to complete the unpleasant task as quickly and efficiently as possible. Daniel and Constance rode in the trap, and a large farm cart lumbered along behind them, driven by a couple of farm labourers.

They pulled up outside and the younger farm hand hopped down and helped Constance out. He held the heads of the pony and the horse whilst Constance and Daniel mounted the steps of Somersham Court and rapped the large brass knocker. The front door was opened by Mrs Phillips who had always been in the employ of Lord Edgerton and thoroughly enjoyed the drama of the day.

'Mrs Phillips, stand aside. We are here to collect the personal effects of Mr and Mrs Matthews.' Before she could reply, Daniel continued, 'No doubt you will have had your instructions from Lord Edgerton.' Before she could reply Daniel continued, 'I am Daniel Matthews, brother of Thomas and have every authority to carry this out.'

Mrs Phillips stood to one side, taken aback by the dismissiveness of the callers. Of course, she knew what was to happen, but it was supposed to be in two days' time with Lord Edgerton present, not today during his absence. She returned to the kitchen and thought about her options. She had decided to prepare her own meagre possessions for a quick dismissal and crated up as much of the food and drink that could be reasonably carried in a handcart. She wasn't going to arrive at her sister's house of sanctuary empty-handed.

In no time at all, Daniel had found her, in his hand were several pages of paper. 'Now, Mrs Phillips, you and I are going to start at the top of the house and check the contents against the inventory. You will witness their presence and condition.'

'I'm not signing no papers like; I just keep house, not nothing like that.' She paused and then triumphantly announced that she couldn't write her name, not that anyone present believed her.

'Don't worry, Mrs Phillips, when the inspection is finished you just make your mark and these two men will witness it.'

The stout young farmhands stepped into the kitchen to stand behind Daniel.

'Now, if you please, let us not waste any more time.'

Before leaving the kitchen, Daniel commented to Mrs Phillips, 'One of the farmhands has noticed that there is a handcart by the back door. It appears to have a large number of cheeses, bottles, and smoked meats on it. I hope it is a delivery waiting to be unloaded and I trust not about to be pilfered from the premises.' Daniel's eyes bored into the unnerved woman's face.

Her manner immediately changed and she quietly accompanied Daniel and Constance to each room which was scrutinized and checked against the inventory. Needless to say, nothing was found to be damaged or missing.

Mrs Phillips glared at Constance, as though challenging her to find fault in her work.

'Thank you, Mrs Phillips, everything is in order, which is only what I would expect from a housekeeper such as your good self.' Constance, forever the peacemaker, tried to placate the unpleasant woman.

'Daniel, what about the paintings in the drawing room?' Constance answered her own question. 'I never want to see them again and it is not for me to have them removed to Old

Manor Farm.'

She could see Daniel struggling to recall which paintings she was referring to, so she added, 'The big oil painting over the fireplace and the portrait of Somersham Boy. There are four small oils that Ned Versey painted before he left. I want to keep them.' She stopped to think about it. 'No, just three of them, I don't like the one with the packhorse in the woods, there is something about it that makes me uncomfortable.

Daniel was getting impatient. 'There is a little cupboard under the back stairs on the second floor, put them in there and lock them in.' Constance now just wanted to get away.

So Daniel and his companions took the paintings to the cupboard, having firstly wrapped them in felted cloth. He felt a certain degree of sadness committing his brother's image to the dark, knowing it was unlikely to see the light of day for some considerable time.

It was a sombre little procession that left Somersham Court for the last time. No one looked back at the once again unoccupied house.

Chapter Twenty-Two
October 2021

The message that Mr Smith had left only whetted the appetite of Sergeant Tindall; he was convinced Adrian Albini was a person of great interest and inconveniently missing. However, the Sergeant did not think Miles had any knowledge or information about their investigation. The jury was out as far as Lucy was concerned; she was potentially a link to tracking down her brother.

Unfortunately for Miles and Lucy, Mr Smith considered them both people of interest, only his interest was more dangerous, with the possibility of gratuitous violence and mindless destruction. Miles was more concerned than Lucy, she was so wrapped up in her concerns for Adrian she seemed reluctant to believe he could possibly have anything to do with wholesale forgery and money laundering, never mind the consequences of crossing a ruthless gang of art thieves.

Miles walked the dogs down to the stream and then around the outside edge of the meadow. He loved to watch these dogs, built for speed and chase, run for the sheer joy of being able to. He needed space to think and decide what to do. It was obvious that Adrian had crossed swords with the wrong person.

He was still thinking about it when towelling the dogs' legs and paws before letting the animals into the house.

'Excuse me, Mr Mortimer, I wonder if I could have a word?'

Miles didn't want to have any words with anyone but despite that, he cheerfully encouraged Dick to speak.

'The Land Rover parked by the stables is an old Series Three and they leak like sieves, especially through the roof. I wondered if I should put a tarpaulin over it to keep the worst of the weather off it. And maybe turn the engine over and move the wheels so the weight isn't consistently on one part of the tyres.'

'Excellent idea, Dick, thank you. I should have thought of that myself.'

'There are also the dog beds and suchlike in the back; should I take them out and get Betty to give them a wash to stop them going mouldy?'

'No, I'll do that. I'll give it a good clear out and then we can get it covered.' Miles thought it was something he could do to distract himself from his current dark thoughts.

He went to find Lucy. She was hunched over a laptop talking to someone about cross-passages and inglenooks. He didn't interrupt, but she told the caller to hang on whilst she spoke to him. He explained briefly Dick's idea and his offer to clean it out. She smiled, gave him the thumbs up and went back to her call.

He went down to the kitchen to seek Mrs B's advice on which of her many sprays he should or could use. Miles did not dare to touch her grooming box of cleaning equipment. So armed with good advice and a selection of sprays together with appropriate cleaning cloths, he made his way to the Land Rover. He cursed himself for not bringing the keys, but found it wasn't locked. That didn't surprise him.

The dog beds were beginning to smell musty and though there wasn't any obvious sign of water getting in, there was a pervasive smell of damp. Miles climbed inside and sat on the boxed-in wheel arch. He felt cramped in the back of the vehicle with his legs crunched up and tried to imagine Lucy being born in there. He had heard of home births and water births but imagined Land Rover births must have been nigh on unique, well in England anyway. When he scrambled out, the metal floor didn't feel quite right. His curiosity was now aroused and he took a closer look. He ran his hand round the edge and was surprised to find that the metal was not continuous with the wheel arches. Instead, it had a detachable metal sheet, the sharp edge which gave him a minor cut on his finger confirming it. Upon careful examination of the vehicle frame, he found a small, slim slot that seemed out of place. A sturdy, long-handled screwdriver found a mechanism that released the metal plate. Miles was not prepared for what he found, for wrapped in cloth and padded by foam cut to size was a frameless painting, still held taut on its stretchers. Even to his untrained eye, he could see it was of age and quality. His first reaction was to rush to find Lucy and show her his discovery. But something stopped him. Mr Smith and Sergeant Tindall; both were looking for Adrian and something of value he had. There was considerable risk in returning it to either of them. Miles needed time to think. Returning the painting to its secret compartment, he took the dog beds and rubbish bag back to the house.

All his years of risk assessment and holding his nerve in the money markets allowed him to think quickly and formulate a plan with the highest chance of giving peace of mind and security for the future. Miles thought about how this discovery might affect Lucy and he decided to keep Lucy in the dark for the time being. He needed to control the situation for all their sakes.

The next day, Mr Smith rang and was not in a patient mood.

'Good morning, Mr Smith. I suggest you talk to me, not Lucy, as I believe I can assist you.'

'Mr Mortimer, how can *you* help?'

'We are both successful businessmen, albeit in different spheres of work. We both understand the laws of supply and demand and how to negotiate a mutually satisfactory agreement.' There was silence on the other end of the phone. Miles continued.

'I believe I'm in a position to supply you with something you want, but I demand something in return.'

'I see, how much?' Mr Smith sounded almost disappointed.

'There is no financial element to this. However, it will rely on trust on both sides.'

'Continue, you interest me.'

'You are looking for a painting, possibly two: the original and maybe a forged copy. I can only assume you have neither you wouldn't be so persistent in your searches. I believe you didn't find anything at Adrian's home and that you had his studio torched out of pure malice.' Miles took the silence as an indication to keep going.

'My house presented a totally different challenge; nearly always occupied and with dogs to raise the alarm. As I am sure you now know, I have a firearms licence and therefore have additional security. The phone engineers' ruse was neither subtle nor imaginative. The surveillance equipment was soon found, as you will already know from the recordings. I'll not be returning them to you as they are stored off-site, with a detailed statement in case they are needed in the future.'

'So what do you want?'

'I do not want the police involved, yet it goes against the grain to assist in nefarious criminal activities. What I really want is for all of you to go away and leave me to live in peace, with the assurance that nothing unpleasant happens to anyone or anything I care about.'

'Surely your duty as an upright citizen should make you contact the police.'

Miles could hear the sneer in his voice.

'Indeed, they only plod around houses looking for things and when they don't find what they're looking for, they at least don't torch the property!' Miles was getting bored with dancing around the subject.

'I know where the painting of the Spanish lady with the heavy lace headdress is. I do not know if it's the original or a clever fake. I will exchange this image for another image. I want *you* to make the exchange. You get the painting and I get a copy of your passport and matching driving licence with your likeness on it. Don't try to send someone else; I know your voice now and it's quite distinctive. We will meet in public. I suggest the little café in Halesworth in the pedestrian part which has outside tables. You can bring one person with you and I will have one person with me. Once the transaction is complete, you will never contact me or anyone associated with me. The copies of your documentation will go into safe

storage along with the bugs you had planted in my house.'
Miles waited to hear the phone disconnect, but the silence
remained.

'I can work with that, but I don't like it. Trust does not
come easily. But God help you if the police are informed of
this arrangement.'

'I have no intention of being charged with perverting the
course of justice, thank you very much. Nor handling stolen
artwork. My silence is guaranteed so long as you leave us
alone.' Then Miles added one more point.

'I am not responsible for Adrian Albini's actions, either in
the past or the future. I will not be held accountable for him.'

The conversation did not run on much longer, only to
agree on time and further details of the proposed exchange.

Miles' level of adrenaline had risen considerably during
the telephone call. He phoned Davy and arranged to meet up
with him that afternoon. He gave him minimum details but
explained he wanted a "minder" during a meeting and that
Davy needed to be as discreet as Miles was about Davy's *al
fresco* activities.

Twenty-four hours later, Miles' car pulled into the
supermarket car park in Halesworth. He may have had nerves
of steel in the city exchanges in London, but facing a ruthless
criminal was a totally different matter.

Davy was carrying the carefully wrapped, but empty,
parcel close to his chest. Miles wasn't going to risk a street
snatch by Mr Smith's goons. The previous day, Davy had
taken the picture, carefully wrapped, to the meeting place and
asked them to keep it behind the counter until the next day.
Davy had the kind of charm that melted knicker elastic at a

hundred yards. Consequently, the picture was stored with due care in a corner out of sight by a willing young female.

Thankfully the weather was kind to them, as sitting outside in the pouring rain would have made them conspicuous. It was a crisp, sunny, late autumn morning. Miles sat down, the shop window behind him, whilst Davy disappeared inside and returned with two large mugs of steaming coffee and a couple of sticky pastries. Mrs B's comment about carbohydrates being a sedative came to his mind.

Mr Smith was a nondescript-looking man in his mid-forties, possibly early fifties. His companion was a different matter: a tall, broad-shouldered young man with a hard hatchet face framed by wiry, wavy brown hair. Both were immaculately dressed. Despite the obvious grooming and quality clothing, the knuckles on the young man, just summed it up. The letters of LOVE and HATE had been tattooed on the left and right hands. *Probably ex-army or prison or both,* thought Davy.

They sat at the table and Miles offered for Davy to get coffees for them. The idea was dismissed with a small wave of the hand.

'The goods?' Mr Smith pointed to the large package next to Davy.

'No. It's close by but that's an empty parcel, just in case you decided to change the terms of our meeting and did a street snatch.' Miles waited for a reaction. There wasn't one.

Mr Smith's companion had suggested the idea in the car on the way up from London, but it had been dismissed. Mr Smith had already decided to play straight with Mr Mortimer. It was the simplest and quickest resolution to his problem.

'Ron, go with Mr Mortimer's friend and collect the goods.'

'Show me the copies first,' Miles stated.

Two sheets of folded A4 paper were put on the table but Mr Smith left his hand on them until the painting was retrieved from the shop. They each inspected their exchanges and were satisfied.

It had been difficult for both men to trust a stranger to keep to their bargain when covering up a police matter with an illegal transaction. Yet the alternative was too uncertain to chance. Miles and Mr Smith shook hands and went their separate ways.

The whole episode made Miles feel sick to the pit of his stomach, but as far as he was concerned, he was covering a crime for the greater good.

§

He was not, however, prepared for the events at home. He was tired, hungry and felt physically dirty having made a pact with a violent criminal. He wanted a hot bath, a decent dinner and to watch nonsense on the TV with Lucy curled up on the settee next to him. Lucy had other ideas. She was packing her belongings with a view to loading up the Land Rover.

'Why?'

'I've taken advantage of your hospitality too long; I can't stay here any longer. I need to work and pay my way. I have a friend, Sarah, who's a conservator and is working on restoring tapestries in Devon. She needs help as her assistant has broken her arm. I can stay with her whilst we work.' Lucy tried to sound nonchalant and matter of fact.

Miles neither knew nor cared what a conservator did. Why would Lucy take work hundreds of miles away for at least six weeks? If the broken arm was to be believed.

'Lucy, haven't you realised by now that I really like having you here; I enjoy your company, I want you to live here. Why do you have to go?' He wanted to say, why do you have to spoil things when we have finally got together?

'You don't understand. I am not here because you invited me to come and live with you. I am here because there was no alternative; my home is uninhabitable. My life is in total disarray, I can't think straight; Adrian is missing and could be dead; I have little money and I'm not paying my way. The insurance money on the bungalow could be months off, assuming they will even pay out because it was arson. I have to live somewhere until it is rebuilt, but I don't want to rebuild. I want to sell it as a building plot to some idiotic Londoner to build an eco-home or mini mansion with wrought iron gates.'

Miles did not respond to the "idiotic Londoner" comment.

'I know everything is up in the air, which is all the more reason for staying here and letting me help. You know, there is no shame in asking for or taking help from someone who really cares about you.' Miles tried to keep the desperation from his voice.

'You are not listening! I don't want to be beholden to you. If the circumstances were different, if Adrian had gone to live in London and was willing to sell the place, then I would be delighted to accept an invitation to come and share your life. But that isn't the situation. I'm not a charity case.'

'What if you were my wife?' Miles regretted saying it the

moment the words left his mouth.

'But I'm not, and if you think a rash proposal is going to work, then you're a bigger idiot than I thought you capable of being.' She saw the bewildered look on his face; her own heart was breaking as well. Why can't he understand? She didn't want to be there just because she had nowhere else to go. The circumstances had to be different. It had to be a positive invitation to move in with him, even get married, not because she was homeless and penniless. Lucy felt she had lost everything in her life in a matter of weeks; her pride was all she had left.

Lucy put her arms around him and whispered gently into his ear that she did love him and did not want to hurt him but needed time away to get her life sorted out. She kissed him gently by the corner of his eye, only to taste the salty tears forming.

'Would it help if I got the Land Rover filled with petrol and checked the tyres before your drive? At least I could do something practical.' Miles turned away so that she could not see he was close to tears. He had spent a nerve-wracking day committing a criminal offence to protect her, and now she was leaving him.

'It must be over three hundred miles to Devon. You can't expect the Land Rover to make the journey in one day; it will be a nightmare, especially with the dogs with you. It isn't fair on them, cooped up in the back for hours on end.' Miles was clutching at straws now.

'I've done it before and I stop regularly. They will sleep most of the way, especially after the run they have just had. Stop worrying. I can look after myself.'

Miles didn't doubt she could, but he wanted to look after her and she wasn't going to let him. He wanted her to know he had just sold his soul to a criminal boss and his thug to protect her and she was leaving without even discussing it with him.

Once Ozzy and Marble were settled on their clean dog beds in the back, she promised she would text him when they arrived. Miles waved them off as the Land Rover disappeared out of the drive.

Mrs B came quietly up to Miles' side and put her hand on his arm. 'She'll be back before you know it. She loves you too much to stay away for long.'

CHAPTER TWENTY-THREE

October 1721

'Come on in, Michael, we will speak in the parlour, less likelihood of interruption.' The lawyer was struck by how tired and worn-down John looked. Once they had settled in the chairs on either side of the desk, Michael knew there was no way of raising the subject gently.

'John, I have received notice from Lord Edgerton that he intends to terminate his lease of Somersham Court and invoke the penalty clause...' Michael went on to read the reference number and the words of the legal agreement.

'By God, he has a nerve! By all means, terminate the lease, that would suit me to be rid of any association of that perfidious man and I can and will repay the remaining rental. But to imply that my son has performed an act that brings disrepute on him is downright libellous.' John was offended to his very core. His son and been assaulted, robbed and thrown into a foreign canal. How did Edgerton think that brought him or anyone into disrepute?

'There is an article in the *Ipswich Journal,* very carefully written, that implies that because the body was not found, there's the possibility that Thomas has absconded with the gold in collusion with his younger brother.' Michael resisted telling John that this explanation was gathering momentum in the coffeehouses and trading organisations.

'I travelled to Holland with my cousin, we spoke to the innkeeper, an Englishman well-versed in the way of life there. He was reluctant to speak ill of Thomas, but he did say that Thomas did not take advice well and strayed into areas no foreigner should go. We visited the moneymen that Thomas was expecting to meet, but they were less than helpful and very dismissive. We also visited Daniel's trade connections, who had raised the alarm in Amsterdam. The authorities could not find any trace of Thomas, other than the torn patch of his waistcoat, the ripped letters and the linen wrapping he had hidden the money in. It was the authorities that declared the most likely fate of my son.'

'Indeed, I know of your efforts to establish events, but quite simply, John, can you repay the lease money?'

'Yes, I can return the outstanding amount on the rental when the lease is terminated. But I will never repay all of it. It would be tantamount to me agreeing that my son was corrupt and had stolen the money. It is a vicious falsehood!' John's tired face now blazed with anger.

'Is this your reply to Lord Edgerton then?'

'Yes. Only if he can prove his allegations are true, will I adhere to his clause.' John folded his arms in front of himself in defiance.

There was a gentle knock on the parlour door which Alice opened, her brother, Seth, standing back in the shadows.

'My apologies, husband, but Seth has visited and has some urgent news he wishes to share with you.'

'Do you mind, Michael?'

The lawyer shook his head; he was quite curious to meet Alice's brother.

'Seth, good to see you. Come in and join us. May I present to you Michael La Trobe? He acts for me in matters of law.' The two men shook hands. The lawyer's soft hands felt crushed by the large, strong, calloused hand of the blacksmith.

'Speak plainly, brother.'

'There are rumours going round that Thomas has made off with a lot of Lord Edgerton's money and that you are expected to make good the theft. And that will bankrupt you. Traders are being advised not to do business with you as your finances are under strain.' Seth felt better once he had blurted out the words, he neither believed nor condoned.

'Michael, please explain.'

The lawyer outlined the clause in basic terms.

'Being robbed and killed is not bringing anyone into disrepute other than the thugs who carried out the attack!' Seth was outraged. 'I came here today, in part to tell you of the rumours, but also to pledge my support to you and all the family. And not just my support, but all those whose accounts were settled when Sir bloody Stanley Jacks reneged on our agreements. Whatever happens, you will never be turned from our doors.'

John sank down in his chair. He could take the calumny in his stride, but the kindness was hard to bear. 'My thanks to you, Seth, your words put strength in my heart.'

'Is there nothing you can do, sir?' Seth pointed his question towards the lawyer.

'There is little defence against slurs and innuendos, to recourse to law is expensive and rarely brings satisfaction to either side. The only people who gain are the men of law! Now I must take my leave of you, John. Do you have any instructions for me other than to refuse Edgerton's application?'

John shook his head and stood to shake his hand.

'I'll show you out, sir.' Alice opened the door, her heart even heavier now she had an understanding of the situation.

Seth and John lit their pipes and looked at each other, not knowing quite what to say. Seth broke the silence.

'Well, brother, I know little of commerce and business. I have a trade where for the most part I am paid for work done. I avoid working for the landed gentry because most of them are empty shells: all show and no substance. They leave unpaid accounts from tailors, vintners, grocers and tradesmen of all walks. I would rather shoe working horses than fancy chasers. A working horse is needed by its owner; a good job done for a fair price, cash on completion.'

John smiled slightly and took another taper to his pipe to get it going.

'If I was you, I would sell the damn house. If needs be, sell some land to give you capital, then farm sufficient land to provide a modest income for the family. Forget trading overseas and hobnobbing with the burghers of Norwich. Go back to your roots. Alice and Daniel will support you and even thank you for it.' Seth could see his words were falling on deaf ears.

'I'll go and make my peace with my sister for she is affronted that my reason for coming was to see you and not her. Women!' Seth shook John's hand and clapped him on the arm in what he hoped was a reassuring way. He left the parlour, stopping at the door to look back at John. He wondered how much more pressure his sister's husband could take.

Seth was not the only visitor that day.

§

Alice had settled Ellen by the kitchen fireside. Her tears had nearly stopped and Ellen's words were now more comprehensible.

'My father will not give me permission to marry Daniel.'

'But he has already given permission, why would he withdraw it?'

'He says Thomas is a thief and I should not marry into such a family and have a criminal brother-in-law,' Ellen reported, verbatim.

Alice was furious. How dare that penny-pinching old bastard, who would not waste money on doctors or medicine and was probably the cause of his wife's illness and ultimately her death! If she had been a feline, her claws would have unsheathed with murderous intent.

'Do you want to marry Daniel and live here with us?' Alice asked calmly.

'Yes, but until I am twenty-one, I must seek permission.' Ellen blew her nose noisily.

'Well, this is what you must do. Return to your father and tell him that you will be marrying Daniel on your twenty-first birthday and that for the next two years you will live in his house and perform your duties as he demands. Just state you will marry Daniel Matthews the minute the law allows it without the necessity of his consent. He is free to change his mind at any time but being forced to stay unwed will make being a loving daughter difficult.'

Ellen looked amazed at Alice's suggestion. To speak back to her father was not in her nature. 'Do you think it will work?'

'It might. Either way, you need to stand up to bullies, play them at their own game. If he throws you out in a fit of rage, come here and we will take you in as a ward for the next couple of years. Men think they own us women; they do, but we can make their lives hell as retribution.' Alice had never made anyone's life hell, having never had the necessity. But she would give the miserable mean-minded Master Holsey a run for his money.

'Come, Ellen, you must be getting home. Go put a cold cloth across your eyes to reduce the redness and swelling. Crying is assumed to be a sign of womanly weakness, so don't show that you are so distressed. I will accompany you, for I need to have words with your father.'

The two women made the journey in no time, during which Alice gave Ellen her first lesson in understanding and managing men, a far greater skill than household management.

Master Holsey was standing by his door, his mood not improved by the lack of prepared food on the table when he had returned from work. Alice felt Ellen physically shrink at the sight of her surly father. The young woman jumped down from the trap and scuttled into the house having mumbled an apology to her father.

'Mistress Matthews, what brings you here?' His gruff voice was meant to sound intimidating.

''Tis obvious, I have brought Ellen home. We would not want her to be walking the lanes alone for we care much for her safety and happiness.' Alice spoke lightly and with forced friendliness. Before he could reply, she added, 'Indeed, Master Holsey, I would crave a few minutes of your time to clear up some misunderstandings.' She was about to alight from the trap, but he walked up close and stood nearby.

'As you are aware, we are a house in mourning since our son, Thomas, was robbed and killed in Holland whilst there on Lord Edgerton's business. Despite our pain, we have been told that rumours are circulating that Thomas is not dead and has stolen money, like a thief in the night.' Alice watched the stonemason's face carefully.

He made no effort to respond.

'I am sure you will remember how distressing it must have been for you when malicious rumours started after your lady wife died; how her death had been brought about by your refusal to pay for any medical aid for her and you had let her die a prolonged, agonised death. How anyone with any sense of decency could have passed on to neighbours such a dastardly rumour, we will never know.'

Holsey's body language changed from haughty to nervous.

'Forgive me for reviving that memory, but it only demonstrates how such vile tittle-tattle can affect the innocent. I think anyone doing such a thing should be openly denounced and publicly shamed.'

'As you say, Mistress Matthews.'

'I have to return now. The one happy thing is that Daniel and Ellen will be wed, hopefully sooner rather than later. Our whole family cannot wait to welcome her into our home and lives, for she is a credit to you. We are so pleased that you agree to their wedding being celebrated from Old Manor

Farm. So I wish you good day and look forward to you and Ellen visiting us to start the preparations for their special day.' With that, Alice gave him a beaming smile, not that it reached her eyes, and shook the reins to get the pony to walk on.

CHAPTER TWENTY-FOUR
June 1722

John Matthews was a broken man, in mind and body. Despite the best efforts of his family, his spirits could not be lifted. Six months had passed since Thomas' disappearance, and life had settled down into a pattern that suited them all.

Alice was feeling the aches and pains of her years, but Daniel's wife, Ellen, was learning all the skills needed to run a good household, and Constance's gentle nature kept the youngsters in check while teaching them their letters and numbers. Joseph was blossoming as a young country boy and spent many hours with his Uncle Daniel out and about on the land.

The accusations and innuendos about Thomas' disappearance with Lord Edgerton's gold still rumbled on but failed to affect the closeness of the hardworking tight-knit family. There had been a marked change in their income and status in the community, other than trusted friends. Considering that Constance, Alice and Daniel had never sought social betterment, this was a benefit, not a loss. Ellen's father had shown a reluctance to let his daughter marry into a family who counted a suspected thief amongst them. However, Ellen offered her father the choice of a sour, uncaring spinster of a daughter costing him money living at home, or a loving, caring, married daughter living elsewhere at her husband's expense. His love of his purse had soon won him over.

Ellen and Daniel had married quietly, and she fitted in well with the Matthews' household; an industrious, pragmatic young woman made a much welcome addition. Now that the news she was with child had been met with great excitement, the family looked to the future and put the past events behind them.

There was no doubt that Thomas and Lord Edgerton's missing gold had impacted their lives. Not as many people were prepared to do business with the Matthews family; some had gone as far as to shun their company. However, most of their tenants and farm labourers respected and trusted them, and they had no desire to leave. Somersham Court had been sold at a loss, but there were sufficient funds to see them through bad harvests and keep them all in a modest lifestyle. Daniel was aware that the house had been sold under its value due to malicious rumours spread by Edgerton and his cronies. However, the new owner had spotted a bargain and that is exactly what he had got.

That morning, everyone was about their daily tasks except for John, who was slumped in his favourite chair by the fireplace in the hall. Billy and Bess, the children of one of their tenant farmers, sat at the long table being taught basic mathematics by Constance, using dried beans as counters. Their concentration span was almost at its end as Billy, who was not as quick as his younger sister, was beginning to try Constance's patience. A welcome interruption was made by the kitchen maid who knocked and then entered.

'Master Matthews, there's mail for you and he told me it

has come from America. Not that I know where that is. The post rider said it was prepaid and urgent.' She walked the length of the old hall, passing Constance and the children without acknowledgement.

The old man did not stir but continued to stare into space.

'Master Matthews, please, sir, take this.' She thrust the travel-stained letter in front of him. He did not stir. Constance had slipped out of the room to look for Alice and Ellen and had sent Billy to find Daniel as quickly as possible. The maid left the letter on the corner of the long dining table, gave a quick curtsy and left the room. Young Bess did not like being left alone with the strange, old man so ran out of the hall to find more friendly company.

As she came in, Alice wiped her hands on the apron she used when breadmaking and went straight over to her husband. She spoke in quiet and gentle tones as she explained that a letter from America was important. She didn't know why, but it was so extraordinary that it had to be. She helped him to the large carver chair placed at the head of the table. He pushed the letter towards her.

'John, dearest, you know my eyesight and lettering is not good enough for me to read it.'

The old man just shrugged.

'Maybe Constance could read it for us.' This idea did not sit well with her daughter-in-law; she did not want the attention or responsibility. Her apprehension was saved by Daniel striding into the room with his wife at his side.

'Mother, what's all this nonsense about America?' He saw the untouched letter and went over to pick it up. He looked over it carefully; it had been pre-paid, which in itself was unusual.

He broke the seals and unfolded the sheets into a readable shape. He cast his eye over the first page and then went as pale as death as he grabbed a chair to steady himself. Quickly recovering his wits, he pulled the chair out to sit on it.

'The letter is from a preacher in America telling us that Thomas is dead and buried at sea.' His delivery was not intentionally brutal, but he was in shock, for the statement was so blatantly untrue. Only he and one other person knew the truth.

Daniel looked at the assembled family members now all sitting down. His wife, Ellen, looked surprised for she had only heard the ugly rumours put about by people. Constance's naturally pale face was now ashen and yet unmoved.

'Son, please read the whole letter,' John's dry and shaky voice instructed.

Daniel did as asked, but his voice was unsteady.

Thomas could not have been on that boat heading for the Americas. He knew that the conversations being recalled in this letter could not have taken place; he knew where his brother's body lay and that was not at the bottom of the ocean. It could only be Carver who had written the letter.

But why?

The letter explained that its author was a minister and preacher of Calvinism invited out to America to join with other like-minded revival preachers to turn the people of America away from materialism, reject worldliness and open their minds to the consequences of living sinful lives. The writer who had signed the letter "Reverend Jones" described how Thomas had fallen ill and sought absolution for his wicked and sinful life. The preacher had listened and then promised that once he made landfall, a letter would be sent to inform his family of his demise.

There was a message for each member: contrition for the way he had treated Constance, affection for his mother, respect for his brother's work ethic and regard for his father. The explanation offered was that Thomas and Daniel had arrived late in Holland and that whilst waiting for a response to a note of apology, Thomas had unwittingly wandered into a tavern of ill-repute. Subsequently, he had been plied with local gin, unaware of the strength of the liquor. Consequently, he had been in no condition to defend himself against the robbers. The letter described how it was the reaction of the robbers that caused the life-threatening injuries and changed his course of life.

Thomas had been roughly held whilst they checked his pockets and body for a money belt, his great coat and waistcoat getting torn in the process. They had taken childish delight in ripping up his letters. But then the mood changed after one of them had scraped at a coin and started shouting and swearing at him. He did not understand a word, then the kicking started and he lost consciousness. He assumed they had rolled him into the canal. The cold water jolted him back to life for just long enough to convince him he was going to die. He was pulled out of the water by a passing barge. It took many days for his memory to partially recover after the concussion. What the robbers had shouted at him was *ze zijn nep* "they are counterfeit". He gave the bargemen a false name and was put ashore. He joined a group of French people who were French Huguenots making their way to the docks to emigrate to the Americas. Thomas begged them to take him with them but never recovered from the beating and died at sea.

There was a stunned silence; tears started to run gently down John's face and he left the table to return to his fireside chair.

'Well, Constance, you can prove you are a bona fide widow now.' Daniel's words sounded harsh and crass.

Alice stood up and looked at each one of them in turn, trying to read their minds.

'We have not received this letter. The chances that it was even written are minimal; the chances it made its destination more so.' No one spoke, but the letter was pushed from one person to another as each read the passage pertinent to them. They all started talking at once about how guilty they felt for the uncharitable conclusions they had made. No one noticed that John was now clutching his left arm and the rocking movement was more convulsive. It was not long before John Matthews breathed his last breath, just as Constance spoke.

'But what happened to Thomas' hound, Somersham Boy?'

'I doubt anyone will ever be able to answer that,' replied Daniel.

CHAPTER TWENTY-FIVE
December 2021

The six weeks in Devon working with her conservator friend had been the right decision, even if Lucy had doubted it at the start. The Land Rover made the journey stoically; the regular stops kept the engine from overheating, the dogs getting restless and Lucy being shaken to pieces. The steady forty-five miles an hour on motorways was annoying to the other car users but she soon got used to the huge continental lorries thundering past as their slipstreams buffeted the old vehicle. Like intrepid explorers of yesteryear, Lucy battled on whilst the dogs slept on their newly laundered beds.

Sarah lived just outside the village of Bampton in a small, converted barn with a large outbuilding which she used as a workshop. The two women had shared a flat whilst at art college and had been close until Lucy became obsessed with Denis and turned her back on family and friends. But they had always kept in touch, albeit sporadically.

Lucy loved the peace and tranquillity, and the cosiness of the valleys and trees of the countryside were so unlike the open spaces of East Anglia. Sarah was not happy about the two dogs, but Ozzy and Marble were on their best behaviour and soon accepted them, just so long as they didn't go anywhere near the workshop.

Miles had to restrain himself from phoning and messaging her daily. The last thing he wanted was to stalk her. So one evening he sat in his study and wrote her a traditional letter, ink on paper complete with envelope. Lucy was thrilled to receive his letter and wrote copious pages in reply. She wrote of their work and how she had spent most of one day vacuuming strips off an old tapestry with a special brush of goats' hair, washing the sections so carefully and stitching supportive linen scrim to the now clean and dried sections. She could express herself better in the written word, and with each letter exchanged Miles began to understand why she had gone. There was something very strange about starting a postal courtship having already lived and loved together.

The weeks flew past and Sarah's permanent assistant soon had the plaster cast removed from her arm and was back to work on light duties. Though Sarah was delighted to have Lucy there, living and working with someone had become rather claustrophobic and she looked forward to having her house to herself again.

Miles had nearly finished the letter when he decided to make the invitation before Lucy decided to move on somewhere else. He suggested that Lucy and the greyhounds return to Somersham Court for Christmas. Much to his relief and pleasure, she wrote back immediately that she would love to.

§

Mrs B was beside herself with "I told you so" and excitement that there would be company for Miles as she and "her Dick" were thinking of visiting relatives for Christmas. Miles was also pleased as it meant he had Lucy all to himself, and if it went pear-shaped there would not be any witnesses to his humiliation.

Lucy did return. Skye and Fergus were thrilled to see their canine cousins. Mrs B had killed the proverbial "fatted calf" and helped Lucy put up some pagan greenery round the house more in keeping with the festival of Yule than the tinsel of modern Christmas.

All the problems that blighted Lucy had been argued and counter-argued in their correspondence, which had put a rather practical slant in their love letters. Lucy had reconciled herself to the idea that Adrian was missing, but no body had been found, so there was hope. Davy had made a statement about seeing the dark shadowy character leave the bungalow at the start of the fire. Whilst giving his statement to the sergeant, he was relieved that a close friend had "lent" him his wife to pose as the *al fresco* lady. Though the cause of the fire was still deemed as arson, the focus was no longer on Adrian, which would have invalidated the insurance. The burnt wreck was now advertised as a "wonderful opportunity for development" and had received a lot of interest at a high price.

Mr Smith appeared to be respecting the agreement.

Christmas Day came and they walked down to the church through the meadow and the woodland. The little church was packed, Christmas the only time it ever was. The candles burnt in the candelabras and the warm golden light added to the atmosphere created by Christmas carols and readings.

The vicar stood by the door, offering greetings to the congregation as they left. Spotting Miles and Lucy, he said, 'Thank you for attending the service, hope to see you again soon.' If he had been honest, he was rather hoping for an invitation to Somersham Court for a mince pie and sherry.

'Indeed, I hope to see you again soon.'

Lucy threw Miles a quizzical look.

As they walked back through the woods, they reached the kissing gate he had had installed in place of a stile, so Lucy's three-legged bulldogs and blind lurchers could get through.

He went through first then blocked the gate to stop her from following. 'There is a forfeit for coming through my gate.'

Lucy gave him a kiss, then pushed again, but Miles would not budge.

'I want more than that.'

Lucy's mind boggled; it was far too cold for anything too saucy outside.

'You can't come through until you promise to marry me.'

Lucy froze, and Miles felt like the world had frozen in time too. His heart raced almost as fast as his stomach churned.

'Yes, I will.'

Miles was so thrilled that he pulled the gate towards him with such force, he trapped his finger in the latch. The romance of the moment was completely lost as he filled the air with angry expletives. Lucy laughed.

§

'Oh, come in, do come in, indeed we *are* seeing you again soon.' The vicar looked so stereotypical that he was out of place in the modern world. No brightly coloured shirt with dog collar, no jeans, no trainers, just oversized grey flannels and a baggy beige cardigan with carefully darned patches on the cuffs worn under a Harris Tweed jacket of similar wear and tear.

He beckoned Lucy and Miles into a study which also served as the parish office. There were stacks of papers, articles and files on every possible surface. A large partners' desk had sufficient desktop space for a leather blotter, which was much used, as evidenced by the myriads of ink markings on it. On the opposite side of the room was a smaller, modern desk which had a PC and printer on it, obviously not used by him. The vicar waved his arm at it.

'Since my wife died, I have struggled with the parish. She was tireless, running the PCC, chairing committees, chivvying up support, organising everything and everyone, including me.' The vicar was obviously mentally exhausted and sliding into depression.

'Come and sit down. Can I offer you tea or coffee?' The offer was made out of politeness rather than hospitality as it would involve him making it himself.

'What is a PCC?' Miles was having serious second thoughts about getting married by him. It crossed his mind that they should wait until a new incumbent was found, preferably one that might smile a little.

'Oh, the Parochial Council Committee. They look after the management of the parish, well, they should, but the Churchwarden died and we cannot find anyone to volunteer to take his place. Our treasurer is in her eighties and I am not too sure how long she can cope. We don't have a verger but there is a wonderful lady archivist called Karen in the village who keeps us in order and works wonders, but she has just told me she wants to move to Dorset.'

Miles looked at Lucy and tried to convey "let's get out of here" messages to her.

'That's awful, you must miss your wife dreadfully. What will happen here then?

'The diocese has decided to turn the church into a festival church; it has too much historical interest to be sold off. There's the graveyard to consider too.'

'What's a festival church?' Miles had a mental picture of a mini-Glastonbury on his doorstep and he did not like the image.

'No daily services just matches, hatches and dispatches!' There was a hint of a smile on the old man's face.

Miles warmed a little towards him.

'Depends on when you want to marry, but it could well be the last marriage rites I'll ever perform unless you want to bring in a younger, trendier vicar?'

Lucy shot a warning glare at Miles before speaking again.

'We would love you to perform our marriage ceremony. We have no need for anyone happy, clappy or trendy; just kind and sincere.'

Miles just smiled at her, his impulsive and sentimental but slightly tactless Lucy.

'Oh, how exciting. But I have to ask some basic questions of suitability before we can proceed, if that is all right with you?'

They both nodded in agreement.

'Mr Mortimer, have you been married before?'

'Yes, I married my late wife, Helen, in 2010. She died of Leukaemia in 2018.'

'Miss Moncrief, have you been married before?'

'No.' Lucy saw no reason to expand on how she had changed her surname and lived with Denis pretending to be his wife.

'Well, that's all straightforward. We can get the ball rolling once you suggest a date.'

'The 24th of June, Midsummer's Day,' they both said in unison.

The vicar took down copious notes in a large notebook, writing with a fountain pen in large and florid handwriting. This really appealed to Lucy as she appreciated the traditional use of ink and pen.

Once they had been through all the questions the vicar needed to ask, he got to the spiritual part of the interview Miles was dreading. Lucy came to his rescue.

'We talked about this and came to the conclusion that we both believe in Christianity as a humanitarian philosophical religion, but we both have problems with buying the idea of the old geezer sat on a cloud judging us all and deciding who goes to Heaven or Hell.' Lucy thought of adding that everyone is responsible for their own version of Heaven and Hell during their lifetime, but she did not want to provoke a lengthy philosophical debate.

'We've both been baptized into the Church of England. Is that sufficient?' She failed to comment that neither of them had been confirmed. She certainly wasn't going to tell him that she kicked up such a fuss at the first confirmation class about wine and blood, never mind bread and flesh. The whole idea had freaked her out. Her mother was madly in love with a new gentleman friend and was too absorbed in her own life to take issue at Lucy's refusal to be confirmed.

'Would you like to be confirmed prior to your marriage?'

They exchanged looks and they declined as the idea was

not met with any enthusiasm.

'Have you discussed the future? How do you see yourselves in say twenty years' time? Are you in agreement about children and money matters?'

Lucy blushed and Miles looked taken aback.

'We have a lot more to talk about and agree or disagree on, and I'm sure we will have given the important topics a good airing. If we can't agree, then we can always cancel!' Miles gave him a happy, joking smile.

'Well, I suppose it's better to cancel than make a vow you can't keep,' came the vicar's deadpan voice.

As they were leaving, Lucy turned to the now happier and slightly more cheerful vicar and asked if she could help with any paperwork. She explained that being self-employed gave her some spare time and as a historian she had some idea of the archaic ways of the Church of England.

'My dear girl, I would welcome all the help I can get. Your timing is perfect; I think there is a leaky underground water pipe in the graveyard. Though the ground is only soggy at the moment, it could get a lot worse.' Lucy had a vision of corpses floating to the surface and rising up out of the ground like a bad zombie movie.

'Could you manage a faculty application?'

Miles was intrigued. What was a faculty application, and why would anyone need to apply for one? Lucy mentally groaned because she knew it meant working with the diocese and its administrative team. She had had dealings with them several years ago about access to church property as part of a project she had been involved in. Now she wondered if her red wine-fuelled monologue on the history of the church's repression of women was going to be remembered by the rather precious deacon.

As though a mind reader, the vicar continued. 'We have a new deacon and she is very helpful, but she talks so quickly I find her hard to follow.'

Lucy smiled and sighed an internal sigh of relief. 'Of course, I'll help prepare the faculty, but I'll need some guidance from you as I am not up to date with procedures.'

'I shouldn't worry about that, my dear, nothing has changed for decades and I doubt anything will change for decades to come.' The vicar's face cracked into a broad, rather naughty, schoolboy grin.

Indeed, once she started, Lucy found the whole process unnecessarily complicated and with no sense of urgency. Her patience was being pushed to its limits by the bureaucracy and the definition of the faculty; was it an emergency or a full one? All she wanted was either a template for a "statement of significance of need" form, or maybe an exemplar so that she could ensure that the application was done in the correct format.

Lucy slammed her phone down on the desk, thankfully the mobile had a shock-resistant cover on it, otherwise it would not have survived. She looked out of the window, as though seeking inspiration from the wide Norfolk sky. She could not help but smile as Dick trundled an old-fashioned wooden wheelbarrow out of the gate to the walled garden, towards the compost beds constructed just round the corner. A man at peace with his life and lot; his demands on life were few but the rewards were many, measured not in monetary terms but in contentment.

Picking the phone up, Lucy hoped that the next call would not be so frustrating. It wasn't as she got through to the archaeology department quickly and found a helpful and enthusiastic member of the team. She explained about the suspected leaking pipe in the graveyard and reported her own findings. The nearest marked grave was a single female occupancy with a provisional date of 1721. The gravestone was indistinct, but it tallied with the burial books held at County Records. It was agreed that Lucy would monitor the situation until a visit could be carried out by the archaeological department.

She decided that she had earned herself some tea and toast as a reward for finally getting the situation under control.

No sooner than she had settled in the kitchen, the landline rang.

'Lucy, Lucy, there has been a catastrophe in the graveyard!'

Lucy couldn't speak immediately otherwise she would have spattered toast and honey all over the phone receiver.

'The walls of the trench have collapsed and the grave to the north has fallen into the trench.'

Lucy did not think this particularly catastrophic and her patience was wearing a little thin. But nothing prepared her for this next thing the vicar said.

'It looks like three sets of remains have fallen through.'

'What?'

'There are two skulls and what looks like part of a baby's ribcage, though my anatomy knowledge is limited.'

Lucy quietly and calmly explained that as "bones of antiquity" there was a particular order in which things had to be done next and that she would be at the church in about fifteen minutes.

'Leave it to me. Just make sure no one touches anything and, if possible, put a tarpaulin over the trench. Don't worry, it will be fine. These things happen, especially in graveyards.' Her attempt to lighten his mood fell on deaf ears.

She phoned the Norwich Police Station and explained the situation. There was little excitement for the discovery, as CID was stretched just dealing with twenty-first-century problems let alone old bones. However, there was a bit of interest in the mention of a multiple occupancy grave. They assured her that someone would be down to do a brief assessment of the site and its findings.

Lucy's next call was to a friend at County Records to ask for anything on an Annie Morton who had died in 1721 and was buried in St Nicholas' churchyard. She explained her interest and why it was rather pressing. She certainly caught their attention when she explained about the leaking pipe and the wall of the trench collapsing to reveal two adult skulls and a small ribcage. Once she had made all the necessary calls, she rushed over to the graveyard.

Indeed, just visible in the mudslide were the smooth tops of two skulls and nearer the foot was the reported small ribcage. However, to Lucy, it didn't look right, too straight-sided and not rounded, as you would expect of a baby. One of her calls had been to the county archaeologist, Flora Robinson, to inform her of the discovery; it was Flora's responsibility to validate the findings and she promised to keep Lucy up to date.

The days passed slowly for Lucy and Miles as they were fascinated by the find. They were hardly surprised when the Norfolk constabulary declared them bones of antiquity that required no criminal investigation. Flora and her team had visited and carefully removed the bones for further investigation, but they quickly established there was one skeleton of probably an elderly woman, a much taller, younger male and not a baby but a dog, a hunting type of hound.

Lucy put the three paintings side by side on the coffee table and was scrutinising them in case there was something she had missed. She leant forward to pick up the bottle to refill her glass of wine. Then she turned to look at Miles who was writing notes for his upcoming lecture.

'I know what this is now!'

'Know what?' Miles was mildly irritated to have his thought flow interrupted, until he saw the look of triumph on Lucy's face. He asked her to explain.

'Annie Morton was interred on the 25th of March 1721. We know this because of parish records. She was a spinster who left her estate to the parish. So it isn't a double grave of a husband and wife. Pretty unlikely she would have owned a hunting hound, let alone be buried with it.'

'How do you know it's her grave?'

'There's a headstone but it's weather-worn. I bet using modern equipment the details originally carved on it will bear me out. I'll ask Flora.' But this wasn't the point Lucy wanted to make. She continued.

'Look at the date of the burial, then turn it into Roman numerals: XXV, III, XVII, XXI. Ignore the V, they are on the three paintings we have. The V is a red herring, probably V for Versey. Months ago, Adrian mentioned that Clive Millar had had an apprentice called Edward Versey, it was in the record of indentures. I reckon that there are four paintings in the series. The fourth one is probably a painting of the church with Annie's grave centre stage. The hidden message is that something happened in the house. He wanted the viewer to leave the garden by that gate and walk over to the wood, travel through the wood and arrive at Annie's grave.'

'Aren't you getting a little fanciful? I thought you historians hated assumptions and guesswork based on rather sketchy details.' Miles thought the pun would amuse her. It didn't.

'Sometimes you have to have a possible theory to work on, then test it out against the facts.'

'OK. What could have happened here that prevented him from being given a decent Christian burial?'

'Murder. I think we are looking at the late Thomas Matthews.'

'But your research showed evidence in the newspaper archives that he went missing in Holland, along with a lot of gold belonging to a trade syndicate. There were some quite nasty innuendos that he hadn't been robbed in Holland but had done a runner.'

'Flora sent me a text yesterday; the full report isn't ready yet but she said that the male's neck had been broken and the hound's skull had been fatally traumatised.'

'So Thomas Matthews never went missing in Holland. He never even left the parish but was killed in this house and his body hidden in the newly dug grave of Annie Morton. The dog was Thomas' greyhound, the same one as in the portrait,' Miles mused. 'Well, now we know what happened to Somersham Boy!'

Author's Note

This book would never have come to life without the unwavering support and encouragement of my wonderful friends and family. Especially Claire, Penny, Karen, Anneli and Don – you each played an invaluable role in making the dream of publishing a book, a reality. Thank you.

Writing a book is an intimidating challenge on its own, but turning a manuscript into a finished, tangible book is an entirely different experience. The journey involved countless steps – from proof readings and plot checks to book cover design and marketing – and there were many moments where I couldn't have continued without the steadfast support of those around me.

I am especially grateful to the incredible team at Cranthorpe Millner. Their professionalism, patience, and unwavering encouragement kept me going, even in my lowest moments, when my confidence faltered. I truly could not have navigated the complexities of this process without them.

Jay D. Waveney
August 2025